POP

Kitty Aldridge was born in Bahrain in 1962. She trained as an actress in London and has since worked in film, theatre and television as an actress and writer. *Pop* is her first novel.

Kitty Aldridge

POP

VINTAGE

Published by Vintage 2002

2 4 6 8 10 9 7 5 3

Copyright © Kitty Aldridge 2001

Kitty Aldridge has asserted her right under the Copyright, Designs and
Patents Act 1988 to be identified as the author of this work

This book is sold subject to the condition that it shall not by way of trade
or otherwise, be lent, resold, hired out, or otherwise circulated without the
publisher's prior consent in any form of binding or cover other than that
in which it is published and without a similar condition including this
condition being imposed on the subsequent purchaser

First published in Great Britain in 2001 by Jonathan Cape

Vintage
Random House, 20 Vauxhall Bridge Road, London SW1V 2SA

Random House Australia (Pty) Limited
20 Alfred Street, Milsons Point, Sydney, New South Wales 2061, Australia

Random House New Zealand Limited
18 Poland Road, Glenfield, Auckland 10, New Zealand

Random House South Africa (Pty) Limited
Isle of Houghton, Corner of Boundary Road & Carse O'Gowrie,
Houghton 2198, South Africa

The Random House Group Limited Reg. No. 954009
www.randomhouse.co.uk

Grateful acknowledgement is made to the following for permission to
reprint previously published material:
'Love's Been Good To Me'. Composed by Rod McKuen. Used by
permission of Ambassador Music Ltd.
'Make 'Em Laugh'. Words by Arthur Freed , music by Nacio Herb Brown
© 1952 EMI Catalogue Partnership and EMI Robbins Catalog Inc, USA.
Worldwide print rights controlled by Warner Bros. Publications Inc/IMP
Ltd. Lyrics reproduced by permission of IMP Ltd. All rights reversed.
'Oh Carol'. Words and Music by Howard Greenfield and Neil Sedaka ©
1958, Screen Gems-EMI Music Inc, USA. Reproduced by permission of
Screen Gems-EMI Music Ltd, London WC2H 0QY.

While every effort has been made to obtain permission from owners
of copyright material reproduced herein, the publishers would like to
apologise for any omissions and will be pleased to incorporate missing
acknowledgements in any future editions.

A CIP catalogue record for this book is available from the British Library

ISBN 9780099428329 (from Jan 2007)
ISBN 0 099 42832 6

Penguin Random House is committed to a sustainable future for
our business, our readers and our planet. This book is made from
Forest Stewardship Council® certified paper.

Printed and bound in Great Britain by Clays Ltd, Elcograf S.p.A.

For Mark

Pop

She is looking up at a tall man in shambolic clothes. He is racing-dog thin with a long mischievous face, whiplashed with creases. The railway-station wind lifts his remaining hair. It is hard to say how old he is; old, seventy perhaps. But he moves with the quick fluidity of a youth and hangs a lean on one hip like a gunslinger. When he is not squinting he has the openly amazed expression of a child. His eyes are a shocking shade of blue; they steal almost all the available light. Maggie follows, up into his eyes like the light. When she wakes she'll remember this is not a dream. They are leaning into the wind made by the arrival and departure of trains, underwater limbs, as they struggle for a deliberate movement, tipping in the undertow. Maggie remembers how her mother screamed in a wind, like on a roller-coaster ride, arms out and mouth wide. No one is screaming today at Birmingham New Street station but she hears it clear as day, ringing in her ears, pulling her awake. Maggie is thirteen. Unlucky for some. That summer there was a freak heatwave.

There is a broad shaft of sunlight on the ceiling, fin-shaped, like the sail of a boat. Maggie watches it sway as the curtains twitch in a breeze. She is shipwrecked beneath on an ancient foam settee,

1

which makes an assortment of sighs and pings as it struggles to hold itself together. It plucks a bass string and exhales as she sits up. She waits while the old man strikes a match repeatedly against its box. Next of kin. The words seem senseless, jumbled up, waiting to be solved. The Grand Daughter, like a fable or a fairy tale. The cigarette in his mouth is quivering. His nervousness cables down his legs and sends ripples shivering through his worsted trousers; he looks like a man facing the gallows or the tundra. Finally he succeeds in creating a flame inside his cupped hands and blows some fluffy spirals that bend into frowns as they rise, smoke signals to a distant cavalry indicating all is not well. The cough comes next, sodden as a Staffordshire bog and forcing him into a series of violent bows. When he recovers he notices Maggie.

'Alright mate? You coming?' In thickly bending Midlands vowels that start off squatting under his tongue then flatten out the sides of his mouth.

Cigarette ash falls gently dust to dust on to his lapel from the Player's Navy Cut between his teeth. He pulls on a hat and swings a rolled-up *Daily Mirror* left and right to part the greenish front-room curtains. Blazing sunlight hurls itself in.

'You coming then? Where's that bloody hound?'

Maggie waits to be sure this is what he has said. Blowbroth appears from nowhere, panting and leering, like a griffin, a mongrel in actual fact, bizarrely constructed, made out of discarded bits. Maggie stares.

'Come on then if you're coming, lass.'

The Plough and Harrow

August 1975. The heat has intensified and previous records are broken. The newspaper declares it is the hottest summer since 1911. Next year this year's record will be broken and people will wonder where will it end. They walk three abreast the length of Clarendon Road, heads down and stride for stride, a plume of smoke ribboning out behind them. The old man begins to whistle through his teeth as they sweep past the Baptist church in man-dog-child formation, blazing the smoke trail in their wake like the Red Arrows. Maggie crosses herself swiftly on account of the whistling, praying not to spend an eternal damnation in Sutton Coldfield. Single file through a shrieking glass-panelled door at the Plough and Harrow. Inside there's a warm reek of yeast and furniture polish. The sun blasts through the tea-stained lace skirting the lower half of the windows and bleaches the net of smoke draped over the regulars' heads. The old man's pint is already pulled and streaming on a beer-mat. The landlord's heavy arms are spread like girders either side of it as he lifts his big cement face.

'Arthur.'

'Morning, Ken.'

'On the house, mate.'

'Ta.'

Hushed and quick like passwords.

'Your Carole's youngest?' His eyes rolling in the cement, peeping, embarrassed.

'And eldest. Just the one,' replies the old man.

'On the house, mate,' murmurs Ken, presenting the pint and

3

squeezing the old man's forearm. 'Terrible business.' Shaking his head. 'Awful bloody business, Arthur.' He brightens to Maggie. 'Okay, love?' Then clouding again, like a tragicomic mask, 'Terrible business,' to the old man.

'She sixteen then?'

The old man looks at Maggie. 'Oh ar, mate, she's big for her age.'

Ken winks. 'No problem, Arthur. On the house, alright?'

She considers the contradiction in the old man's remark. She was big for her age, it was true; tall enough to pass for sixteen anyway, tall enough to lift a glass of ginger beer from the bar without spilling it. She watched the world from the top of an athlete's skeleton that had begun elongating during her eleventh year. Gigantic hands and feet sprang out of her sleeves and trousers. She particularly despised her hands; they swung heavily at her sides, puce with shame. The old man's accidentally truthful remark was apparently lost in Ken's bountiful sea of sympathy; glad he was, to conspire in its illogic.

The sun burns against the windows, wood creaks. The old man goes up in a roar of flame, the smoke falls around them, silence. The two recline their matching skeletons in identical poses on the padded ruby banquette. Just the solemn ticking of an oak clock while their lives race off without them.

Later they ate tea together in an airless kitchen. An old tin thermometer, wobbly on its nail, recorded eighty-five degrees Fahrenheit. The old man filled a kettle from a tap that sang out soprano notes with the water pressure. When the kettle whistled on the gas ring, he poured boiling water over a sieveful of tinned peas. These were folded into corned beef from a tin and shared between two pale-blue plates. His eyebrows swung up and down philosophically as he ate.

He only spoke twice.

'I'll answer to Pop, mate. That's what your mother called me.'

And, 'Do you follow football at all?'

Clarendon Road

Maggie heard him weeping again. He had cried the previous day too.

'It could be worse,' Pop's friend Dolly Minski had whispered to her from an old smoker's snap-and-crackle throat. 'Far worse.'

'God only knows you can bet on that, there's always something worser than the flaming worst.' Maggie watched Dolly's sugar-babe-pink mouth make shivering shapes as she hushed comforts into her face, while Pop gasped on the stairs. Her breath was a warm breeze of Campari and garibaldis. Grey veins looped across her liver-flecked hands. She might have been referring to the widowed old soldier who'd become penniless and forgotten in his high-rise, and resorted to eating dog food after his pension book was stolen and he'd been too proud to report it. Pop had mentioned the story the day before in the car on the way from Birmingham New Street station; it was all he had said during the journey. He'd read it in the *Daily Mirror*, said it was a bloody disgrace. After that he was quiet so Maggie counted buses and then lone dogs, seven and four, keep the kettle boiling if you miss the beat you're out.

They had stopped abruptly at an angle, some feet from the

pavement outside 99 Clarendon Road. He said, 'Here we are then,' and burst into tears.

She watched a child dragging a gargantuan dog along across the way.

'Sorry, mate, Christ alive.' He blew some trumpet blasts into his handkerchief and swiped at his eyes.

'Right,' he had said eventually, dew shining in his nostrils. 'Welcome to Sutton Coldfield. Jewel of Warwickshire.' She gazed at him steadily. A splinter of hair had reared up from his head and stood out like an aerial.

'Strictly speaking it's not Warwickshire any more. S'posed to call it West Midlands now, as decreed by Ted Heath and his flaming diddymen. We're all in bloody Birmingham apparently, we just didn't know it. Right. Welcome to the West Midlands, mate. Fat lot of ruddy difference it makes, eh?'

And he opened the door into an oncoming Volvo.

As they reached number ninety-nine he had tried a courtier's smile, hauling up his moustache, sparkly with mucus in the grimy sunlight, and leaning conspiratorially close.

'There's a dog, mate. He don't bite.' He rolled a ball of keys in his palm, searching for the correct one.

'He don't know he's a dog, best not tell him, eh? Fancies himself.' And a loud hiss followed by a silent rocket of laughter shot out of him, leaving his chest wheezing with whistles. It folded his eyes and uncovered long, ivory teeth that looked as if they might play a tune if you tapped them. He hauled in another breath, releasing chords of musical notes from his chest, an accordion load, and choked on the congestion it caused. They stumbled over the threshold that way, to the fanfare of his strangled gasps and hacking cough.

Blowbroth

Blowbroth and Maggie sat opposite one another, impassive, like Fischer and Karpov in the chess final. She in her pale silence that sent people elsewhere, alarmed, irritated, off her back anyway. A protest, her small power, brand new. Beyond the debris of ashtrays, devastated armchairs and hillocks of *Daily Mirror*s, she watched Pop hurriedly lighting another cigarette. The smoke curled curiously towards her. She blinked through it, small quick eyes buried under a shelf of fringe grown right over them and halfway down her nose. She had white, bloodless skin, hardly freckled, just the odd long blue vein rising. Yards and yards of legs and arms making right angles, so much person and practically nobody in there. He coughed, shook the box of matches and whistled six notes from the White Horse Inn theme.

'Maggie. Young Carole's bab,' Pop explained to the dog and coughed again, louder. Blowbroth lay nonchalantly across a mutilated armchair, watching her with yellow eyes, thumping a slow rhythm against the arm with his truncheon tail. She watched him back. She hadn't known there was a dog. She had never seen anything like it before. He was a derangement of breeding, a riot of genes, the work of a madman.

A spiffy little terrier's head, cocked ready for argument, schemed under an outsize pair of rotating Alsatian ears. Under these, two round amber eyes, flecked with gold, blazed a maniacal indifference. The body was roughly spaniel with a long lurcher's spine and a corgi's legs and finished off with the truncheon tail that followed him around like an exclamation mark.

Maggie shifted her stare to the regiment of beer tankards and toby jugs that filed along the mantelpiece, their faces gloating back at her. Blowbroth's stomach whined and pinged in the pause and he raised his eyebrows at her returning glance.

Pop swiped his thinning hair back with gold nicotined fingers. 'I could make a brew,' he said loudly, and then fading. He glanced around for the kitchen. 'I'll have to put the kettle on, mate.' He strangled his cigarette, dropped it, still smouldering, into an Ansell's Bitter ashtray and traipsed like a condemned man into the kitchen.

'Tea. *Camellia sinensis.* Evergreen. Native of Burma,' he briefed. 'Once upon a time the stuff grew wild, Rajasthan, in the north, mate, wild as bloody dandelions. There aren't any milk, alright?'

The smoke from his discarded cigarette curled upwards in a tall twisting rope. Maggie had seen a picture of a brown-skinned boy sitting at the top of just such a spellbound rope. Blowbroth's gaze had slid to her bell-bottom jeans with the flowers winding up the leg, and finally rested on the belt buckle, a sunshine-yellow smiley face, beaming out at her disintegrating life. A wind scooped up some clouds outside, lifting away the tiara of light from the mantelpiece, and the room darkened, deepening all the mauves and browns. A smell like preservation and dilapidation – yellowing paper, dog hair and dust – hung between the numerous towers of newspapers and slain furniture. An enormous ashtray big as a dinner plate, loaded with fag ends like logs, heaved out a stench; under the debris bold letters stammered 'Llandudno'. Cupboards and drawers slammed in the kitchen. Blowbroth folded himself in half to scratch his ear.

'Woof,' Maggie murmured. He snapped back around, fast as a lizard. Yellow eyes crackling with suspicion.

'Sugar, mate?' Pop peered around the door jamb.

'Yes,' she replied. Yes what? her mother enquired in her head.

Pop sidled in and bowed to rest the tin tray on top of a medium-sized newspaper tower. Two mugs, one smattered with pink flowers, the other chanting VILLA VILLA VILLA in urgent capitals, held steaming tea. Pop spooned dazzling white sugar into one.

'Say when,' and his hand trembled avalanches over the side.

'When,' she replied and Blowbroth flashed her again with his two yellow beams. The tea was scalding, sweet and brown.

''Twas Eve's mug, that one, mate,' Pop said and Maggie's lips hovered at the floral rim. Her grandmother had been dead for years. She remembered nothing of her except the cool coiled rosary that poured out of her palm into Maggie's like rain. 'No one else ever 'ad that mug.'

She peered into its murky depths, searching for signs of the old woman's illness, and the colour of her death stared back. The cancer had strangled her liver while her eyes turned black. Her seamstress's fingers fretted across the blanket as though she were still stitching. Pop had filled his wife up with sweetened tea until her breath was hot and rank. As her face began to shrink against the pillow her neat mouth murmured what could have been prayers. Closer though, Pop would hear that she was pleading, begging the ceiling for mercy in short, wispy sentences, repeated over like a benediction. At night she screamed.

He slurped up a slosh, slapped down his mug and tucked a cigarette between his lips. He looked at her squinting into her cup, hair all over.

He thought of the phone call to social services the day after the police had visited, the letter in his hand, the thin echo of his voice in the phone box. 'Sorry mate, can't do it. It's not possible, don't think so, no, it's not right at all, sorry.' And how he'd cursed himself afterwards for the way he'd sounded, like a coward, spineless, unheroic. He hurried back to the phone box to call them again, said he'd changed his mind about having her after all, and they said okay they'd send someone. So he set about convincing her, this woman who came with a file, with long thick brown hair falling over the pages as she wrote on them. Then the day he drove to Birmingham New Street to collect Maggie, how he'd cursed himself again and his child her mother, and her father and the Department of Health and Social Security and regretted his urge to prove himself a hero and regretted it still.

'Paper?' he mumbled, offering her the *Daily Mirror*, folded neat as a napkin. 'Highest unemployment since the war. Hope you're not after a ruddy job, mate.'

Sittingbourne

Only a few weeks earlier in temperatures of eighty-four degrees Fahrenheit, the hottest July day of 1975, Maggie M. Merriman had walked from her house in Kent across a melting black tar road through the eye of a softly barrelling storm of meadow-thistle seeds. She walked in a straight line. Waxy seals of warm tar pressed from her heel into a dock and daisy verge on the other side while tufts of thistle floated down to the road and were held like feathers. She wanted to see how much water was left in the thin stream that leaked across the housing estate. The rushing-water skirts laced with froth that had snatched her waist and swayed her hips now fell limp around her ankles. The dock-clad bank was turning as crisp and withered as dry tobacco. Dashing left and right were jagged cracks, splitting the earth into jigsaw pieces, pausing at the black roads oozing and stinking now as ancient peatbogs, and hurrying off again on the other side. Everything was shrinking, liquefying, disintegrating under a great gonging sun rolling in a big tin sky. Grasshoppers creaked in the grass and paused, bees big as airships purred past, weaving through the thick air. Distant car engines and the clang of hammering swam lazily, lost and distorted.

She slid her thumb over the dial of her transistor radio, slowly, to tantalise the silence, until big-city soul music rolled out like reinforced concrete. A vast juggernaut of sound, anthem to New York City, roaring its optimism across the rows of empty driveways and out to the houses on the edges of the estate that were wobbling in the heat haze, pushing back the neat lawns and shrubberies and Austin Maxis until the mighty do-right multi-storey voices were high and wide as a Manhattan sky.

Further upstream there was a copse of tangled wilderness where foxes, adders and voles hid, and across the stream from that a large field dashing with rabbits, containing an enormous square-shaped horse wearing a blank expression. Guarding this boundary that marked the front line of the advancing new housing estate was a squadron of yellow diggers and bulldozers that rested for long intervals between bouts of Jurassic destruction. Clumps of scrub, brush and nettles rose defiantly in their path only to be chewed into pieces by the hungry metal teeth. There were some thuggish-looking trees with amputated stumps out of which new shoots sprouted spikes. When the sun bowed low behind them they stood like warrior gangs, threatening retaliation. In spite of the army of machinery and batches of hollering families – each with its hot metal car and coiling hosepipe – the corner of surviving countryside remained infested with wildlife. The heatwave sent all the local creatures cringing to the stream. The corpulent cats with their addresses on their collars caught fistfuls of mice. The podgy boy with thin calves found a dead grass snake in the road and paraded it up and down dangling on the end of a stick, until his elder brother got hold of it and tied it around the rear-view mirror of his Ford Capri that loud-hailed Black Sabbath and Thin Lizzy like an election campaign. The women backcombed the sweat of the day into their hair every evening and a group met regularly around a biscuit tin to tap teaspoons and roll their eyes. The missing link had been discovered, its name was Lucy, it was three feet tall and it had lived in Africa. Fat lot of help that was then.

Maggie pounded rhythms on the big oil drum that stood abandoned on the wilderness boundary, leaving smears of rust the colour of ox blood to dry on her palms. She liked to hang upside down from a particular alder, her long feet hooked over a horizontal branch, watching the inverted square horse with the catatonic gaze. *Tears on My Pillow*, Johnny Nash, the radio played the same songs in any position. The disc jockeys prattling in their eerily glad voices, chuckling at their own drollery, their quips, the one-liners, off the cuff.

Droll quips, one-liners, catchphrases, Maggie kept a store. Her heroes were the past masters, the middle-aged comedians with their thick skin and long faces, grave under the weight of serious comedy. She watched their Saturday-night slots and their Royal Command performances, kneeling before the small screen, respectful and attentive, not laughing but listening. Ken Dodd, Dick Emery, Les Dawson, Larry Grayson, Eric and Ernie. She had the walk and the talk, the seems like a nice boy excuse me missus innit marvellous shut that door and it's goodnight from him. Could knock off *Bring Me Sunshine* slick as you like with all the dainty skips and wing elbows; floated arms and legs in shop doorways like Harry Worth; slunk across the common as Max

Wall, a perfect crouching squat, past the cricket practice, like a chair had been whipped out from under her, snapping glances left and right. She kept jokes stockpiled in categories in her head. She Tommy Coopered with dabbing hands and tucked chin, checking the effect in reflective surfaces, practising at the mirror, experimenting on her mother, who stared unblinking right through her and out the other side as if Maggie had accidentally hypnotised her with the quick just-like-that moves.

There were blood-curdling screams and blue-murder yelling from the estate kids. A troop of them would thunder-charge past on foot and Chopper bikes, leaving a roar of profanity, belches and vile insults burning in the air, a legion set off on some terrible crusade.

With a cynical audience of some eight or nine looking on, Maggie drew a breath, pinched her nose and pushed against the pressure, in the hope of making her ears bleed to prove to her crowd of disbelievers that she had X-ray vision and sonic hearing. A boy with alligator eyes calmly watched her fail and then pulled a trembling caterpillar of snot from his nostril, stealing her moment and crushing her power. To consolidate his superiority he swung it into her hair.

'Ha bloody ha,' Maggie said. 'Nice one, pop-picker.'

'Ughh,' cried everyone else and ran away.

'Oi, scuse me, missus!' Maggie called, trailing after them, hauling some back. 'What a wonderful day for sticking a hosepipe up your trouser leg and singing . . .'

It didn't really work without the tickling stick, but she pressed on anyway. At the end they listened to the sound of a car reversing. Maggie snickered, high-shouldered, rocking forward to prompt them. A couple of them brayed nervously, eyes sliding to check the others. She often told jokes she didn't understand; it was awkward when she was asked to explain. This was one of those times. 'Ooh you are awful,' she piped shrilly instead, 'but I like you,' and pushed herself into the scaly male fern.

Then her mother died unexpectedly. Exactly a week after her thirteenth birthday. Misadventure they called it, as though she'd been a compulsive thrill-seeker. Maggie knew better. She knew something they didn't. She kept it to herself. Miss Adventure. She added seven and thirteen in case the sum revealed an answer. Twenty was the age her mother had been when she was born. The whole universe is mathematical, her father had told her. Everything under the sun is maths. You can solve anything at all numerically. Maggie had difficulty with numbers but she knew now absolutely and quite conclusively that thirteen was unlucky and that life was a serious business, joking aside.

Her mother had believed in destiny, in kismet, a cherished word she spoke with precise lips and amazed eyes like a word from a magic spell. She had long ago disposed of the Catholic girl she'd once been. She and Maggie no longer went to bow their heads at Mass. These days she was in touch with the universe and all its mysteries, karmicly, astrally, the Kabbala, the kismet, the *que sera*. She liked to tease the gods, however; she chose not to look when she reversed out of the driveway, she carried a rabbit's foot instead. She liked to test her luck. She had written her own obituary which included things she hadn't yet done. Second thoughts were the only thing she feared.

'No regrets on my deathbed, thank you,' she intoned daily, like a baroque message for the milkman.

★ ★ ★

She and her mother had driven to the seaside town of Rottingdean to celebrate her unlucky anniversary. For a treat, they had eaten fish and chips and giant banana splits in a deserted restaurant.

In the old days when they had lived a few miles away in Lewes, the trip had been made as a family. Maggie's father, the family's only other member, would be splayed behind the wheel of their Ford Cortina, his elbow slung through the open window while Tammy Wynette and George Jones sang *We Must Have Been Out of Our Minds* on cassette. Maggie's mother, wrapped in a short violet raincoat, still and strange as a mermaid, gazed through black sunglasses at the bedraggled countryside, her sighs clouding tiny haloes against the passenger window. Her father joined the chorus with high-pitched American vowels, not at home in his Maidstone mouth. Gear changes with the key changes, up and down. The smoke from their cigarettes twisting into a single cloud above the dashboard and hanging there. An elbow each out of the windows now, wing fins, and Maggie, halfway across the back seat to be opposite the music, their impartial pilot, watching the runway of road rushing between their heads towards her.

Rottingdean. Maggie had conjured images of beaches littered with the corpses of devout men in cassocks and whirling seagulls screaming over the prize of their eyeballs. She had been disappointed that first trip to discover a lonely place, cheerfully sedated, patrolled by the elderly and the infirm, whose only resident fiend was the cruel whipping wind. The whole of *The Twelfth of Never* while waiting in the queue. Three heads pointed south, east and west. Crunching tyres over the stony-shingle car park, past the nodding attendant, rosy skinned in his official coat, shiny coins in his hand, nice day for it in his mouth. 'Rottingdean', now cut prettily from coloured paper, hung like a new-year decoration in her head. Ahead of them, filling the windscreen, the grey-blue chop of the English Channel, an undecided two-tone sky above. Car doors to be arm-wrestled on one side and torn out of hands on the other. Then the japey punch in the face, the clout of salt wind, right on the nose, an English wind. Bop. Biff on the conk, right where you stand, no funny business, smack dab on your hooter, fair's fair. And the Channel's rushing roar from France behind, foaming at the mouth and on to the beaches where we are not afraid to fight them, our mortal enemy or anyone else for that matter. Thick swipes of salt clotting everyone's hair and seasoning cheeks. Whipped off the sea on a swerving wind that shoves to get past, cuts voices into ribbons.

They bought a beach-ball splashed with the colours of the rainbow and Maggie carried it, solemn referee leading her wordless team of two to the beach. Her father was expert with a football. She and her mother watched while he dribbled and headed and juggled. Maggie saw her own amazed eyebrows rising, reflected in the bluebottle lenses of her mother's sunglasses. Underneath, her mother's drooping mouth, waxy with lipstick, an avenging shade of plum. He urged Maggie to tackle him but every time she did he'd twist and buck and the ball would spin away with him while she fell through empty air. Her mother shouted through the wind at him to grow up for crying out loud, Christ sake, Jesus. And eventually he headed the ball in Maggie's direction and lit a cigarette.

She mimicked his prancing for a while, a bit of Pelé, a bit of Best, and then flicked the ball into a funnel of wind which carried it like an asteroid down the beach. She tore after it, swerving through the straggle of some other family, crashing through their shrieks, sprinting in a perpetual falling motion with the wind at her back until her legs began to fold. It flew faster until its blur of spinning rainbow colours disappeared off the edge of the earth. She paused to acknowledge that it had gone and that they were now ball-less as a family, which deprived them temporarily of a recreational reason to be on the beach as a team. This left them with the contemplative ocean-gazers whose lives were falling apart.

She walked back against the wind, crouching into a Max Wall to lift their spirits. 'Very funny,' her father invariably commented. She planted long feet towards them and crunched across the stones on bent knees, rubber-necked, furtive and urgent. Far up the beach she could make out the solitary cigarillo shape of him at the water's edge. She raised her arms in a big semaphore shrug to inform him of their loss before she noticed he was turned towards the ocean, staring out at its hazy infinity. Several yards behind him, huddled behind a windbreak, sat the purple bruise of her mother, swaddled in her violet raincoat with her Dunhill Longs, repeatedly attempting to strike a match in the cross-wind. Above them, from a rushing sky, the seagulls' songs fell down.

Not long afterwards Maggie's father disappeared into the world in search of himself. Retail had made him ill. 'This job is gonna kill me,' he muttered through a cupped hand. He had ulcers, asthma, paranoia, and now his hair was falling out. He said, 'My life is a joke,' as though he'd been the comedian in the household all along and everyone had forgotten to laugh. Every Saturday morning he'd soaped the Cortina and blasted it with a jerking hosepipe like a firefighter. He drove it away, still dripping, Glen Campbell's *Rhinestone Cowboy* blasting through the driver's window where he kept his elbow.

Her mother knew he'd gone when she discovered the empty space in the wardrobe where his snakeskin-effect boots had stood. The divorce papers duly arrived. Then there was a postcard for Maggie from Tennessee. She looked for it on her twirling globe. A little below Tennessee she noticed the word Birmingham.

She thought of the way he used to shave with his head on one side and sing. *I have been a rover, I have walked alone . . .* Counting how many good years he had left in him . . . *Once in a while along the way love's been good to me . . .* The music was always in his ears and some line about believin' or the Delta in his mouth. He'd just got born in the wrong place, that was all. Maidstone when it should have been Mississippi.

There was a girl in Portland . . . And the one about God didn't make the little green apples, and it don't rain in Indianapolis in the summertime. It rained in Sittingbourne alright, until now.

Her mother caught the incurable disease known as tiredness, diagnosed by the GP as exhaustion, dash, depression, and they were in real danger of becoming an unremarkable tragedy as a family. She said 'Christ' frequently in a variety of voices. She let off ghostly cries that lifted Maggie's hair from her scalp, breathily faint but unstoppable, like a person's last breath. Like the final distant wail of a suicide falling through twenty floors' worth of rushing air.

She played her father's country records, including his entire collection of Bobbie Gentry, on repeat in her room until she knew the words to *Mississippi Delta*, *Natural to Be Gone*, *Greyhound Goin' Somewhere*.

She lay face-down on the talc-flecked carpet like a domestic-murder victim, half dressed in shorts and a pyjama shirt amid a detritus of Big Hits LPs. Every now and then she got up to check her profile in the mirror. She railed chorus harmonies at her reflection, singing back at herself in perfect sync like Anni-Frid and Agnetha before sliding to the floor again. The window held a square of swimming-lesson blue, an uncorruptible sky, sapphire as Our Lady's robes. She listened to country records until she could drawl the verses in a preacher's-daughter whine. *Your Cheatin' Heart*, Hank Williams, *He'll Have to Go*, Jim Reeves, *I Can't Stop Loving You*, Ray Charles, *By the Time I Get to Phoenix*, *Galveston*, *Wichita Lineman*, Glen Campbell, *She Thinks I Still Care*, George Jones.

Songs about people who were always walking out and walking back in again. Songs about people who were sorry and about some who weren't. Songs about people who were looking for love, about some who'd found love and others who were trying to avoid it at any cost. Songs about drinking to remember and drinking to forget. Like one of these her mother turned to bottles of Southern Comfort and Cinzano Bianco for restoration.

The heatwave was the daily news; no one talked about anything else. There were announcements, bulletins, dos and don'ts. Some people's pets died and then some people died, it was war. First hosepipes were banned, then baths, then lavatory-flushing, washing was discouraged. Broken-hearted gardeners wept over their borders.

In the beginning the heat had been celebrated. Wire chairs and gaudy cushions were dragged into gardens up and down the country. Paddling pools, ice lollies and dimpled flesh turned the south of England's sober suburbia into a poor man's Riviera. Doors and windows were flung open so that family mealtimes, complete with accusatory arguments and other hair-raising intimacies, were aired operatically alfresco, continental-style, for the whole neighbourhood to hear. Whiffs of food, howls of boredom and casual cruelties floated about, bobbing like garbage in polluted water, washing over fences and up shingle-effect driveways, betraying secrets from within. Then as the drought became official, the celebrating ceased and the carping began.

Maggie watched all the green fade until the estate was dusty dry in shades of sand and tan, the colours of the places in the songs that had called out to her father and claimed him: Memphis, Nashville, New Orleans, Baton Rouge. There he was, or thereabouts, Tennessee, Mississippi, Louisiana, wanderer cowboy from Kent, hound-dogging around the southern states of America while right here in Sittingbourne his little housing estate had turned with a chameleon's accuracy to the colours that were in his soul.

Connecting the sections of estate turned desert were the black treacle roads they called drives, melted and pungent as the day they were laid, forcing cars to creep along, lacing the whole area with the smell of a burning oil spill.

Everything became eerily still as though a tragedy had struck. As though the brick boxes contained dead families slumped around *Love Thy Neighbour* and *The Benny Hill Show*; as if they had suffered an alien invasion or a chemical leak. She caught the occasional glimpse of a person hauling Tesco bags out of a car boot or yelling at a galumphing dog, always sleek and stupid breeds, red setter, Dalmatian, Afghan. But mostly nobody dared move lest the sun zapped them, just some lone child bouncing through the heat haze on a tangerine space hopper. She heard isolated sounds, strangely amplified, a distant car engine, a solitary dog bark, the clatter of some metal object to the ground, a door slam. An absence of birdsong and a doom-laden stillness hanging in its place. Maggie watched *The Clangers* in a stupor while the growling diggers ate the field, bite-size pieces at a time.

She was playing *Ode To Billie Joe*, it just so happened, on a June day like the song says. A general stench of tanning oil, petrol, dog shit, barbecues, tar, dustbins and creosote. Everybody gasping in their brick boxes wishing they were dead. Her mother had been drinking Tia Maria with ice and was now collapsed on a sun lounger in the back garden in a shiny gold bikini, burning slowly crimson as though she had been struck suddenly by mortal shame. Some of the asphalt roofs on the estate were softening, turning to goo like marzipan houses. The faint sound of Jonathan King's *Everyone's Gone to the Moon* drifted into the bedroom where Maggie lay murdered on the carpet as usual, asphyxiated by boredom. From the window she'd seen her mother sprawled below, as if King Kong had dropped her, an afternoon shadow slanted across her legs, amputating them at the thigh. The entire family now in white chalk outlines and no Kojak strolling around with a lollipop to solve it all.

She sat in front of the fridge in her underwear with the door open, her back to the shelves, while it moaned and shuddered in protest. She drank Tizer from the bottle until her lips were stiff with sugar and unleashed great blasting belches that sent the cat skidding in terror. In the next room on the stereogram, Bobbie Gentry sang about the Mississippi delta, the Tallahatchie bridge, biscuits, black-eyed peas. Her mother's face appeared suddenly at the window. Something flew in Maggie's chest; the shock rushed through her skin, prickling down to her feet.

'Hey, hiya Mum, okay?' to reassure herself, not expecting her to hear. The face swam through the glass, eyes floating adrift in their sockets, cut loose from their brain. Maggie could hear the scuffing of her mother's feet below the window, struggling for balance, saw her start to smile, slow and slippery.

'Hi, sweetheart.' Her mother's mouth made shapes and Maggie listened to the hum of her voice on the glass. Then she pressed against it and blew a gauzy cloud. Her mother pulled back and grimaced before opening her mouth wide as if in amazement. From one of her punch-drunk eyes, an escaping tear. She choked and held out her tongue like they used to at Communion before they all went off the rails, and then the noise came. She'd started to make the noise a while before Maggie's father had booked his ticket to America and may well have speeded up the whole process with it. It would start as a high-pitched whine in her head and fall through her as though she were a deep-dug shaft, finally roaring out like a blitzkrieg of heavy artillery, obliterating anyone in the line of fire.

Maggie watched impassively from her ice cave. Suddenly her mother appeared to notice her. She tapped twice smartly against the glass as though she had not had Maggie's attention until now. The fridge trembled and began a low, steady hum in the key of G, as though they might all burst into song like the Partridge Family.

'Piss off!' her mother shrieked and waved her arms at some invisible interloper. This action sent her spinning out of view for a moment, and then came the skid of her feet towards the back door.

Her mother had a way of yanking down door handles for her exits and entrances that suggested the priming of a rifle, swiftly followed by a resounding slam, effecting the explosion of the shot. The simulation was only half performed today as she struggled, swaying like a seahorse, to remember why she had come in at all, and so the door hung unfired and forgotten.

'Swarms of wasps!' She was shrill with outrage. 'Kill you if you're allergic.' She wheeled around in an apparent search for something until, tiring and losing interest, she paused long enough in front of Maggie to take her in. There were a few moments' silence between them, in memoriam, followed by a 'Christ' as she left, and finally a bawled 'God' from the next room, before the cha-clunk of the handle and the boom of the slam.

Maggie sat in the humming vibrations until she became aware

of a saline prickling and something cool lapping. Underneath her a lake of urine stretched like the Caspian Sea across the yellow swirls in the linoleum, pointing accusing fingers in all directions around the room.

Four Oaks

At midday they walk, a mad dog and two tall Englishmen, to the Fox and Dogs under a big trembling sun. The heat nails them into the earth, hammers them down like tent pegs. Maggie sways under her blindfold hair, narrows her eyes against the glare that leaps off metal and glass. Cortinas creak, windows burn, streets lie deserted. An exotic new dust, straight out of a spaghetti western, lines the gutters, coating windscreens and dying gardens. She strides stiffly on locked knees to miss the paving cracks.

'Right. Okay, mate. This'll do.' Pop turns and points with his cigarette towards the bus stop.

'Due south, Sutton town centre, Villa Park and Birmingham, mate. To the west, Walsall, Wolverhampton and Welsh Wales. To the east . . .' he swings his arm suddenly, swiping over her head, 'Atherstone and Nuneaton. To the north-east, Tamworth.' She doesn't listen, but nods once or twice, head down to hide her embarrassment. To be here or to be there, lost in the wildernesses of Walsall or Wolverhampton – there is very little in it. She is cheered by the wanton carelessness of not paying attention. He continues dispatching directions east and west. It is her bearings he is concerned about. Maggie supposed her bearings were lost without hope of recovery. On he drills, north pole, south pole, beggar man, thief. This is what he can do, he can offer her the comfort of map co-ordinates. You are here. He is pleased with his geographical dissertation, the accuracy of it, the enlightening orientation. The education of Maggie M. Merriman.

'Okay, mate?' he says and slaps her on the back.

They take a short detour around the Dugdale estate for Pop's fags at the newsagents on Bodington Road, next to Hall the general grocer and the Charisma hair studio with its posse of hood dryers lined up in the window like gossiping daleks. There is a single sycamore on the green at Dugdale Crescent that makes Maggie think of hangman. They set off again. She tears open a raspberry Mivvi that is already melting, spotting the pavement with a trail of red.

Blowbroth checks the Little Sutton post office where Dolly Minski is often found, leaning on the counter winking indiscriminately, chatting to her friend Dor the postmistress, purveyor of all local gossip, news and scandal. But not today, just the boy who is not right, always by the greetings cards in a Villa shirt grinning broadly, making vowel sounds. Pop is gleaming like a navvy in his shirtsleeves.

'Father Forgive,' begs the notice outside the Baptist church in long, pious letters.

'Christ alive, it's hot,' Pop heckles as they pass.

The Fox and Dogs is a cool, spotless oasis containing only a devoted few. A ting of till and beer glass, a low murmur of conversation, a gathering at matins. They scrape back two wooden chairs beside the dartboard. The horse brasses blaze on the walls, ignited by the sun; the bar is polished, the ale taps gleam. Pop exchanges jeers with the landlord, his high brow shiny as his brasses, tea towel over his shoulder should anything dare to dull.

Maggie and Blowbroth watch the apple in Pop's throat bouncing like a stopcock as the cold dark ale slides down.

He lights a cigarette. The pub is silent as a library.

24

'Brian Godfrey, Mike Ferguson, Dick Edwards,' he creaks in a high-pitched strain in deference to the peace. 'They all drank here, '68, '69. Knew them well enough to speak to, mate.' Girl and dog wait patiently. Maggie blinks under her Berlin Wall of fringe. He tries to think of something to interest her. He is surprised to realise that he wants to. Unable to think of anything suitable, he presses on.

'Three great Villa players,' he creaks again, at an even higher pitch. The shiny landlord looks up.

'Never passed a ball in his whole damn life, Ferguson. Brian used to say, "When we're tired we give the bleedin' ball to Fergie, mate." Never passed a ball.' He pauses to release an explosive cough that rings off the horse brasses. 'Players lived locally in those days. Tommy Docherty put a stop to it in the end, fans complaining, y'know, saw them drinking the night before, that kind of thing. No pleasing some people. Great, but not the greatest, not for my money anyhow. No, the greatest player we ever had, mate, was Billy Walker. And Pongo Waring of course, and if it's a hat trick you're after you can have Harry Hampton, mate, the Wellington Whirlwind, score a goal with his bloody teeth.'

He clears his throat. Well, what did she expect? He watches her. Bored probably, hard to tell through the hair. Bugger it. He twists round in his chair.

'Ready for me this year then, are you?' he calls to the landlord.

'Ready or not, Arthur, here you will come, I fear.'

His face reels back, bright with glee, and he jerks his head towards a felt-tipped poster on the door. 'Read that out then, mate.'

Maggie lifts her hair and murmurs through the higgledy words:

PUB quiz. SaturdAy 23rd August 8pm.
1st PRIZE £5 AND a gallon of BEER.

The dog looks from her to Pop and back.

'One for your annals this year, mate,' he calls out to the landlord again. 'Catch me if you damn well can.' And he winks a shining eye at Maggie.

The Slang

A diamond-winged buzzard, dark as an ink blot, is circling high in the aquamarine, far above the earth, like the turning of time.

Girl and old man are leaning back and sliding, which is the only way to do it along The Slang, with its sudden plunging drops and about-face inclines. Always changing its mind, the meandering sand-soil and gravel path at the bottom of Grange Lane wanders through barley and wheat fields until the Hillwood Road, where it halts abruptly opposite the White Hart as if it's dashed in for a drink and never come out again; which is, Maggie guesses, the other reason they are on it. The official reason for this expedition, however, is to see a blind horse in the flesh. A field trip. The further education of Maggie M. Merriman.

Pop is pleased with himself. All lasses like horses: it's like kids and Santa Claus, done deal. The breeze is hazy with airborne seeds. Giant cow parsley sways against their shoulders and the arching stems, like ballerinas' spines, of pendulous sedge grasses droop around their knees.

The air drags sound around lazily, noise registering moments after the connected action. From as far away as Lichfield and the Driffold, an engine, a shout, distorted and distant as though pushed through water, lulling the earth to sleep.

'Every inch of his field, knows it like a map in his brain,' he calls over his shoulder. 'Every last inch. He can't be moved.' She feels the sun baking her hair until it smells sweet on the dry bone of her skull.

'Wouldn't shoot the bugger, not the heart. Flat refused.' He turns to face her, leans closer. 'Milk eyes it's got, like a spook,' he hisses and grins ecstatically with saucer eyes before they continue, a comma of his cackle floating over their heads. She wants to see it, is looking forward to it now, the optimism sends her glance up to the sky. The sun scorches her face, twists it into a squint as she scans for the buzzard. It flaps its wings once, slowly, like a swimmer turning, such a perfect circle, one o'clock, two o'clock, three o'clock. The skin across her temples chills, tightens, and blushes a dark rose. Her head hums, full of heat and dust. Ahead, Pop's pink pate bobs like a luminous lifebuoy in a sea of cigarette smoke. The heat has put a tune in his heart.

> *They're digging up Father's grave to build a sewer,*
> *They're digging it up regardless of expense . . .*

He pauses repeatedly mid-verse to cough. Great choking blasts barrelling across the fields, on their way to eardrums waiting in Lichfield and the Driffold. When the attack subsides he relights his cigarette.

'Bloody choke you to death this barley will.'

The television mast, tall and precise as a tuning fork, is looming behind them. Pop mounts the stile at the boundary of Hillside Farm, cigarette between teeth, eyes narrowed, and winks as he dismounts on the other side. Blowbroth scrabbles under it, quick as liquid, demented by the sudden countryside, gripped by a pastoral violence and quivering with instincts. His sneer is dissolving to reveal the malevolent, hard-nosed rat catcher he actually is.

The path that will take them down to the farm is decked high on both sides with a wild and teeming tangle of hedgerow and nettles, strung between birch and oak and hung temptingly with dark, swollen blackberries and pale catkin tails. They troop idly through its magnificence; a bower made for a bride and groom; smoking, stumbling and coughing. Pop disappears behind a tree to urinate.

'Twenty gallons of water a day a mature oak draws. That is a fact.'

While she waits she spots an abandoned bird's egg, powder blue, slightly cracked, in a tangle of brush. It is cool as a church. When he reappears, she holds it high under his nose for inspection. 'Mistle thrush,' she gambles.

'Hedge sparrow,' he counters, one eye closed. Bugger it.

As the streets darken to mauve then to black and blue Pop snaps on a lamp, surprising a fly, and hands Maggie a book so heavy she and it almost go through the floor. *Encyclopaedia Britannica* it says, a vomit of letters; it lies across her knees, stopping the flow of blood.

'Ask me anything, anything at all, love, any subject you like.' He leans against the mantelpiece, his arms stretched out like a fighter at the ropes. 'Okay, commence.'

The pages fall left and right under her fingers, drawings of cloud formations, maps, a nebula, Descartes, Derbyshire.

'Devil's Island,' she says finally.

'Group of islands off French Guiana, penal colony, next.'

A veil of smoke falls over her head.

'Diaghilev.'

'What about him?'

'What's he then?'

'Ballet bloke . . . er, don't tell me, Russian.'

'Eros.'

'God of love, a lad, shoots with a bow and arrows, Greek.'

Maggie gazes up at him.

'Okay, mate? Just getting warm.'

'I want to go home.'

They look at one another through the drifts of tobacco mist. His eyes are wide, his mouth flutters the shape of an answer that he doesn't have. He thinks about points in the First Division to steady his panic. 'How about a biscuit?'

Her eyes drift. 'Okay.'

Kitchen cupboards slam-crash as he hurries, panic rising again. Flaming kids, he thinks, surprising himself, bloody hell. Then, steady on there, mate, steady on, arranging the biscuits on a plate in apology, tripping out with it held high next to a steward's grin, swooping the plate before her. 'Any one you like.'

She takes one and so does he and their munching fills the hole in the room and raises the dog. Blowbroth slides in beside the plate, boss-eyed and drooling. Pop racks his brain for a topic of conversation and to his complete amazement nothing comes, so he helps himself to another biscuit and crunches and blinks through the discomfort. He tries again, skimming through subjects, items of interest, but nothing makes it into his mouth and he has to stuff another biscuit in instead. Maggie does too and the sound of gnashing custard creams is horrible, then bearable, then comforting. By the time the plate is empty he no longer wants to speak about anything. He picks his teeth and relaxes until it is completely dark outside.

'Good company you are, mate,' he says finally and realises it is true, actually.

Malc

Pop had a rival and his name was Malc. Malc had won the pub quiz three times in a row, a hat trick, which was a local record. He was on the brink of irrevocably ruining Pop's life. To cap it all Malc was a cheery bloke whom everyone appeared to like. Big and beery and sort of busted up as though bits of him had given way or snapped off. His clothes strained at their fastenings, a shelf of belly swung left and right, bumping people out of his path, sharp hair grew out of his ears and nostrils and the index finger of his left hand was missing. When he and Arthur occupied the same few square feet there was a crackle and snap in the air like you were ringside at an Ali–Frazier fight.

'Hail fellow, well met. Been swotting up, have we?'

Pop slowed his walk, poked out his chest, clamped his hand on his hip. 'No need this year, mate. Only got you to beat.' Laughter. One-nil.

'Hope you're still laughing on the night, Arthur.'

'Depends how funny you are, Malc.' More laughter.

'Oh ar, no bloody points scored for crummy jokes as far as I know.'

'Oh I dunno. I see you haven't done so bad, mate.'

And so on. Round and around they went until the beer unravelled their arguments, derailed all trains of thought.

'Run along, son, run along now,' Pop tushed, wafting his hand at Malc's table.

'Who the 'ell are you? Dixon of Dock Green?'

'Ask me again when you can do your trousers up.'

'Is your name Dixon?' Malc pressed.

'Question for *you*,' Pop resisted. 'Are you drunk or are you sober?'

'I'm asking, do you live in Dock Green? I'd like to know.'

'Things in heaven and earth we're not s'posed to know. You've got a lot to learn, Mr Hat Trick, son.'

'Are you a teacher? What do you teach, eh? Old dogs new tricks?'

A dry laugh, just the one, fell out in the corner. It was enough to take the fight out of Pop.

Pop's world was small in scale in spite of all the grandly sweeping statements and infinite store of reference and anecdote. His day folded neatly around three pubs, the Pint Pot on Tower Road, the Fox and Dogs on Sutton Lane and the Plough and Harrow on Slade Road, once known as Muffin's Den in the days when the highwaymen rode, making a triangle that placed him back where he started again, three pints of ale wiser.

His other passions included Sutton Park, Aston Villa Football Club (whose home matches his elder brother had taken him to see as an infant, travelling backwards in the bicycle basket) and explaining little-known facts to the uninitiated. When stuck for a fact he could produce a statistic, palindrome, insult, quote from obscure literature, or weather forecast without pausing to think. He was a creature of habit. It never occurred to him to live any other way, and he hid his deep mistrust of anything new by feigning a mocking disinterest. He was wholly insensitive to the needs of others, although he would on occasion reward a long-term listener's patience by interrupting himself with an intermission of jokes, rhymes, songs and broadsides. But mostly he held conversations as though the form were word association, as though at the close one party were the winner and the other the loser. His face shone whenever he spoke and clouded when he was required to listen, his eyes narrowing with suspicion, alert for the trick, the dupe. His mouth would flurry word shapes while others spoke and behind his eyes the oranges, cherries and lemons spun in a blur of likelihoods, current form and points per subject. His stash of scores, dates and tropical diseases was alarming.

This information was both his sword and his shield; it would lead him inexorably through the chaos to the Holy Grail, the promised land, the end of the rainbow. His vanity encouraged him to improvise when in trouble and he was never beyond leaping in with someone's punch-line, finishing their sentence, or offering superior adjectives as they attempted a story of their own. By the end of that week Maggie was entirely accustomed to her mediating role, keeping score between Pop and some cornered innocent, while she read on the back of a crisp packet the address to which complaints should be sent.

The Pint Pot

A blanket stitch of neat gardens and little gates hemmed the curving ribbon of Tower Road. Their feet slapped the hot pavement in a steady spattering repetition, reminiscent of rainfall, badly needed now, a distant memory for most. Blowbroth was ahead, nosying around, pausing at tyres and gates, sniffing other people's comings and goings. The Pint Pot on the corner was a small black and white Tudor house, its unlikely trade within was advertised by a scarlet panel declaring 'Ansell's' and 'The

Pint Pot' in large gold letters under a foaming gold jug. Their arrival brought the total number of customers that morning to seven including the landlady, which filled it comfortably. They stepped out of the raucous sunshine and din of birdsong into a dark stillness. Inside it was impossible to tell the time of day, or the season; it was like moving out of time. In the shadows the tiny interior was crammed with what chairs and tables it could hold. Rearing up on all sides were sheer cliff faces of Staffordshire pottery, stacked on shelves climbing as high as the ceiling. Dishes, ducks, jugs, spaniels, urchins, shepherds, serving girls, geese, cottages, penguins, figurines, pheasants, whole corps of toby jugs, bulldogs, teapots. An infinity of china, turning the room into a whirling grotto. A huge porcelain Dalmatian, his spots a suit of clubs, glared down at Blowbroth.

Pop's pint was pulling as they cleared a path through the obstacle course of tables and chairs. He ordered a ginger ale for Maggie.

'Thank you, my dear. Good morning,' he chimed courteously to the landlady and dropped a coin into the box for the lifeboatmen.

The landlady was vast, as big as a yeti. Under her chin her throat swung like a bison's. She moved slowly and deliberately and didn't trouble herself to smile or speak. One of the china-stacked walls was a partition that hid the off-licence shop on the other side, an even smaller room stuffed with bottles and crates. When the bell above its separate door tinged she lumbered through, disappearing behind the wall, and appearing wordlessly again, her approach heralded by a chorus of groans from the floorboards.

Pop's pint stood tall and commanding. Honeyed amber, swirling with secrets and crowned with a spun halo of cobweb froth, it smelled a thousand years old. If you didn't know better

33

you might believe it was planet earth's elixir, an ancient and magical potion brewed in the Garden of Eden. Maggie dipped her finger in. It was bitter as sand.

The other men sat each in his own cocoon of smoke, alone with his thoughts like an Orthodox order at meditation. The cash till was the only thing to shatter the peace. She caught a glimpse of white belly flesh, the old boy in the wrinkled grey suit, the zip yawning while he considered the wall. She looked away. Pop was shifting in his seat and flinching his glance around. He was going to speak. She turned her crisp bag over to read the free offer and address.

'Incredible really, that we can get on with the Russians in space but not down here on earth, funny that.' The other men looked over from their smoke pods. Maggie spotted a china Pierrot on a shelf, in a heap with his head in his hands.

'Russians?' one of them eventually said.

'Apollo Eighteen and Soyuz Nineteen, joint flight and link-up in outer space, mate,' Pop explained exultantly. One-nil.

'Oh ar,' someone said.

'No gravity in space,' another mumbled for a bonus point.

'Difficult language, Russian.' The man with the cap again.

'Not if you're Russian it ain't.'

'A Russian ballerina defecated last year.'

'Morning, Dusty.'

Another old boy in a short mac letting in an explosion of sunshine. The door closed and he blinked his way to the bar.

'No language barriers in space, are there?' A small reflective pause, no conferring.

'What ruddy language do they speak in space then?'

'Some universal tongue.'

'Don't be bloody daft.'

'Latin.'

'*Latin?*'

'Eh?'

'Oh ar, it's often used in important ceremonies. Occasions of state. International summits. Investitures.'

'*Utcumque placuerit Deo*, mate.'

No one replies, the final word is his. A blinding victory. He grins left and right, brimming, mouthing the Latin words silently to himself again. Checking the bar to see if the yeti noticed. Ordering a round, on him, to be sure.

Maggie May

Margaret Mary became Maggie May in 1971 after the Rod Stewart song reached number one in the hit parade. Her father used it once and she was never Margaret Mary again, she was a pop song, number one no less.

Her father called her by the song title for the rest of his life. It could have been worse. Rod sang to her in flapping shirtsleeves throughout her ninth year and when she became ten, the transistor radio she'd longed for in the window of Rumbelows – loving it until she licked the glass – was hers.

Maggie May Merriman, in the doctor's records and on school reports, a fact then. Initials that accurately spelled out a person with little to say, unless it was attached to a punch-line. Maggot, they called her in the playground. She watched them through the cords of bell-rope hair that hung across her eyes.

'My mother-in-law's so fat,' she murmured in the dinner queue at lunchtime, feet apart, hands in pockets; not easy Les Dawson, deceptive technique, timing almost imperceptible. When she'd finished she glanced at their dazed eyes and slack jaws. 'What?' said Julie Hart, gap-toothed, standing on one leg. Someone blew a ripping fart noise which set off a chain of convulsive laughter, instant as nerve gas, right along the line all the way to the custard vat.

Girls sat in pairs, silent as old men, over cat's cradle or swiping at jacks. Maggie liked to keep the little rubber ball in her mouth, which made her look sniffy and imperious. She sat on the oak stump, stiff and stony as the Red Queen, while girls sprang with flying hair over French skipping elastic and under the lasso of a long rope that dashed the ground with rhymes and songs. She hardly remembered the boys, the names but not the faces. There was a glamorous one who could stand up on his Chopper. David Harper, Ian Jolly, Steven Bone, they thundered from left to right and back in a rip of noise.

Maggie had inherited her father's and grandfather's height and long bones. She was built for shelf-stacking, for scaring crows. The jokes deflected the jibes, caught them mid-air and sent them back on a punch-line, boom-boom, mortar and grenade. She'd watched transfixed as Donald O'Connor danced up the walls . . . *just slip on a banana peel, the world's at your feet, make 'em laugh make 'em laugh make 'em laugh* . . . and a great round peg crashed into a great round hole.

She and her mother watched *The Golden Shot* together. It was the night before she died. Her mother's sharp elbow draped around her collarbone, as if they were a couple. The petite brass-haired hostess beamed cheeky-lovely out of the television set, the place her mother would have given all her limbs to live in. She watched it with a terrible longing that atrophied into envy as she drained her third drink. If she could have crawled in through the grey square of light like a big, plastered Alice amok in Wonderland, she would have.

Maggie's mum was the estate's very own famous actress, whom no one could actually remember having ever seen in anything.

She never missed a quiz show, so sweet was the torture, but especially not *The Golden Shot* because she was convinced she'd met Anne Aston at an audition once. Miss Aston floated the contestants on and off, charting their course with pointy toes, indicating the scores with pointy fingers and most importantly measuring the arrow's distance from the bullseye – 'It's close, Bob' – at the centre of the apple. Maggie's mother inspected Anne's appearance each week – 'Christ alive, what's she wearing *now*?'

As far as Maggie could tell it was the same Peter Pan face and biggish knockers as the week before, but her mother noticed small things. Even during the clattering excitement of a bullseye hit that sent the lights around the apple flashing and the pirate's chest creaking open to reveal more light bulbs, she remained fastened to some detail of hair or wardrobe. Maggie watched Miss Aston's artful-dodger grin for clues. Her mother issued terse commands in a low voice as though she were in radio contact. 'Oh God, straighten your hem, Anne, smaller strides, Christ sake. Pause and smile . . . PAUSE, ANNE!' For the glowing Bob Monkhouse a sigh, a shake of her head and a simple mantra. 'So professional, so professional, people have absolutely no idea what it takes, no idea, so professional.'

Her mother had calculated that if she had Anne Aston's job, life would be a cinch. That this job, or one very similar, perhaps for a rival channel, was the key to everlasting peace of mind. She got it into her head that Miss Aston took it all for granted. 'Try mine for a day, you brassy cow,' she scolded her.

She placed trembling bowls of alphabet soup on the floral tablecloth. Her mother made 'bob' and 'gob' out of her letters and then 'stir'. Maggie saw an *h* and realised if she could find a *c* then she could show her mother she'd made 'Christ'. Maggie made 'sin' and then found *g*, *e*, and *r* to make 'singer'. The Greek key design around the bowls in two-tone brown and marmalade sent her giddy. When she glanced away it continued to blaze for a few seconds across everything else. The hot soup made them sweat and the rising steam made their noses run, so that they sniffed loudly one after the other, like a polite conversation.

Her mother took her hand and squeezed it. 'Love you, sweetheart. You're my little baby. You're all I've got.' And she started to cry as she realised that this enormous, elongating child, staring gravely at her out of a bony, bloodless face, was it, was what she'd got.

The Ford Anglia Deluxe Saloon

They walked off the ale in Sutton Park. Along the broad, low-lying path known as the Gum Slade, lined with towering trees rising heavenwards. Beneath the creaking and moaning branches, a requiem led by a murmuring clergy of ancient oaks. The air there was cool, shaded from the sun under vast canopies while sprightlier birches and yews threw shapes across the paths, wild patterns shattering through sunlight.

They had to walk almost everywhere. Pop drove an old pale-green Ford Anglia Deluxe Saloon, but it was prone to mechanical problems and he would punish it by ignoring it for extended periods. He would stroll casually by on the street, past

38

the driver's door, whistling theatrically, as though he'd never set eyes on it before, while its grimy headlights gawped wide.

It worked, strangely. When he sensed sufficient time had elapsed Pop would pounce, quick as a car thief, wielding the little metal key like a switchblade, and the car's engine would clatter into life first time.

'Take machinery by surprise,' he explained, winking. 'Never fails.'

He drove it like a tank, in a state of manic alertness, swiping at the gearstick and wrestling the wheel. Bombasting his way across junctions and roundabouts. He issued commands and shouted abuse at it, window down, turning the heads of pedestrians and other drivers in his path. The interior of the car was a crematorium of ash, like bowling along in a remembrance casket. It flew from the end of his cigarette in the slipstream funnelling through the open window, and the grey flecks danced around like those little water-filled snow scenes when shaken. He ignored the rear-view mirror, considered it a distraction, a causer of accidents. He arm-wrestled every gear, ignoring its shrieks and groans, while his passengers were shipwrecked back and forward.

'Second, you bastard, SECOND! Christ! Not fit for scrap, you aren't.'

On inclines, he leant forward over the steering wheel, Maggie likewise, persuaded by his example, and eventually they fell together with every turn like a yacht race team. Going downhill, Pop's technique was to knock the stick out of gear and coast down in neutral, tobogganing, with the engine quiet and the only sound the tyres peeling along at increasing speed. He preferred to coast to a stop too, so they arrived everywhere in silence, gliding to the halt that would pitch them towards the dashboard and back again as he stamped on the brake. He was incapable of parking and left the Anglia at wild angles, like an abandoned getaway vehicle.

'Parking's for women, mate,' he said with a flirty wink.

While driving, his hands were frantically busy with fag-lighting and smoking, smoothing down his hair, thumping the dashboard to cure mysterious rattles, waving pedestrians impatiently over crossings, shaking his fist at other road users and winding his window up and down. When necessary he steered with his knees. The Anglia could reach alarming speeds if the road was long and straight enough.

The Lichfield Road into Bassetts Pole is such a road. Long and straight through cow-parsley verges. Left and right lush fields lie stained in consecrated colours. Blocks of gold and green, a rip tide feathering across on a breeze. Poppies, tentative on their thin stems, crowding together for strength in numbers until they drench a meadow scarlet, the colour of sacrifice, Amen. Then an ecstatic blaze of yellow rape, like the sun has fallen into the field. Hiding its brightness behind a hawthorn hedge and bursting out again for a surprise, blinding you, ha ha, and racing away over farmland into Staffordshire. The car hurling along in a warm flapping wind, the smell of baking leather and leaking oil. Maggie lets the rush hold her and the wind dry her tongue, all of it sweeter for the wild water-bed suspension and the lawlessness of their miles per hour. Pop knocks out of gear at high speed and they career into the car park of the Bassetts Pole pub, bouncing and skidding in a cloud of dust and shower of stones like Bonnie and Clyde.

The ale is dark and very bitter at the pub in Bassetts Pole. The yeasty tang of it unravels towards the A38, tempting those it can reach with its promise of dank, delicious relief. It is a whitewashed pub with a slate-tile roof, cosy as a cottage, with inglenook fireplaces inside and twisted apple trees in the garden. Maggie blows away the time from dandelion heads, one o'clock, two o'clock, and watches the seeds set sail on the wind. She lies on the Stafford–Warwick border, a post marks the spot, her face full of daisies, searching out four-leaf clovers for luck. The landlord is suspicious that Maggie may be a child in spite of her height, which is why she is face-down on a famous boundary between two A roads. Dogs are allowed of course, curled around the pairs of jumbled feet that point towards the ale taps. She can see the men in her mind's eye, silent and still in the shadows, lifting tall glasses between ticks of the clock, clearing their throats but never speaking.

A plaque is fixed to the boundary post, black slate, cool to the touch.

Erected to the memory of Captain J.H.W. Wilkinson and his comrades of the Staffordshire Regiments who fell in the Great War 1914–1918.

She has seen pictures of those sorts of faces. Long and bony and coloured in sepia, cracked with jollity, just a tick of bewilderment in the eyes, loping lads who will break your heart. Like storybook characters, with strong foreheads and brown curls on top. Cheery lads, mother's pride, sent walking on an empty belly through the mud to meet their executioners. Their faces and the facts she knew. Pop's uncle and elder brother were two such young men walking in that war. He had loved his brother, a gangle-legged youth with Arthur's blue eyes and talking the hind legs off donkeys just the same. A sun-kissed compulsive sniggerer, lying about his age to the recruiting officer.

There were clouds now over the poppy field. Maggie wondered if there were enough for rain. She began combing extra carefully between the daisies for her elusive four-leaf token. If she found one today her luck might change. Timing-wise this would not be a bad thing.

The Plough and Harrow

There is a smell at Arthur's house. Something almost ecclesiastical mixed up with hair tonic, dog, yesterday's hake and chips and the ever-swirling mists of tobacco smoke through which they step daily like explorers. He is reading aloud from 'Gunga Din' by Rudyard flaming bloody genius Kipling.

He reads loudly through his nose with exaggerated emphasis and forgets to breathe which makes him cough. But when he speaks the name Gunga Din, Maggie hears the echo of the metal-and-water words. No matter how many times she tries she cannot speak it like he does with her south of England shingle-shiny girl's voice. It is a name begging to be spoken by a Midlands man.

Pop had plans for Malcolm this year, he said, and they didn't include winning the pub quiz a fourth time. This year he would relieve Malc of his title with a cunning programme of preparation, application and abomination. This year they wouldn't see which way he went. For now, he went to the Plough and Harrow to celebrate his strategic planning.

Maggie recalled an old memory of the Plough and Harrow from her childhood. She remembered him taking her mother inside for a drink. They must have travelled up somehow, she and her mother with a suitcase and a mouthful of whinges. He opened with a flourish the door that said LOUNGE rather than the BAR entrance they used now and followed her mother's shapely legs in, golden in their Wolford's American Tan, smoke rippling over his head. In spite of the beer being dearer, he had chosen the lounge for its carpet and wallpaper, she realised now, somewhere her mother's slingbacks wouldn't scrape. Maggie sat and waited for them on the grass, near a tethered goat, while the air turned lilac and gold and hazy with midges. She listened to the lambs crying from the fields at Fox Hill. The goat had curling horns and a beard and watched her with blue eyes made lunatic by Gothic keyhole pupils.

Pop sprang out of the pub into the diffusing evening light, towing a leak of voices and a smell of ale behind him as he strode across the grass with slicing strides; like it was the egg-and-spoon race, the crisps-and-squash race, her drink slopping over his shoe in his hurry and him slicing back again, younger then, elasticated. Speaking before he was even through the door, interrupting some poor sod. Never quiet, never still, sounding off, always nodding, winking, nudging, howling at some joke, his own probably. She ate her bag of crisps in front of the goat and blew bubbles into the glass of orange in an effort to baffle it. It watched her sideways with a combined look of fear and malice in its Hammer Horror eyes. From inside the pub a cheer of laughter leapt into the rafters and the sun leaked molten brass over the cul de sacs and farms. Swallows hurtled and fell, quick as arrows, for the evening insects while a solitary car engine grumbled up the hill.

The goat began to relax. Its gaze left Maggie and cast about elsewhere. She blew three times, hard and sure as a trumpeter, until she got it just right and then, when it was at maximum volume, taut as a drum, she walloped that crisp bag between her hands with every scrap of concentrated violence she could muster.

The bang was heard in the pub. The previous landlord, sleeker than Ken with oiled hair and scarlet-tipped ears, reckoned they must be popping pigeons up at Roughly Farm. The goat sprang away and ran to the end of its chain where it stood incredulous, outraged, its little beard quivering while it gawped billy-the-brazen at her with devil eyes.

The goat was long gone now. A big grey square of tar for pub-parking where she and he had been, the Anglia at an angle by the door that says BAR. There's a decaying gravestone leaning in the corner by the bin. Before the goat, long ago, this place had been a graveyard. Maggie kneels to search for a name but the years have wiped it away.

Inside, the dartboard darkens as a drifting cloud passes. Pop has bought a round; there are only three of them in at eleven thirty. A man with one leg, whom he greets as Joker, as though he might suddenly produce the other one, sits alone with a pint of mild. Pop is in his tent of smoke, the *Daily Mirror* spread before him like a map. They cough and reach for their shining drinks, sending sunlight skidding round the walls.

'Ah!' he hails at new arrivals, as though they have an appointment, whistling strings of minor notes between.

Maggie tosses cheese Quavers for Blowbroth to catch.

Ken swings in and out, tall and wide as a wardrobe, watchful and wary, granite-headed. He likes his humour dry and his customers well behaved. He'd been commended by the West Midlands police force for his enthusiastic attitude toward capturing criminals. He enjoys murder mysteries, he can't swim, and his wife has left him; none of these is connected as far as he knows.

Pop likes him and makes an effort to impress, but Ken's history with the police, his status as landlord and official bar-room arbitrator, and his natural inclination towards law and order appeal to the infantile delinquent who prances just below the surface in Pop. It is in this mode that Pop often sets about him.

'Oh *bhai*, Ken, *ek* packet Players *dena*.'

Ken always responds slowly and precisely as though he is reading people their rights.

'English, Arthur, in this establishment. Not in the bloody jungle now, mate.'

'Flashback, Ken. Get 'em with the fever. Not a damn thing to be done about it.'

'I don't believe a bloody word of it. Only fever you've got is blue with the Queen's head on and you've bloody owed me two of 'em for a month.'

'*Tea Kai, aur ek* packet *krisp dena*, an' all mate, ta.'

'Beyond me, to be perfectly honest, why you learn all that rubbish anyhow.'

'See the world, Ken. Broaden your horizons, mate. Do you the world of good.'

'Oh ar.'

'Sure as God made little green apples. I'll give you an example. What language, Ken, do they speak in Taiwan?'

'Don't be bloody daft, Arthur. Yes, John? What'll you have?'

'No, go on. Taiwan?'

'. . . bloody believe it. Bloody Taiwanese.'

'No, Ken! No, mate, common mistake. Mandarin, mate! Bit of a trick question actually, bit unfair, not easy for the uninitiated.'

'I don't believe a bloody word of it. Ice and lemon?'

''Strue mate, ask anyone. Got any crisps, Ken, at all?'

'Plain.'

'They'll do, better take a couple. She likes 'em, the kid.'

Blowbroth has eaten three bags of Quavers and several cubes of ice.

'Knock it off, hairy-gob. That's all the savoury snacks he's had down his neck,' Pop points out to everyone.

Blowbroth doesn't react. The cogs in his brain turn over, a

wheel spins, sending a thought to his cortex, and he turns an acid stare on the plastic Sooty for the blind before carefully releasing a noxious stench.

'Afternoon.'

'Morning.'

'Hello, Bren.'

'Alright?'

'Very little joy in driving these days.'

'He's got his new motor, hasn't he?'

'How are you doing?'

'Not so bad.'

'Pint of mild?'

'Ta.'

'These are six and tuppence a pack now. Most of that is bloody tax.'

'They refine the tobacco.'

'Saltpetre,' Pop hurls in. 'That's what keeps 'em burning, mate, the saltpetre.'

'Incredible damn price, innit?'

Pop straightens up, his facts ready in rows. 'You're drawing arsenic through fibreglass actually, that's what it is.'

'They'll not get away with it for ever, people will revolt.'

'If you open it up you've got a bloody great strip,' he perseveres, on one elbow, wide-eyed.

'Remember cork-tipped?'

'It's a piece of cotton wool in actual fact,' but his voice is fading.

Nobody is listening. Pop sits back, gives it a rest, taps his fag over the ashtray, and is still tapping when there is no ash left to tap. He lets his eyes slide over the wall.

Maggie glances away to the man in the corner, freckled hands running with green veins turning the pages of his newspaper

46

with its quivering headline: LIFE ON MARS: CHANCES ARE
1 IN 50.

The Anglia wouldn't start. Pop leant down to its wing mirror
like he was having a word in its ear.

'I'm torching you on Monday. Wanker.' He straightened up
and strode away, past the other cars, shooting a furious fart as
he went.

'Austin Accord, now that's a proper motor.'

They walked to Mere Green. Strolled under an advertising
billboard. 'Ansell's Bittermen. You can't beat 'em,' it bragged.
A crowd of men holding tankards scowled down at the world. A
mish–mash of Bittermen. The doctor, the teacher, the salesman,
the brickie, the petty thief. The hard man at the front, daring
you to drink anything else. The chubby one at the back, just in,
peeking over the shoulder of the ladies' man with the sloping
eyes. They were everywhere. The Ansell's Bittermen. Pop was
a Bitterman; the West Midlands was full of Bittermen.

Pop seemed subdued, his mouth hung. He dropped coins in
the box of the plastic cripple girl on a plinth outside the chemist.
He put them in one at a time so they had to stand there ages while
his charity crashed slowly in bit by bit. Maggie looked at the
brown callipered legs and the blue beseeching eyes and thought
of Jesus on Christmas cards.

Iris

Pop had stayed up half the night with his facts. He knew every West Indian cricket team for the past five years. 'I'll wipe the floor with you in a sporting category any day, Malcolm Denton!' he hollered as he shaved at dawn.

The statement sprang through the open window and bounced off car roofs into the trees. The birds stopped singing momentarily, considering the claim.

The three of them trooped in the man–dog–child formation along Tower Road past the Pint Pot and on past Iris's house.

Iris was Pop's exquisite, unattainable love and he was going to win her at any cost. He told himself the gallon of beer and five pounds meant nothing; winning, that was what counted. He would demonstrate to Iris he had the biggest brain in Sutton Coldfield, that Malcolm Denton's brain was in his arse. This would gain her attention and enable him to push on to the next phase, Phase Two.

Iris was a widow from a well-to-do family; her father had been a butcher and her mother could play the piano. Her husband had been a warrant officer during the war. Iris had been a dance teacher – 'ankles like sand eels,' Pop observed.

Ideas above his station Dolly called it, but he had made up his mind. Iris lived behind a scarlet front door bearing the brass numbers 3 and 1 – which, Maggie noted, in case it became relevant later, was her own age backwards. A polished carriage lamp illuminated the lavish gloss paint at night, the raging shade of Pop's unrequited passion.

The light was already gleaming, pushing back the mauve

evening. It was a larger semi than Pop's, with an extended front garden that rolled out teasingly in front of the shiny door. Frothing nets hung at the windows and there was a smart little iron gate with a catch that made a loud clang whenever Pop entered, uninvited, to venture up the flower-lined path to the knocker. He liked to tap out messages in Morse code to amuse her during her journey to answer it. Iris had operated an LMS signal box at Walsall station during the war. She wore spectacles with magnifying lenses that made her pale eyes enormous, two bewildered orbs staring out as though through water. Pop's Morse messages would often be interrupted halfway through by the sudden removal of the door as she opened it without warning. He had put the strength of her right arm down to the tireless pulling and pushing of all the levers – 'tall as her, some of 'em' – during her time in the signal box.

He had met her at the post office, stepping aside with a flourish to let her go first, raising Dor's eyebrows, flushing Iris's cheeks.

'How chivalrous, thank you,' she had said. And that did it, that moment. The word 'chivalrous' perhaps, and the high colour in her face. She likes me, he thought, no kidding. He knew it was love the day he saw her dashing for the bus through the rain with a Spar bag over her head. He stood transfixed, dripping, as she hurried past. She snatched a glance at him and then another, and he thought, 'Likes to be admired this one, appreciates the attention, lonely probably.'

As they passed the house, their heads swivelled like a turning-out parade. There were no lights on, one empty milk bottle and all her roses were out. 'Begonias'll need doing before long,' he commented as they all swung by agawp.

When they got home Pop poured himself a tot of whisky and stared at his reflection in the darkening square of kitchen

49

window, checking his angles. He drank and leant and swiped at his hair. Courtly love would win her, he reckoned. He would wear her down with romance et cetera, maybe a couple of selfless acts of bravery. He would dazzle her with facts and fantastical tales until she surrendered limply in his arms, something like that. He would move heaven and earth, he told himself, and if she changed her mind he would ruddy move them back again. He reviewed his profile in the window. He could be poet and soldier, scholar and knight, like his famous namesake. He toyed with the idea of challenging a foe or dispatching a rival; he pictured Malc with a staff up his arse, his head on a spike. P'raps he could set himself tasks, like Hercules, or, at great personal risk, obtain precious items for her amusement and what all.

Maggie's silence began to draw the walls in. He didn't have a television. He went to watch at Dolly and Carl Minski's when it was the World Cup or a bloke on the moon. Eventually he shuffled a pack of cards violently.

'Right, there are three ways to shuffle a deck of cards, mate. Full attention? Never take your eye off the dealer's hands, no matter what he does to distract you.'

She watched a blur of cards zagging between his long tobacco-stained fingers and fanning under his thumbs, then slicing up the air in rapid little chops as he demonstrated wilder, increasingly ambitious styles. His eyes narrowed with concentration, perspiration sparkling in the folds, never blinking when one mutinous card and then another cartwheeled out.

They played gin rummy and poker under a hot cone of ceiling light in the front room. Blowbroth groaned the horrible moan of an injured man through the back door. Card games affected his bowels and he was banned from the house during them, due to the foulness of the stenches.

Pop engineered long meditative silences. Just the sound of

their breathing and the occasional rasp and hiss of a matchstick. The smoke arranged itself in horizontal layers under the yellow light, softening other colours like the deep damson of the armchair, which haemorrhaged gently from the left, like the Turner print her mother had hung over every mantelpiece in every house they'd ever lived in. From next door came the bass and brass of *The Sweeney*.

Pop picked his teeth, flattened his moustache, cleared his throat and murmured unintelligible advice to himself. He swung whisky around in a doll-size tumbler decorated with sprinting African men wielding spears in a chase around the glass. He glared daggers through the smoke at his fan of cards and whispered insults at them. When it became apparent that he was losing, he stood up and paced around the room, flashing over his hand to check whether they'd thought better and turned themselves into a royal flush. He continued to mumble threats to his cards, jeering quietly, daring them, come on then, come on.

Finally, as he lost all hope of redemption, he allowed himself a hero's smile, slow and languid, Dirty Harry. Movie-star moods suited him, lending him a temporary maturity. It was only a card game after all; let the little lady win a hand if it meant so much to her. Maggie beat him with a fistful of kings and the conclusion was final, which threw him into an irritable coughing fit. The coughing fits that closed a lost card game were considerably more spectacular than the average, common or garden fit. The irritable variety included a display of sudden, violent jerks, stumbling, thrashing, retching, staggering and a volley of accusations. When he was finally able to draw breath again he demanded to know, quite suddenly, through streaming eyes and a smile shining radiant as a new bride's, where the Golden Temple of Amritsar was, as though he had misplaced it.

'Ooooh, ooooh, oh, oh,' groaned Blowbroth from the garden,

51

as if he knew the answer. Maggie's gaze rolled up to the ceiling to recall the temple's location as easily as her previous address, as though the victory at the card table had awarded her new and terrifying powers.

'Give up?' Pop insisted, his eyebrows making the leaping arches of an M across his forehead, like a clue.

'Manchester,' she tried.

'Wrong!' Pop hymned triumphantly, his fists aloft like an Olympian.

'Wrong!' he boomed in a different voice, searching for the best version.

'Not even warm, mate!' he roared as he let Blowbroth in, who skidded across the kitchen, tail thrashing, and hurled headlong into the mutilated armchair whose position had been changed for the game.

'Drink to celebrate?' And he bowed suddenly to kiss her forehead, bumping his teeth and losing his balance so he had to grasp her shoulder to steady himself. 'You're alright,' he said, as though it were she who'd toppled.

'You're alright,' he repeated, throwing a tentative arm around her shoulder, and dropping his cheek against her head so she could feel his breath in her hair, the distant thunder of his heart in her ear. They shuffled slightly for balance, then steadied as the smoke began to clear.

Pop and Maggie

Maggie woke with the shapes and sounds of words in her mouth, as though she had been talking for some time in her neat bed. She lay still, pinned down by a mild fear combined with a sort of fatigued hopelessness. She thought to call out to her mother, before she remembered.

She felt a warm stranglehold around her throat and sea water in her mouth as she struggled to breathe through the first spasm and rush of tears. Then she realised she was able to make out the long outline of Pop sitting perfectly still at the end of the bed. Weightless with fear, she waited for a moment before speaking his name. He didn't move a muscle. He looked like one of Medusa's knights, turned to stone, his hair flying into the shadows, his oily eyes moving in the gloom, round and frightened as a hare's. Eventually she spoke his name again and he stood up, as though released from a spell. He moved to the switch and a click revealed them each panicking in the brightness as the room shrank back.

'Okay mate?' he gasped in a stage whisper and sat again at the furthest corner of the bed. He wiped his glasses, picked his nails, swiped invisible dust from his trousers. Though nervous, he began to speak in cheerful shouts. His telegraph-pole legs wrapped repeatedly around one another like a corkscrew, as though he might drill right through the floor. I shall now demonstrate the drilling through the floor, okay, full attention, mate. At the end of every sentence he cleared his throat to make room for more words and pulled at his moustache.

'The fella upstairs works in mysterious ways, mate. It's not for us to fathom it. Funny old business. Bloody carry-on. Load of ruddy nonsense if you ask me, half the time. God knows. Except he dun't. Hasn't a clue. Even the blokes with their collars on backwards can't tell you what the hell it's all in aid of. They're in the flaming dark as much as we are, mate, and that's a fact.'

He frisked himself for cigarettes, unravelling his legs to slide the flattened pack from his trouser pocket. The now familiar slide, draw, tap, roll, aim, lock, fire. A sentence would begin before or during the search for a match, adding an exhausting suspense during the business of the fire production, the lighting, the inhalation and the exhalation, by which time he'd invariably have forgotten what it was he wanted to say. Today the ritual was conducted in silence and was strangely comforting. The soft tobacco, crackling sweet as it burned, spun out delicate swirling robes of fog until there were no hard edges or sharp corners left in the room. Apparitions hung swaying in the air and pillows of cloud folded into pleats and floated upwards, transforming the room into a temple. They were hazy, indefinable and wise as pashas in an opium den. The taste of bitter-sweet tobacco leaf settled in the back of her throat.

'She's gone, mate,' he said simply. He was quivering now, leaning awkwardly across the foot of the bed, supported on one elbow, in a gesture of casual intimacy which he clearly regretted but chose to conquer. Neither of them could think of a remark to follow this. He swallowed a curl of smoke. His chest sang a distant note.

'Nothing to be done about it now,' he added eventually. A secret peeped out and vanished in his eyes and he spluttered on a curd of rogue phlegm that had surprised him. 'Right carry-on, anyhow.'

The trembling began to beat a tattoo on the headboard behind. 'Bugger it, damn and blastit,' as a cone of ash tumbled and broke into pieces on the bed covers.

'You'll be alright, mate,' he said, sucking in some more smoke. 'Have no fear, Pop is here,' and his chest gurgled with laughter. 'Don't be afraid, Pop won't be swayed,' cackling now with his head tipped back. 'Never be worried, Pop isn't curried,' rocking with giggles, pulling up phlegm.

'Knock knock,' Maggie said, brightening, but he hadn't heard.

'You're a Landywood,' he continued, patting the mound of her foot. 'Long line of survivors, us.'

He realised his mistake immediately after the cheeky wink, just before he exhaled, when the memory of his daughter's ungainly finale drained him of his will and the smoke that would have jet-streamed out of the side of his mouth evacuated slowly, in sad curls as though an electrical fault had caught in his head and set him smouldering. Discs of tears hung in his eyes.

'Women are fools,' Her mother spoke up in her head. She had sermoned it repeatedly with a preacher's quavering. 'What we put up with. If you wanna get on, get yourself born a fella.' It was typical of her to have passed away during International Women's Year.

Pop tapped the hot ash into the palm of his hand.

'Knock knock,' she repeated. He frowned, still lumbered with his previous remark. 'Knock knock.'

'Eh?'

'You have to ask who's there.'

'Oh ar, knock knock, I know that one, mate. Ask me another.'

Maggie blinked at him, at the sludgy eyes, the teeth hanging out ready for grinning.

'Mum said you were in the war. Did you kill anyone?'

He brightened instantly. He stood up, opened the window and flung out the ashes in his palm. 'Ahh!' as though he thought she'd never ask. The ashes flew wildly back into the room and those that did not stick to him floated grey and weightless as ghosts until they settled one by one like forensic clues.

Khumbirgram

He had left for India after a final pint of ale, whistling the theme from *The Desert Song* through his teeth, in March 1942. Departing the Liverpool docks with the rest of the RAF's 110 Squadron after they were withdrawn from the line in Europe, aboard the HMTL *Johan Van Oldenbarnevelt*.

Filled with natter and joking asides. Pitching on their sea legs across the wide folds of salted grey. None of them knew where they were going.

Two months later the boat docked in Bombay, having stopped for some days at Freetown and Cape Town, and from there the squadron travelled to Karachi and on to their base at Quetta, to await the arrival of new aircraft.

Maggie was soothed by the click of his tongue around exotic words. She waited, only moderately bored, for the tales of flying-ace bravery and daring dogfights. Only to discover he was not a Squadron Leader, or a Wing Commander, or even an NCO. He wore a cloth propeller on his sleeve, just above the elbow, a pencil behind one ear and a cigarette behind the other. He was an earthbound airman, an RAF carpenter. Leading Aircraftman Landywood, AE 848509, was never a war hero in any traditional sense. He considered himself one of the lads, an erk, an ordinary serviceman. Just like all the others from the shipyards, farms, factories and shopfloors, shovelled up like peat coal from the shires, numbered and uniformed, ranked and filed.

He produced a shoebox of curled photographs from a dusty cupboard. Three airmen, one of them Pop, drenched in sweat, grinning, smoking. Crouching behind them the dark humps of the mountain range on the India–Burma border. Maggie's glance flashed from rifle to bony chest to missing tooth. The sun's nuclear glare scorched through the monochrome, turning blacks to greys. A smell of sand rose from the photograph which had now become yellowing scroll, closing like an oyster over its pearly-faced trio.

Tens of thousands of milk-fed boys, eyes front and presenting arms. Grinning in a steel helmet for a photograph in somebody else's country, wishing they were home, some of them.

Pop talked. A freight-train load. Maggie fell backwards and the stories hurtled over her. He had fallen for India the same way he fell for Aston Villa football club – travelling backwards. The train journey from Quetta in the western foothills of the Himalayas to Bengal took three days. The first stage of a journey towards the war in Burma, which eventually carried it east of the Brahmaputra and beyond Chittagong, almost to the Burmese border, from where they were to carry out attacks against Japanese-held villages, bridges, stockades and troop camps and support the 7th Division.

The carriages on the troop train were infested with skittering cockroaches and cooked the men inside like loaves in a bread oven. They slumped about on grimy seats under rattling fans, draped in sodden shirts, mumbling, smoking, shrugging. The air was thick with the bitter spice of sweat and Punjabi dust. Faces hung, creased and shadowed, too hot to play cards, rocked into a bored sleep on the clacketing iron tracks, awakening dazed and clammy with stiffened joints, scenery unchanged, exactly where they left off.

He became fed up with the moaning and the chloroforming stench and sat instead like the closing scene in a film, on the exterior carriage step at the end of the very last wagon. He sat with his elbows on his knees, cigarette smouldering between his fingers until he tossed it away into the dry kindling landscape and lit a new one. India was pulled out miraculously from under him, in between puffs of smoke, like a magic trick, revealing itself as lingeringly as the Mahabharata. A panorama as strange and still as Mars, with not the slightest movement in the fiercest heat, like travelling through the landscape of someone else's dream. The relief as they groaned to a halt alongside a long red gravel platform with its bamboo tea stall and decrepit iron lavatories that separated Hindus and Moslems.

India and his war funnelled into Maggie this way. Poured into her eyes and ears until she could dream its exotica independently, her bare feet swinging silently through miles of flaring images and deep-sea voices. The colour red bled into her hallucinations. The henna dust that floated everywhere, covering everything, lining pockets and boots, coating tongues and teeth, grazing eyes and packing nostrils with fine rust, turning the ivory cattle saffron. The red sun rising on the fuselage of the Japanese bombers, the scarlet bindi and tilak, the cashew fruit, the flowers adorning the Hindu shrines, the ruby sari of a Hindu bride, the smear of every swatted mosquito, and the bright accusing blood of the dying and the dead, all sweeping and merging in her dreams with the metal glare of dazzling sky that could cut a deep ache through men's skulls.

Through the dust-storm thrown up by the trucks she could make out the servicemen, leaning and sprawling, kitbags as cushions, faces livid from the Martian dirt, hot, exhausted. Some at the back sang 'Oh why are we waiting' to the tune of *O Come All Ye Faithful.*

The relief of the darkness. Maggie pushing herself through the heavy wax of dreaming. The fireflies dragging their soft gold and emerald lights sluggishly through the black; gliding paths

58

along the road until they became twinkling runways. Through the billets and the crammed canteen, wading through the dark ink towards the sulphur-coloured pools of light where groups of men are collapsed over cards. Sodden and reeking, shoulder to greasy shoulder under whirring wreaths of insects clacking against the paper light-shades. A din of voices competing with a shrieking gramophone record, macabre in its bouncy rhyming jollity – *It Always Rains Before the Rainbow.*

Smoke hanging in thick pleats as though they are already in battle, streaky faces floating through it. Flash of teeth for a bad joke in the half-light, teeth tasting of chlorinated tea, teeth in skulls for a last-ditch identification. Groups cheering at a dartboard lit dimly by a rancid yellow bulb. Maggie dreaming all their suits of cards, wheeling molten slow behind the airmen under the jaundiced circle of light, orbiting with the host of droning insects, spying the flush, the full house, the *kharab* hand. Behind the NCO whose fan of cards displayed no symbols but only a run of Japanese rising suns, like a bloody line of machine-gun wounds telling his fortune. Like the boy electrician, newly arrived from Derbyshire, AC Jimmy 'Sprog' Roberts, shot in half on the runway during a Japanese strafing. His mother's screams for her only child almost reached them in Khumbirgram.

Sutton Park

They walked, man-dog-child, almost daily, often silently, through the park. Its immensity meant they never seemed to retrace their exact steps. They walked purposefully with solemn faces, like pilgrims. Often in the direction of a pub, like the Parson and Clerk at the Royal Oak gate.

Sutton Park was once the centre of a royal forest and stretched luxuriously over two thousand four hundred grandly sweeping acres. One of the largest areas of natural parkland in England, its splendour included Anglo-Saxon forests where Mercian kings once hunted for boar and bear. Forest once so vast it almost merged with Cannock in the north and Arden in the south. A few miles to the north-east lay the capital of the kingdom of Mercia, now Tamworth, with its Do It All and Ankerside shopping centre. Apart from aristocratic sweeps of forest where Arthgal, Knight of the Round Table, once rode, there were commanding views from Lord Donegal's Ride at the top of Rowton's Hill, as well as prehistoric cooking sites, a Roman road and an ancient well. There was heathland, marshland, ancient woodland and peatbogs composed of the rotted trees felled by the Roman road builders.

Pop stood, grand and grave as one of the forest's own Saxon kings, surveying all around him.

'Sutton Park,' he said in a ragged whisper, struggling for composure, and drew a breath as though he might make a speech. He tore a white handkerchief from his pocket and blew a blast. She heard the scrape of carbon against phosphorus and watched while he folded himself over the fire. Up went the smoke signals, out roared the cough.

'What d'you see, mate?'

Maggie waited, blinded by hair, suspecting it might be a trick question.

He spread his arms and answered for her. 'England,' he breathed. He pointed with his cigarette, drawing smoke lines in the air, to Four Oaks at the northern gate and Royal Oak on the west side. To the Druids' site by the Bracebridge Pool and the Rowton's Well on the hill, with its magical restorative water that cured all known diseases of the eyes. To the ancient slades, the medieval mills and the route the legionaries trod nearly two thousand years before. And south to the pine trees at the top of Wyndley Glade, reputedly the very centre of England.

When Pop was a boy, scrag-necked and cringing, he fished by himself for sticklebacks and miller's thumbs in the Ebrook and Longmoor streams. The park contained six pools, all man-made, some medieval, some from the eighteenth century, built for milling. They were all fed by two strong streams, the Ebrook and the Longmoor brook, which became one before leaving the park to join the River Tame and eventually the North Sea.

Pop had experienced his first smoke and his first kiss in Sutton Park. He'd learned to drive, cadet-trained, marched, slept, written sentimental verse and had even attempted suicide there. It had been a half-hearted effort, more of a gesture. He'd floated like a funeral lily in Blackroot Pool, flagrantly tragic. His bedraggled limbs thrown across the water, his hair trailing in Arthurian tendrils around his expressionless face. It was shortly after they'd buried Eve. The incident got a small mention in the *Sutton News* and aggravated his cough.

His passion for Sutton Park was reignited now in the name of 'broadening your horizons, mate'. His once furtive patrols with Blowbroth, hands knotted in pockets, peering and ducking, cursing and lighting up, smouldering behind trees, sidling past picnics and slashing through undergrowth, were now grand tours tackled in the name of enlightenment. On these he would be found leaning within a legion of medieval oak, discoursing loudly in a rallying voice, or marching at break-neck pace the length of the Roman Icknield Street, carpet-bombing its length with facts. Or grinding over Rowton's Hill in the Anglia, clutch plate shrieking, *en route* to a favourite bench by Meadow Platt; man, dog and child falling through every gear change. In dry weather, on a seat with a view, he could talk and puff his way through an afternoon until dark.

He dropped his cigarette and stood on it.

'P'raps you're a lucky charm. Possible, eh?' He reached out for her shoulders, held her at arm's length to look at her properly. He brushed the hair out of her eyes, hurrying so that he nicked her skin with one of his nails. 'Where the 'ell are you under there? Oh right. Don't say much, do you, mate?' He was gripping her. He winked. 'Okay, love?' Maggie looked down at their shoes, each facing the other pair fair and square, and she blushed. An unlikely alliance, his black and thinly laced, and her Bata plimsolls, once white, the left one turned out slightly.

He hugged her. She landed in his chest, surprised at the strength in his arms. She breathed him in, a bonfire, a hint of Omo. She wanted to respond; she thought about moving an arm. He released her.

'Fancy a pint?'

His long, loping stride looked good from a distance but proved impossible to keep up with if your role was that of strolling companion. Maggie drove her legs faster until her gait was peculiar, before giving up and accepting the rear view of him swaying, pale rider, ahead. A skittish breeze flung a branch in his path and he paused over it. His head bowed low in a saintly stoop, for a moment as though all his sins were about to be washed away.

'Elm!' he yelled and took off again on his stalk legs before she had got there, twirling the branch in front of him like a baton. The elms were all dying from a Dutch disease. She bounced deeper in each stride and threw her weight forward, trying to catch him.

Without interrupting his own charge, he flashed his chin over his shoulder and threw out instructions. 'Bend your knees! Weight forward! Drop through your stride. Breathe!'

He demonstrated some lunging bends with a poker back and square shoulders, not a million miles from her own Max Wall. She began to gain on him with the aid of the plunging walk. Leaves and paper debris wheeled around in the breeze, newly arrived from the North Sea, dragging a clutch of clouds with it, agitating the trees. The sun fell through canopies of leaves, flashing a bright gold mosaic across the path as though they had stumbled on to the Yellow Brick Road. Maggie thought of her mother quickly, then it was gone, like lightning blinking far away.

'Elder! Birch! Noble fir!' His elm branch in the air now, thrusting up to name individual trees. He swung around to find her and spangles of sunlight flashed across his face. She wondered if the same haloes and blessings were dancing across hers.

He strode forward again. 'Ash!' he confirmed another, lancing through its foliage with the stick. 'Oak!' A single uppercut from beneath. He pictured Iris laughing, shading her eyes from the glare to catch a better glimpse of his arboreal mastery. Blowbroth ran ahead. Maggie struggled to plunge lower, while he accused tree after tree of its species, swinging his stick left and right along the forestry parade, like Don Quixote de la Mancha at his windmills.

Carole

Maggie was shocked by her mother's beauty. It hung between them like a third party, brazen, unassailable, while her mother diligently set about trying to destroy it. The skin was as pale as a drowned child's, with only the occasional fork-lightning vein on her temple. Her eyes blinked slowly, muddy grey, damp with booze, the sun-dazzled windows reflected in them. Through the gauze of cigarette smoke she looked like a character preserved in a black-and-white photograph. She'd lick the smoke from her lips, pulling the light on to them. In her neck a strong pulse pushed against smooth skin.

Carole; she'd added the *e* herself.

The morning after she had declared Anne Aston's handkerchief-sleeve dress the worst item of clothing she'd ever seen on British television, her mother died. Seven days after her thirteenth birthday, kismet changed Maggie's life for ever. The world appeared crudely exposed for the first time, its arbitrary cruelty, the informal horror.

The house filled up with strangers and she found herself hiding behind doors, eavesdropping on the drama her mother had caused. The same doors she'd hidden behind when her mother was alive, eavesdropping on the drama her father had caused. She imagined people the length and breadth of England, silenced behind doors.

'Mum,' she said, and listened to the word float away. She remembered being lost in Debenham's as a small child, the terror and anger, the coats and calves of other mothers, wrong ones, the horror of being all alone in haberdashery, the shop assistants with their long noses and Egyptian eyes. This time she wouldn't reappear from behind a pillar with a fistful of ostrich feathers and purple ribbon. This time there would be no lustful reconnection, no warm kisses and breathless scolding. This time it was for ever and ever Amen.

Maggie lay on her mother's side of the bed and breathed. She curled up in her chairs and slid open her drawers. She tried on all her jewellery and snapped a tall blond flame out of her initialled cigarette lighter, chill and heavy as a tombstone. She placed a carrier bag over her head in a self-pitying gesture of solidarity and took it off again. She slung back a swig of Cinzano Bianco and then another and wore her mother's gold chain of nuclear-disarmament symbols and her black-feather clip-on earrings. She checked herself in the mirror, a blurred pixie, tarnishing already in the rancid glamour. Her skin looked slapped, her eyes realigned. There were people talking downstairs. Fearing they might prevent her keeping anything, she folded up her mother's Lurex evening gloves, sequinned headband, collection of chokers, macramé halter top and favourite cheesecloth dress and hid them with some photographs, glitter tights and her mother's red velvet waistcoat with the diamanté fir trees on the back that she wore every Christmas. She tipped all the jewellery into the tights until they swung like water balloons. She grabbed the favourite old floppy hat with the bunch of cherries on the side, a collection of Chanel and Joy perfumes, a china cat, Charlie talc, a suede brush, a gonk in a denim shirt and a set of 'Love Is . . .' drinks mats.

She heard the tune of that wavering voice, passing sentence on the bank manager, Maggie's father, the milkman. 'He can go and hang himself, they can all go hang.' And the terrible boomerang of that carefree curse.

Her bell-bottom jeans scraped and flapped down the stairs, a saw fraying into wood. She struggled to bring to mind hard facts concerning her mother, in case she was asked. Five foot seven, hundred and ten pounds. Shoulder-length ash-blonde hair with a centre parting, grey eyes, medium build, tangerine suede Biba coat (probably), smoking (probably), missing-person facts. Maggie considered how alluring her mother would have looked on a missing-person poster, how she would have pulled them to her, the souls on the street, the passers-by. Miss Brighton and Hove 1959. Maggie had been impressed that she'd captivated not one but two towns.

Missing didn't categorise her mother now; she felt oppressively present. The house contained her as it never had before, rooms full of her skin, hairbrushes choked with hair, prints of her mouth in coral and magenta crushed into tissues at the bottom of pedal bins. Kisses for nobody. Forensics. Her shoes, going nowhere, cool to the touch, waiting quietly to tiptoe out of fashion. But it was the silence that really held her. Her absence hung about like a stink. The air was matted with her, she was woven like a familiar pattern into the space that Maggie moved through, cutting it up with her scything flares, pausing to listen to it collapsing left and right behind her. Perfect stillness but something of her hanging there, like water clinging to glass.

Maggie felt her mother's words lying in her own mouth, stale and second hand. 'Christ,' she said. It sounded phoney, insincere. 'Jesus,' she tried with emphasis. An improvement.

She wondered if she would be called upon to speak at the funeral. A few words. Maggie tried to think of some. She ransacked her brain for something. Her mother's CV popped up. The one she sent out by the crateload. White fluttering doves of paper winging their urgent message to theatrical temples in every corner of England. Announcing her mother's talents, durability and availability for regional tours, summer season, television, ads, panto. They were written in code. The familiar words indicated that her mother was an all-rounder. To Maggie this was quite unimaginable.

Dance: Dip; Ballet/Mod Jazz/Char/Tap. Singing: Sop/
    Alto/Pop.
Acting: tragedy/comedy/farce. (p.t.o. for productions/
    ads etc)
Other Skills: Mime/Puppetry/Stilts/Improvisation/Illusions.

In the accompanying letter that went out clipped to a blazing photograph, her mother summed herself up by explaining that she was a people person; a bit crazy, she supposed; 'way out', others had suggested, dot dot exclamation mark. At the end as though it were relevant she added that she was an optimist, with another exclamation mark.

Maggie decided she would say church if they asked her about funeral location because of her mother's habitual references to the Saviour. She placed all her mother's things in a white vanity case and dampened her wrists with splashes of Chanel No. 19.

The policewoman's hands were warm, with shiny buffed nails and an engagement ring on the left one. She spoke Maggie's name at the end of every sentence. She had two yellow fang teeth either side of the four white front ones. What's the time, Mr Wolf? She wanted to know if Maggie had any hobbies. Mrs Desborough from next door had brought a rose-spattered quilt and a BOAC overnight bag. She stood stiffly in the kitchen between two policemen as though she'd been arrested. If there had been a misadventure she wanted them to know it had not occurred due to any lack of diligence on her part. Her bulbous eyes rolled from person to person like an actor in a melodrama. Smarting with fear and excitement, she was careful not to blink. She suspected that only liars and the guilty blinked, so she made sure her eyeballs remained unconcealed, so upstanding was she.

The ambulance had not started first time and then it did and blared its way na ner na ner down the empty road, watched by the estate's invisible people positioned behind their twitching nets and Draylons.

Na ner na na ner, jeered the siren, I told you so, I told you so. Careering round the corner at the bottom of Ashfield Drive where it turned into Hazel Mead, trailing a jet-stream of curtain-tugging in its wake.

Dolly

Only thirteen more pints of ale until the quiz, Pop calculated.

'Unlucky,' Maggie reminded him. 'Unlucky for some.'

'Plenty of time. *Bahut*,' he said, 'bloke upstairs made the world in seven.'

Blowbroth hung limp across a chair. At intervals a dream would snag in his sleep, electrocuting his slack body.

'Come in, Malcolm Denton!' Pop called, pointing accusingly at the mirror as if Malc were hidden on the other side. 'Your time is up!'

Maggie released another sweet from the Pez dispenser she kept, revolver-style, in her waistband and slid it under her tongue. It fell apart slowly, blowtorching her gums with its chalky acid, watering her eyes.

An aimless fly traced a path to and from the rain-spattered window now shining with a biblical brightness as the sun burned through it. Pop's dome, suddenly illuminated, glowed with concentration at the *Daily Mirror* crossword clues, his breathing hissing out of him in small gassy leaks. A leaning tower of encyclopedias threatened to collapse over him.

'Seven across. The whole shebang in an instant. Eight letters.' Pop's voice, a brick through the trance. Blowbroth opened his eyes, considering.

'Universe!' Pop heckled back to himself and the fly bounced

off the glass again. They sat under the weight of the word for a moment before the slapping of the door knocker and explosion of the bell tore it away. Pop convulsed with the shock.

'Jesus Christ alive, who the flamin 'ell's that?' He tipped from the chair, ducking out of sight like a paratrooper. Blowbroth sprang up, inspired by the tension, upturned snout spinning question marks at the door. Pop stalked out, gasping at the inconvenience as he went.

'Door needs doing, Art, you lazy bugger.' A frenzy of high-pitched barks. 'Shudup you, beyave.' A woman. Deep in the black country. Pop replying nervously, a madrigal of his-and-her voices in the hall.

'Out, pillock.'

Blowbroth re-entered shiftily and snaked on to the armchair, turning two circles before he settled. Maggie snapped the Pez giraffe open and took aim at him with both hands like Inspector Harry Callahan. Soprano remarks in the hall again, bending through the wall. Blowbroth's tail quickened its rhythm at the sound, and his yellow gaze turned on the door, which opened suddenly as if commanded by his stare.

Her voice enters first and then she follows at speed as if arriving on a monorail. Blowbroth throws himself at her winkle-picker heels, while the light shatters around her, like the first appearance of the fairy godmother. She stands in a spangle of colours under a crimped halo of golden perm, held together by a tight dress that runs out above her muffin knees. Her face is stiff with pink make-up, ageing her beyond her sixty-something years. A shiny bag swings from a dappled arm and she tinkles with bracelets when she moves. Pop's friend Dolly, open-armed like she's on at the Palladium.

He jangles the loose change in his pockets, a quick, panicking sleigh ride. 'You know Dolly Minski,' he says. Blowbroth gazes up, hypnotised by the words.

'Don't ply the kid with questions, Art,' says Dolly, spooning the dog off her shoe and discarding her handbag. 'She's had an almighty shock.' She arrives at Maggie in a rush of bosom and Yardley, kneeling before her, firing warning shots from both knees.

'Ahh. Alright, love? It's Dolly speaking to you now.' She winks a feathery tarred eye slowly and pitches to the right, grips Maggie's knees for balance. 'Ahh. You're a good kid, Mag. Oi, come on, Art, don't tell me you've forgotten how to boil a kettle on top of everything.'

She smells of lily of the valley and Silvikrin hairspray and something sharper, like a smack in the gob. She takes Maggie's hand and weaves her bloated fingers between each of the girl's before cradling both in her other hand and pressing it all against her cheek. Pop slopes out, still playing sleighbells on the coins and flinging the flak down the chain of command: ''Oppit then, daft pillock.' Just visible, the dog's stiff tail tip floating after, like a middle finger raised behind his back.

Maggie breathes in the pandemonium of cosmetics and swallows a swell of fear that says she is staying here for ever. Dolly's arms are cool and soft and crashing with catalogue jewellery, a Siberian wind whistles out of her nose while she scans the girl's face. Her little fringed eyes coast in closer, the pencil arches of her eyebrows floating high in their corners, framing her clown face in parentheses. 'Ahh, shhh, terrible blow for a kid, crying shame, thing to do to a knee-high. Still, it could be worse, love, always something worse.' She strokes Maggie's hair, sucks a squall back up her nostrils, and heaves a philosopher's sigh.

70

Streetly Gate

'Meet Thy God,' the Holy Trinity Church noticeboard suggests. The words scud past the passenger window, daring Maggie to try. Pop is horsewhipping the Anglia up the hill on the Lichfield Road and shouting *Three Little Maids* and other hits from *The Mikado* at the road ahead. Popular composers, opera, boxing champions, Tudor kings and queens. She sees a magpie, damn. One for sorrow two for joy, she scans for a second, another is sure to be close; evil birds, thieves and troublemakers, enemy of the songbird, lackey of the devil. She feared their black and white clothes, knew all about their refusal to go into full mourning at the time of the Crucifixion. She can find no second bird in the scenery; left and right there are only sparrows, off-licences and signs to West Bromwich; she will have to nix the jinx.

Pop begins to whine through *One Fine Day* from *Madame Butterfly*. 'Cracking composer, Puccini.' He serenades himself through a hollow mouth which pulls his eyes into the tragic slants of the song's heartbroken heroine. Maggie crosses her fingers and bows over her knees to spoil the magpie's spell. She is still in this crash position as Pop bursts across a roundabout without looking. Curious to see if he can fit the final, trembling eight bars into the exact length of Streetly Lane, he estimates a perfect correlation travelling continuously at forty miles an hour, and succeeds with two seconds to spare and a purple face. They enter the park through the Streetly gate and drive along the road that cuts like a long jetty through a sea of silver birch. He needs to think, he says.

'Fresh air,' he announces, forefinger raised as if it is the answer to a riddle.

They find a footpath through the crowd of milk-coloured trees that turn pewter when the sun falls under Rowton's Hill, and she stops to feel the stillness gathering behind her, streaking her legs with goosebumps. Coins of sunlight slide on the ground. She looks up at the canopies where the sun breaks through and falls in bright shafts like a hundred ascensions. Warm columns are filled with bouncing insects and the pew-pew, hweet-chirr songs of the warblers. There is a smell like in church: sandstone, spores, swelling wood, and a powdered tin dampness like the blood of Christ, slow death mixed up with the promise of eternal life.

At its heart the coppice is fastened with secrets; only the birdsong moves the air. Unseen life rustles and creeps, protected from the sun. At five o'clock it will roll a little further and blast the birch wood from the west until it shines like gunmetal.

A network of exposed tree roots is partially hidden, like a game, under bracken and moss, made slippery by a bright green paste of liverwort that snatches Maggie's feet away. Pop settles himself at the foot of an adult tree in a small clearing that has been prised open by sunlight and waggles the tuning dial on her radio, cutting up the air in choppy yelps, searching for the live report of Villa versus Queen's Park Rangers.

Something that rests in the forest lifts up and flees; shadows drift after it. When he has found the game, ten minutes in, he strikes a match and the smoke wraps itself around the bark. The players are blown out of the little holes in the radio on a gale of chants and song. The emerald pitch unravels through the gaps in the trees and it all raises a hymn to the forest roof. The commentator panics, 'Chance here for Leonard! Ooh my word, just wide,' and a roar leaps and falls away again, cramming the air around Pop, stiffening the trees. He remains poker-faced

72

– never fooled for a moment, he – a silver birch growing out of his head.

Maggie wanders away from the din, walking tightrope on tree roots. She lights a bracken frond to puff on with a match from her box with the yellow swan gliding and is alarmed at how it catches and hisses long gold flames so that she has to jump up and down on it.

A football chant sways through the trees towards her, behind it a horn braying like a mule, three times, and again, four. She strikes another match, waits until it bites her fingers, and then another.

She throws herself into a clump of dark fungussy fern. She saw someone shot on *Kojak*; she's been shooting herself ever since. She likes the finality, the sensation of bruising contact, the peace as the discomfort melts. She admires Mata Hari – Matey-Hairy, Pop calls her. She knows about the accusing kisses blown at the firing squad on her execution morning. She wonders if it can be practised, such brazen courage, and throws herself again and again into the bracken, in homage.

Carl

Maggie wakes and thinks, Jesus, the quiz, and butterflies swarm in her belly.

Carl arrives in a short mac with what looks like a briefcase.

Carl Minski, Dolly's husband, is a small apologetic man, full of fear. He moves with the urgent uncertainty of a person with something to hide, and watches the world through dark little floating eyes that are as damp and perfectly round as an octopus's. He is nervously cheerful in company, fastidious,

73

painfully self-conscious, his face appears almost permanently startled, he is a man born afraid. He imagines unspeakable catastrophes daily as he stirs his milky tea, and he never trusts banks. As long as he has lived he has never held an account at one, preferring to hide his bundles of money under the sink and high up in overhead light fittings, tossed repeatedly with his bowling arm like a fairground game until they land high in the glass lightshade in the front room. Every evening the aroma of warm cash scents the house as the bulbs heat the rolls of fivers.

Carl snaps open his briefcase. He has prepared questions for Pop in six categories; he's spent all week doing it and he is proud of them. He produces a stopwatch too. 'No good the right answer in a slow gob.'

He has included devilish ones; cookery questions, for instance. 'In what order should your ingredients be added for smooth, uncurdled mayonnaise?'

'Don't be bloody daft,' Pop replies.

'It could come up,' Carl points out, eyes widening in panic. 'They had to name the ingredients for a Battenberg cake once. They had who makes the Queen's hats too, another time.'

'Stone the crows, no wonder fat Malc wins it every ruddy year. What's the flaming answer to that then, the March hare?'

'Hardy Amies,' Carl reports with drawstring lips and a firm nod.

Dolly and Carl lived in a small redbrick semi with a pea-green front door and matching sash window on Worcester Lane. The front path was carpeted in velvet moss and yellow buttercups and toadflax sprouted at the sides. Carl was balding, with a scrubbed face and curvaceous hips and soft thighs like a woman. He dressed immaculately in the style of a repertory theatre player: a brightly coloured handkerchief, a cravat, an oddly inappropriate hat. He owned a vast collection of spectacles and corresponding cases. Faced with food he always sang, '*We started off with a bowl of soup and a couple of herrings that looped the loop.*' He was proud of his quick sense of humour and allowed a silent chuckle to squeeze him up and down while his head flooded crimson. 'Nicky nacky noo!' he trilled when lost for words.

Repeated bouts of laughter made him weep real tears. But his greatest ovations were reserved for Pop's punch-lines. Carl never deserted him as Pop squawked another one across a smoke-filled bar, no matter how many times he'd heard it before. He never failed to collapse into a blood-clotting heap, complete with gasps and appeals for mercy, often adding, especially if response was thin, a pantomime of smacking himself on the leg and mopping his eyes with one of his bright hankies. Carl was quietly devoted to Pop. The Duke of Clarendon he called him, after his address. He found explanations for his flashes of selfishness. He was a fan.

Dolly Minski was the first woman Carl had dared to speak to who was not a member of his family. She was a barmaid and Carl had ordered a gin and lime at the Queen's Head. There was an odd logic to their unlikely pairing. Carl was no more unnerved by the Punch and Judy style Dolly adopted after throwing back a few drinks than he was by the overt flirtations, the mini-skirts, the expletives, or the advice flung out to complete strangers through the rolled-down passenger window. The marriage was both the solid object and the unstoppable force, unshakable. Even Pop, whom Carl admired and Dolly cooked, laundered, skivvied for and fussed over, was no real threat. Not even as she stooped, Mae West and diamond-eyed over his appliances in a smacking pair of rubber gloves while she did for him, or strolled the vacuum cleaner with her wrist cocked high as if she had a leopard slinking on a leash. Even as Dolly and Pop leant over their last orders at a table in the Fox and Dogs, heads tipped coyly askew and set alight by the soft lamps, the vows sworn by Dolly and Carl in 1938 at St John's Church, Walmley, stood tall as swords.

Carl was retired but Dolly still worked at a factory called the Yote on the Mere Green Road, where they produced electric fires. She was never still. In spite of her tar-filled lungs, tight skirts and winkle-picker heels, she was always careering off and about. Even on the bus, at the front of the top deck where she liked to sit, the little frosted mouth going yap yap yap, and the arms pointing and drilling into her handbag. On foot, she wheeled along with an Embassy No. 5 in her teeth like a little blowpipe, poking a path through the world. Very little persuaded it out, not rain, gale, or conversation. She hummed scraps of tunes almost continuously, pausing only to speak. Usually breathless with the humming, the smoking, the heels and the pencil skirts, she was clumsy and had spectacular accidents. Never glancing down to judge the height of kerbs or steps sent her stumbling over most of them, beads and bracelets crashing into strings of curses.

'Shite,' she sighed while people gathered round.

'*Well, hello Dolly* . . .' she railed at people she liked in a quavering vaudeville, complete with cabaret-style gestures and lavish winks for the men, each verse torn open by splits of laughter and the grind of her steel-tipped stiletto. Dolly was a party all on her own. She liked nothing better than to wet herself laughing on the knee of a man even louder than she was.

Hill Wood

Black rooks circle the tops of the elm trees like falling ash. In the early-morning mist, before the sun blasts away the night's cool canopy and the air turns hazy in the heat, they float high in grim, flapping groups. The melancholy sound of their cawing drops through the trees on to the farmland and into graveyards below. Pop is subdued so early. Still folded with sleep, he pads through the floating fog, his dreams breaking off and falling away. He has no socks on; it's too early for Dolly to have delivered clean laundry. The glare of white flesh, soft and nude above his shoe, makes Maggie stoop, trying not to see it, glad no one else is about yet.

They are silent, just their footsteps and Blowbroth's throat-clearing, the ever-present gagging cough. At turns and corners Pop pauses and breathes, 'Nature is afoot,' a whistle in his teeth as the milk float whirrs round. The fields and lanes are squirming with life. It's easy to glimpse shrews and voles, or even the slender spine of a hare or stoat flashing away. Pheasant and grouse come crashing out from their coverts and dash away to a new one, cackling and calling their rusty-hinged 'go-back, go-back, go-back'. There are songs from warblers, larks and thrushes, and the cool, calming repeat of the cuckoo. Blowbroth has the scent of a local vixen in the still air and there's a whiff too of fungus. Pop speaks them out like a roll-call of mythical characters, the Blusher, the Death Cap, the Deceiver and the Dryad's Saddle, in the shadows, little groups in pale and ghostly attendance. On the cool bark of the shadier trees, a lick of lichen, bright emerald, and always a sweet girlish scent of wild grasses. Across the fields comes the shriek and laughter of a green woodpecker; his crown is the bright warning colour of freshly spilled blood. The three stroll aimlessly like sleepwalkers through empty Warwickshire, old and still as a prayer. Maggie finds some early berries in the hedgerow on the Hillwood Road and eats them while Pop sways ahead. Hedgerows and brambles are stuffed with old ramshackle nests, musty as hymnbooks.

There are grasshoppers big as frogs leaping on great hinged legs and marbled white butterflies bouncing on wafer wings. It no longer matters where they are going so long as they are moving. Their walking is not arriving or leaving, rather just walking in order to be still. Their steps make a steady rhythm, keeping time. Tick-tock. Pacing some purpose out of a blank day, their legs moving the minutes round like the hands of a clock. They walk until they are the same as the road markings and fields, a treadmill of hedge and verge, a straggle of cloud trailing behind them, the spires of Staffordshire rising on their horizon. They walk themselves into the ground.

Iris

He is working on a plan to win Iris, a campaign. It must be reasonably dangerous and full of clamour, he reminds himself, and should include somewhere in the final stages the recovery of a precious object, some sort of Grail or what have you, not necessarily holy these days, a gift really. First he must grab her attention; imperative, that. He must organise deeds in order of importance. He could be willing to risk his life, he decides; it depends on several factors, but particularly that he should not have to actually die. He dreams of the wounds he would sustain, of the ministering she would do; he can't help but see the brightness of his blood, the tenderness in her eyes, and finally in spite of himself, he pictures his pale hands crossed over his chest, ready to sleep the eternal sleep in a hollowed oak trunk like the great King and Knight of the Round Table.

Five orange poppies have opened overnight and are hanging

their faces over Iris's fish pond. Pop and Maggie pause just past the gate to look. A flash of pearly blouse sends them lunging behind the creaking curtain of weeping willow that hangs over the ornamental wall. The figure floats, watching. A splash of spectacles in the shadows, blinking one lens then the other.

> A wandering minstrel I, a thing of shreds and patches,
> Of ballad songs and snatches and dreamy lullabies.

The song leaks out of Pop in croaking wispy whines, until the figure inside the house dissolves in the murk. The air hushes through the willow sending the thousands of miniature leaves fluttering like fans. Pop grows still, pulling the world in around him, and hardening his stare at the house as if he means to hex it.

> My catalogue is long through every passion ranging,

hardly moving his mouth at all, a whinge curling out the top of his head.

> And to your humour changing, I'll tune my subtle song,
> I'll tune my su . . . uuu . . . btle song.

Dropping into his gravel-pit chest and raking up a cough.

The willow shifts again. Clacking timber fingers scrape looping messages on the pavement. Maggie looks at Pop squinting between the branches. She walks the last two hundred yards to the post office to buy a stamp, without bothering particularly to be on or off the cracks. Past Blowbroth, stationed by the pillar box, rolling his eyes at old women, and on to the end of a small, orderly queue. She chooses a postcard of the Parade in Sutton Coldfield, with its bustle of shoppers and cars and bright yellow pansies on the roundabout.

Dear Dad,

Did you know that Aston Villa have got an unbeatable midfield?

Another thing, Villa striker Brian Little is actually quite little in real life. Way out man (or is that just the exit?) Guess what? LOG. What number is this word? That's right, 501 upside down. What do you call a deer with no eyes?!!! No idea! Keep smiling, PEACE AND LOVE, Maggie May.

And she draws a smiley face.

The address box is blank. She sticks the stamp high in the corner and props it on the nightstand.

> *Will you come to Abyssinia, will you come?*
> *Bring your own ammunition and a gun,*
> *Mussolini will be there*
> *shooting pellets in the air,*
> *Will you come to Abyssinia, will you come?*

The song escapes through the kitchen window downstairs into Warwickshire. She sits on the bed and tries to imagine what the neighbours must say. He is clanking a tankard around under the wailing tap. If the kettle was boiling on the gas ring at the same time, screaming through its whistle cap, it sounded like a massacre was taking place at number ninety-nine.

'Hah! Vermin!'

Maggie tiptoes down in anticipation of blood or rats. He is bowing low as an Elizabethan before the sink. Both arms fanning out at his back, fingers crossed. He snatches a breath and straightens abruptly, sending an enormous piebald magpie flapping out of a tree.

'*Chor kahi ka*!' he yells in Hindi and spits a great gob into the sink before twirling around, head cocked, grinning solicitously.

'Never trust a magpie, mate.'

He produces Player's with a flourish as though there is more trickery to come. Maggie watches his quick fingers, tan as a wrangler's, pulling out a cigarette and match, winking, leaning like he's Butch Cassidy or something, and going up in a roar of flame.

'*Pica Pica*, never did anyone any good, bloody crows really anyhow. Best to defuse 'em before they go off, if you know what I mean, spoiling some bugger's day, bad luck they are unless you defuse 'em, bloody fact – bow, spit, cross these.' He holds up his pair of crossed fingers as though they were fragile instruments of bomb disposal. 'They're buggers, magpies. We'll lose our first damn game of the season at this rate, or worse, you can never tell.'

He peers up at the sky. 'That's five or six in the last three days, none in pairs neither. This is not good, mate. Mark me, this is no damn good at all.'

The Gracechurch Centre

The local library didn't have a copy of the *Guinness Book of Records*. Pop was determined to gen up on the latest record-holders, which meant a journey into town. The car was in disgrace so they strolled to the bus stop.

He could donate a purchased copy to the library afterwards, he thought, with an inscription p'raps. Dor could mention it to Iris. He could donate more than one, lots even; a Girl Guide would pull the cord and blue velvet curtains would part to reveal his name, applause, photographs. The bus arrived, groaning and hissing.

The Gracechurch Centre shopping precinct in Sutton town centre was all brown slab and tan brick, a monument to the right angle in shades of mud and dirt. It had been opened officially in 1974 by an earl on a piece of scarlet carpet in front of W.H. Smith, while a throng looked on through a sea of prescription glasses. It was therefore not quite a year old, this great dung-coloured emporium, not yet blackened and sticky with gum and lager, but already ringing with the babble of its impatient shoppers.

Pop and Maggie sat obediently on one of the slatted benches beside a parallelogram of brick troughs newly planted with nervy-looking shrubs. Pop checked his receipt again, peered into the carrier bag at the book to check it was still there. The same orange brick was used to form a boxy plinth out of which a Martian sculpture reared up in the direction of other universes. No one took any notice of it. It made Maggie think of cat's teeth and alien invasion, grotesquely swollen at the base and tapering its white curving arms into a knot at the top like a giant shuttlecock. It was riddled with slanting holes like moon-beetle eyes and offered up a metal egg at its summit. As she stared she saw baby reptiles with gnashing teeth plunging out of it and had to blink to wipe them away.

The stone rectangles and herring-bone tiling were full of voices, even at night. The whole construction mumbled and whispered like an ancient mausoleum. Only the occasional beam of sunlight, splicing its angles, honeyed the gloom.

Pop picked his nails and watched women's legs scooping

past. Left and right prams clattered by, bearing bug-eyed babies. Blowbroth lay with his ear to the ground, smelling the granite and raising a wobbling black lip at other dogs.

'Gew on, Little, on the inside, son!' Pop barked, surprising everyone. The words sprang across the paving towards Dorothy Perkins. Instructions from the substitutes' bench. Falling on deaf ears. Brian Little scored twenty goals last season, a personal best. One more than Ray Graydon, a direct wide player, the top goalscorer in England during the previous winter. Great things were expected of Little this season.

The women's legs flashed to and fro, charging at shops, galloping over the stones, conspiring in little groups behind the Martian obelisks.

'Nothing to stop the midfield now, mate, like to see 'em bloody try!' Pop's announcements wafted the shoppers further away from their bench.

He is not wrong. Ron Saunders is transforming the fortunes of Aston Villa. From the moment Ray Graydon's right leg won Villa the League Cup, it was clear the Saunders magic was working.

A groaning child flung itself down under their alien monument and lay there thrashing like a human sacrifice. Maggie spotted familiar legs hurrying away, Wolford's American Tan. She stared. The same drifting stumble, the head at an angle, lost in daydreams of retribution and people to blame.

They bought pies from Tesco and a box of five beefburgers, captured on the waxy yellow packaging sizzling under a shining halo of onion, making Maggie's cheeks ache. She scanned the bus stops and phone boxes but the woman had vanished.

They walked home across dusty pelican crossings to the distant cry of an ice-cream van. The beefburgers sent out a reek like the sweat of twenty men as they melted in their yellow box.

'Women can't play football, they've no sense of direction,' Pop said as they waited for the lights to change at the crossing on the Parade.

99 Clarendon Road

Maggie woke from a thin grey sleep in the ancient horsehair bed and lay listening to the springs under the mattress playing watery tunes, as though someone was hidden there, plucking a harp. There were mornings when the pale citrus light and columns of dust bid a fairy-tale welcome. When the sound of next door's flushing loo, dogs barking, and Pop's rendition of '*Come into the garden, Maud, for the black bat night hath flown*' from the kitchen below were firm and comforting, good as a promise.

The very first morning she had heard him creaking up the stairs with a cup of tea wobbling in a saucer and the distracted quavering of '*Oh Rose Marie I love you, I'm always dreaming of you*'. He had knocked and waited before entering. 'Brought you a cup of tea, mate,' and the stagy creep forward, so's not to spill a drop, despite the moat that already swilled in the saucer. It never happened again, just that first morning. Now she got her own tea and that was fine by her.

Ninety-nine Clarendon Road was an end of terrace redbrick house built in the 1930s. The front door and margins of its sash window were painted a glossy Southampton blue, as though Maggie and the ancient mariner indoors might set sail any minute. A veil of storm-torn net hung inside the door's broad central panel of glass. There was a spill of black tar for Pop to

84

park his car on which he never used and at its looping border clods of grass, daisies and feverfew grew. Years earlier someone had planted forget-me-nots under the window and they still flowered faithfully in dainty groups. Local cats sprayed under a rowan tree that stood where Pop's parking tar met the pavement and all along the fence boundary too.

Maggie picked the violet-blue cornflowers that grew along the front path for the stone at Eve's grave. Their finely laced heads, dainty as needlepoint, fell against the drooping nines of the date. She liked the graveyard with its lush grass, winding paths and gnarled, leaning trees; walnut, horse chestnut, willow and yew, their long, laden branches reaching down to the sleeping rows beneath. At its east side a new development of boxy, orange-faced houses gawped morbidly at it through square windows. She watched the clouds, reflected in the glass, sliding across.

Maggie struck a match and lit the gas. She had started to cook. She liked to stir; she liked the blue roar of the flame. So spectacularly bad was his cooking that any half-hearted effort by anyone else appeared to produce miniature masterpieces. She experimented with tins of sardines, pilchards, cubed vegetables, Fray Bentos, onions, Smash and curry powder, and wore the burns as proudly as merit badges. She was disappointed when they started to heal and always glad for an opportunity to swing them about in front of people during some pointless task. She liked them when they were almost in the shape of letters and sometimes left her hand against a hot handle to create one.

Tonight they would have chops and rice with a cider sauce. She opened the windows so the neighbours would know she could cook fancy dinners. He sat in a cloud of swirling smoke like the Wizard of Oz, shouting at the stories in the *Daily Mirror*.

'They can't hear, you know, Jesus Christ alive.' Maggie was

pleased with her remark; she didn't pause to deliver it, just walked straight into the kitchen, didn't even look at him. Cat spit. He'd felt it too, lowered the paper, stopped breathing for a moment. He knew he only had himself to blame. He had chastised himself more than once for having a child on his hands at his age, a lass at that, and him over his three score and into his final ten. It'd crossed his mind that Iris might be put off. Remarkable, mind you, that he had it in him, he decided. He allowed himself to marvel a little at his own stout-heartedness, reckoned if there were a flaming God after all, this'd do him right by the church rabble, get him his ticket for upstairs alright. It would turn out fine anyhow, mind you; she'd be gone soon, they always did, remarkably unreliable females were, couldn't seem to help themselves, gone as soon as look at you most of them. He ran through his roll-call; mother, sister, wife, daughter, all of them gone one way or another and left him to ponder the mess left behind. This one, the grand-daughter, 'd be the same in time. Take the club with her, mind you; great thing, a football club going down father to son and on and all – a girl would do these days, handed down the generations. Club won't up and sod off at the first excuse, club is standing there a lifetime, not just your own neither. Might lose a game or two, sign the odd clodhopping wanker p'raps, on an off day, it does happen, but you'll not wake up on a flaming Wednesday and find it's disappeared into thin air.

He pulled a breath over the thought of losing her. Laid his long fingers across his forehead while his ribs panicked in and out like bellows. Keep the head, tall fella, nought lost just yet.

'Smells alright,' he called out to her in the kitchen. 'Ravenous, I am,' he added, more to himself really.

She poked her head out, sharp as a cuckoo. 'You'll have to

wait,' she responded gravely, pink from the steam.

'Right you are, mate.' And he winked. 'Any afters?'

The Fox and Dogs

It was Saturday night and the landlord at the Fox and Dogs had his wife Sheila helping behind the bar. Sheila had hair the colour of champagne; it burst out of her head in tight bouncing bubbles. She displayed her gold necklace chains on a plinth of bosom and always asked everybody how they were. Men often remarked upon her lovely smile; those who were hit by it often behaved irrationally, raising their voices, arm-wrestling their neighbour, like a bewitchment really. Tonight the smiles were coming thick and fast and all the men were shouting and pointing at one another, things like, 'You know what your trouble is, don't you?' 'If you believe that you'll believe anything,' and, 'I'll sort you out later.' Everyone bought rounds continuously to stand in front of the smile; each bloke had about three pints lined up at any given time. Pop, Maggie noticed, was not immune. He strolled by Malc's table, both hands around a clutch of pints, fag in teeth, talking.

'Ask a question then, go on, tough as you like, try me.'

'Okay then, Arthur. What does it take for you to shut your bleed'n'ole?'

A ground-swell of laughter, but Pop didn't give up.

'No, go on, anything you like, come on.'

Malc narrowed his eyes, suspicious now. 'Why, pray? For what reason, might I enquire?'

'So I can bleeding well answer it, that's why.' More laughter, higher tidemark.

'You know what your trouble is, Arthur?'

'No mate, enlighten me.'

'You don't know half as much as you think you do.'

'True enough, mate. Ask us a question then and we'll see how I can't answer it.'

'Bloody daft, ridiculous. You ask me one.'

'Eh? No, I asked you.'

And off they went, around and around to nowhere.

Later on as they were leaving, Malc bid him goodnight in the car park with a parting shot. Pop was light-hearted, unprepared:

'The ousel-cock, so black of hue, with orange-tawny bill . . . ta-ra then, Malc, *Midsummer Night's Dream*, Act Three.'

'You've no business being in charge of that kid, mate, I'll say that.'

Pop stopped and turned and all the humour and swagger and beer was gone instantly. He stood and looked at Malcolm and Malcolm stood and looked at him. Someone came out the door and drifted away and there was a call of 'goodnight' from somewhere. Pop took a step towards Malc and raised his finger. 'I am warning you never to insult me or this lass again,' he said.

''Strue though, in't it, Arthur?' His face black from the shadow.

'If you speak like that once more I'll knock your block off, so help me, I will.'

And he walked away knowing if he didn't he would, there and then. Maggie and the dog scurried after, light-toed with excitement, rushing under a big tin moon to catch up.

'You're all mouth, Arthur Landywood, and no trousers, 's your problem.'

Malc's words followed behind them, lead balloons, continuing as they crossed Little Sutton Road, though the rest were indecipherable. Maggie struggled with the trouserless-Pop picture in her mind.

He walked with his head down, but on Clarendon Road the glow of moonlight revealed his face fallen in. She matched his marching pace and let her face fall the same.

Lob o' Lob

Old Bob 'Lob o' Lob' Roberts could usually be found at the table by the door at the Pint Pot with his giant box of cook's matches, whatever the day or the weather. Distracted, agitated, he guarded his post on the threshold like a watchful hobgoblin. He had dazzling white eyebrows that he pulled vigorously and a huge head with corners. His cloudy blue eyes watered when he spoke, his face reddened and his voice wobbled. Like Lewis Carroll's rabbit, he checked his watch frequently, demanded to know what time other people had. It always astonished him.

'That's not the flaming time, it's a bloody impossibility.'

Pop wondered if he might have a jinx or a hex for Malc. Something to throw him off his stride a bit, something harmless that would nevertheless prevent him from answering too many questions entirely correctly. Lob o' Lob said he did. He said it was a simple hex, utterly benign, a mischief really. It would manifest itself in his mouth, running about his teeth so that the answer would not get out right away, or would be scrambled if it did.

Pop nodded and handed Lob some money. Several green notes that Lob counted with a quivering thumb and a licking tongue.

He rarely talked about his sighting of the phantom thought to be the murdered Mary Ashford. So disturbed was he by it, the local rumour went, that he could not persuade himself to describe it to anyone. Miraculously however, he managed a few details for Pop and Maggie after a couple more pints, repeating himself and rolling his eyes for effect.

'Inexplicable,' he theorised. 'There's more to this world than meets the eye.'

Bob Lob had no colouring. He was not considered officially albino though every part of him was white. Only his little blue eyes, rimmed in pink, stood out, like a man drained of colour after a nasty shock, so it was assumed the phantom had spooked him. Lob folded his arms, raised his eyebrows and shook his head through the facts.

Mary was a farmer's servant who had attended Birmingham market with butter as usual on the day she died in 1817. In the evening she went to a dance at Tyburn House, a pub on the road to Tamworth. She left in the early hours of the morning with a man. The following day she was discovered raped and drowned in a pool on Penns Lane. The man, Abraham Thornton, was brought to trial for her violation and murder, but was acquitted. Mary's brother then invoked an ancient statute to 'Appeal for Murder'. Thornton responded by himself invoking an almost forgotten legal right which had not been excercised for centuries, whereby the accused could challenge the accuser to a duel. The challenge was refused and Thornton was free to go and live in America. The vicar of Dudley composed the lengthy epitaph for Mary's gravestone.

Her ghost – having chosen Bob Lob o' Lob as its witness one peaceful May night, the eve before the 158th anniversary of her death – appeared dramatically after closing time, sprinting towards him down Penns Lane in a long dress. Bob described his vision with one hand on his heart, the other extended as if he were in the witness box, with horrified affection.

'Beautiful lass, lovely, no more than twenty if a day. Terrible, just a kid. I thought maybe they'd had fancy dress at the Dog and Duck. Rooted to the spot I was. She came running and wailing and when she got close, still running now, splashing through the brook, spoiling her dress, I could smell what she'd had to drink. She ran straight into me sure as I'm sitting here and damn well disappeared, vanished just like that. Poof.'

'Oh ar. Bloody carry-on.' Pop's jaw was slung sideways into the palm of his hand as if he were sceptical and captivated simultaneously. 'What'd she been drinking then, Lob?'

'Stout, mate. Strong as you like, filled her boots.'

Pop seemed genuinely unsettled and drained his pint.

'And what had you been bloody drinking, eh?' On a spring of laughter as he got up for refills.

Bob Lob knew all the words on her gravestone off by heart. He claimed that after the sighting that night he just knew them the next morning as if by magic. He recited them slowly and carefully with a grim expression while Pop cackled to the landlady.

'As a warning to female virtue, and a humble monument of female charity, this stone marks the grave of Mary Ashford, who in the twentieth year of her age, having incautiously repaired to a scene of amusement without proper protection, was brutally violated and murdered on the twenty-seventh of May, eighteen-seventeen.'

Then with increasing emphasis and an added falsetto pitch of emotion:

Lovely and chaste as the primrose pale,
Rifled of virgin sweetness by the gale;
Mary! The wretch who thee remorseless slew,
Avenging wrath which sleeps not will pursue;
For tho' the deed of blood be veiled in night,
Will not the Judge of all the earth do right?
Fair blighted flow'r! The muse that weeps thy doom,
Rears o'er thy murdered form, this warning tomb.

Maggie sat as still as she could, hands in her lap, boiled and chilled with shame, considering whether the death could turn out to have been her fault. She stared dumbly at the beer-mats while Bob Lob shuddered. He dried his eyes and leant towards her. 'It's a vile world, shorty, not much cop.'

Bob Lob told tales of other hauntings, his hairline and ears turning red under the glare of the attention. The head that haunted the Wylde Green Road in search of its body so appalled him that he began to tell it a second time, revolting himself all over again. At the part where the 'poor bastard' was unable, due to a severe speech defect, to answer the questions posed by an advance party of the Duke of Cumberland's army in pursuit of Bonnie Prince Charlie, Bob Lob shook his head and found he couldn't go on. He could frighten himself to death with a story, even if he'd told it before. By last orders he'd be trembling like a greyhound and scorched in the face and neck from the shock of his own gruesome ramblings.

The ghost Maggie wanted to see was the one who wore a pink cardy and used the public telephone box in Station Road, Erdington. Various witnesses had spotted her countless times making endless telephone calls. Pop had a fondness for Spring-Heel Jack. He was in the lore of the Midland canal folk and featured in stories of the industrial Black Country. He haunted the spoil heaps and cinder banks and possessed astonishing athletic skills like Olga Korbut. Feared most of all by Black Country children were Rawhead and Bloody Bones, the ghosts of the old pit shafts and mine workings, who stole naughty children from their homes and carried them off to their dirty lairs. Kids were threatened with abduction unless they behaved. Lob o' Lob complained they didn't take a blind bit of notice these days.

The Meadows

Maggie watched her mother's elbows and haunches brush gloomy shapes behind the shower curtain. It shrieked left and right on its metal rings while she sang *The Look of Love* or *Yesterday Once More* through the downpour. Her voice was loud against the water and perfectly pitched. Her face would fill up with wonder when she sang; she closed her eyes and felt her way through, like you had to be blind to get there. If the song concerned an injustice of any kind (they almost always did) she would belt out the hook line with clenched jaw and fists. At full tilt Maggie could feel her mother's voice ringing through every timber in the house. Bawling out every last short straw and bitter disappointment on behalf of everybody who knew what they felt like. Back of the stalls and beyond. Maggie thought of the three little pigs and feared for the foundations. She imagined their dusty bodies buried under a rubble of roof tiles and ceiling plaster.

'Mum,' she said out of a tentatively small mouth during the chorus of *Downtown*. And then forgot her own question in the distracting glare of the neon lights so pretty and everything much brighter there and her mother's gleeful promise rising – '*you can forget all your troubles, forget all your cares . . .*' The tender songs made her mother's voice catch in her throat, lilting and rasping, soft as a shore lark, sending Maggie's ribs in all directions, making her scalp tingle like it did when her mother's long nails grazed through it. She often stopped and sang a phrase over, repeating and perfecting. When she'd had a few drinks she sang at her boisterous unafraid best, holding on to notes long after their appointed time until they sank with plummeting vibrato into the next verse. Her mother sang, she imagined, because it was all she could think of to do under the circumstances. Her voice reeled, clinging and falling through songs as though they were murdering her slowly with a quick knife and a flashing red cape. Her style was borrowed, but added to that was her own brand of luck-be-a-lady-tonight desperation and it was this that made you listen. The better she sang the worse Maggie felt. One night, *What Kind of Fool Am I?* boomed through the house with such blasting gala-night force, she felt almost compelled to applaud at the end. Instead she lay in the rushing stillness and waited. The creeping silence seemed to have swallowed the diva alive.

Her sandals slapped the tarmac, squirming under her like wax, until she had completed a tour of the whole estate, a daily ritual, her job almost, the Meadows Estate Ranger. She chose herself an official hat, her mother's Biba wide-brim, and trudged with her arms hanging lifeless at her sides. The roads and paths were soft and stinking as a primeval swamp, charred and black like a million years of bones and forest. The heat soaked up through her rubber soles so that her feet slid and throbbed inside the straps. The metal aerial and dials on her transistor radio burned and flashed in the dazzle. There were no trees anywhere on Ashfield Drive, Hazel Mead, Pine Close or Springfield Chase – they'd chopped them all down. Instead the occasional tiny sapling had been planted, evenly spaced in the grass verges, each tied to a stick and pissed on by the estate dogs, offering a fragile promise for the future. At high noon there was no shade. Maggie hoped she might faint in the heat, anything. She thought of an ambulance siren tearing up the silence, shaking them all out from behind their reflecting windows. She wiped her forehead and watched the houses wobbling in the haze as though it were all a

94

dream. Sahara girl. She let out a shout; it was swallowed quietly by the ghostly collection of echoing houses and empty curving road they called Drive.

Emboldened by the lack of response she let off a scream, also disappearing like water into the blank windows and runways of liquidising tar. Still no evidence of life.

'NUTS,' she raged. 'WHOLE HAZELNUTS.' The thunder of aftershock in her ears 'CADBURYS TAKE THEM AND THEY COVER THEM IN CHOCOLATE.' The crack of sound in the air seconds after; an ash willow rustled, shaking the yelling from its leaves. The empty houses, cul de sacs and parked cars remained unmoved. She wondered why there were no birds. She tried to look at the sun to see if she could make herself go blind, but its glare squeezed her eyes shut while she staggered left and right.

She switched on her radio. Van McCoy's summer hit, *The Hustle*, blasted full volume, the DJ talking megaphone-loud like an estate announcement in a happy-wow voice. 'HEY! HI! OKAY. YEAH. BIKINIS ON GIRLS. WOW. JANE FROM FARNHAM, ARE YOU THERE?'

Beyond the stream and its grassy banks Maggie could see a Triumph Herald float backwards out of a driveway. She watched while it hummed up the hill. She couldn't see anybody driving it.

Maggie peered into people's windows and gardens. She sat on their scorching walls and stared at their cars. She paused behind dustbins and fences to gawp and listen, eavesdropped in the shade provided by stumpy conifers. She pushed her head through a garden hedge once to discover a family eating in a circle on the other side. She tore out again, grazing her ears, the Polaroid of their amazed faces still damp in her mind as she ran away, stooping like a stoat at the sound of their laughter.

Sometimes when no one was around she pushed open letter-boxes and sniffed other people's lives, the seconds counting down her fear as she lingered over the sight of a discarded shoe, an electric cable, a wet towel hanging on a banister. She strained to read the handwriting on envelopes on the floor, trying to recognise the calligraphy, searching for her name. Occasionally she posted things, leaves, sweet wrappers, jokes sometimes, written in big biro words on notepaper and dashed with exclamation marks, and then raising the stakes, a gangrenous tennis shoe found by the stream, size ten. She thought she saw a face sometimes, floating at different windows inside, watching her, in the windows of her own house too. She squinted up self-consciously, waiting to catch her mother's platinum shawl of hair and pale expressionless face. When she did, it made her start and she waved stupidly, a sudden, frantic gesture as though one of them were setting off on a voyage.

There was a craze among girls for notepaper, luscious pastel pages, marbled in lilac, rose, swirling caramel. Pink 'Love Is . . .' notelets with the little naked people with the heavy eyelids and their amorous aphorisms. Misty pages with galloping horses stampeding in the margins, all with matching envelopes. Maggie hunched over them, biro poised, squirming with concentration. Finally she wrote 'Hello', then 'S.W.A.L.K.' She drew a smiley face. She couldn't think of anyone to send it to.

Sometimes her father would say to her mother, 'Me 'n' Maggie May are going by the store, back in a while I guess,' as though he were starring in some twenty-verse Tennessee song. After he'd smoothed back his hair and flattened his sideburns in the hall mirror that turned into an umbrella stand on its way down like a Lewis Carroll hallucination, he'd shuffle dog-gone down the front path. On he'd swing, past the hooligan mob of hydrangeas whose blunt blooms punched the air or hung like spewing drunks while their litter of petals turned brown as tobacco. Out on to Mean Street (mistakenly signed as Ashfield Drive) wide angle, big screen, narrowing his eyes against the sun while he checks for good, bad and ugly in Drive, Mead or Closeville that morning. Pausing for his good-guy close-up next to the Cortina, flinching as Clog Woman from over the road at number twenty-three whose husband never comes home, yells through her kitchen window at Scab Boy who has eczema. Scab Boy stops bouncing on the orange space hopper and turns towards her shout.

Maggie knows what her father is thinking as he gazes out at the location he chose for his life; she knows he knows this is Mars. The landscape, as far as the eye can see, is a carpet of repetition, like an endless roll of wallpaper spinning out across the county, yard after yard. Brick box, turf, shed, partition wire, repeat. Items representing and underlining the owner's individuality are scattered over the pattern, like splashes and smears, spoiling the uniform: wagon wheels, ponds, gnomes, frosted lanterns, rock gardens, slices of varnished wood decorated with sprigs of heather or a horse's head and the name lavished upon the brick box. Heathfell, Wildens, or the ones constructed from the initials of the occupants, Cretna. Footpaths network the drives if you are brave enough to enter the labyrinth on foot, sometimes producing sudden dead ends, or workmen under a toadstool of smoke. On Saturdays the area is littered with children bouncing, yelling, bicycling. Men mow their slice of grass and throw buckets of foaming water over their Fords and Vauxhalls. Inside, the women swear and tear food from ice compartments in snow-covered boxes.

Maggie knew her father knew it didn't happen this way in

country songs. In a country song you solved your problems on the porch, with a beer and a guitar and a woman who probably wasn't your wife. You drove to the store in your truck while the radio played songs about lives worse than your own under a big American sky in the land of the free and easy. He had taken advice from Merle and Glen and George and Johnny. The songs told him he had to walk tall and then keep right on walking and not pay any mind to what folks might say.

Mathew Rowley

Bad news lay in wait at the Fox and Dogs. The magpie had worked a malevolent mischief. A newborn baby had been found in a box by the bins near the Baptist church on Grange Lane in the early hours of Sunday morning. It had been there all night, dressed up for the occasion in soft pastels, neatly tied and wrapped, all tucked up cosy by the bins like Top Cat, with the lid on in case it rained. Making its rescue harder and its rescuer heroic: Mathew Rowley, nicknamed Lard. He thought someone was drowning kittens. He looked bewildered and ashamed in the local paper; it made the nationals too. Pop read them all at the newsagents and discussed it with every customer all afternoon. The heatwave had ensured the baby boy's survival. Girls are much more likely to survive hypothermia, it said in the *Daily Express*; no one at the newsagents knew why. The police called him Moses and he was taken to the Good Hope General Hospital on Cemetery Road. The mother was upset, it said in the *Daily Mirror*, and her name was Dawn. The *Sun* said she was a silly cow and a disgrace to British mothers.

Pop was inconsolable. He fretted and fussed, berated himself and others. 'Why? It don't make any sense at all.'

He stormed and paced, furious not to have rescued the infant himself, unable to come to terms with the decision to go to the Plough not the Dogs on that night, which would have led them all past the bins. He hung his head in his hands and let himself have it. Here was a golden opportunity wasted, the single gesture that would have clinched everything gone by the wayside. An act of heroism that would have guaranteed his place in local lore for all time, an accolade that even Iris could not ignore, damn and blastit. Ye gods, what was he thinking of? Where were his wits? his timing? his instinct? An infant to boot. He blamed the distractions of the quiz, and from there it was only a short hop to Malcolm, whose fault it swiftly became. 'Fat lot of good a hat trick is to a bab in a bin, mate. Things more important than a flaming pub-quiz title. Million times I must have gone by those bins,' he murmured with saucer eyes, incredulous at his bad luck.

He tore some foxgloves from the hedgerow and made off with them. They swung on the end of his marching arm, trumpets quivering, all the way to Tower Road, where he laid them, a fall of arrows, on Iris's step, a memorial to his missed opportunity.

'That'll have to do her for now,' he said as he strode away and Maggie turned to look at them, dumped on the shrine, waiting for the goddess who was never satisfied.

At home he pulled the encyclopedias from the top of the pile and dragged them to the kitchen table. He hunched over them, fag in teeth, sleeves rolled up, like there was a single irrefutable answer to the one big indefinable question and he would sit there all bloody day and night until he'd dug it up.

Maggie let herself out. She took enough coins for the bus and a 99 cone. Blowbroth followed, dragging an elastic line of saliva. She ran for a while and hid and even changed buses, but she couldn't lose him.

There were swings and roundabouts near Powell's Pool and a paddling pool by the Town Gate, donkey rides too sometimes, on a morbid-looking beast with green teeth. She and the dog sat by the Wyndley Pool to watch the people falling in and the kids getting slapped.

.

Pop preferred the west side of the park, the Streetly and Royal Oak gates. It was quiet there, deserted usually, and he could point and lecture and stride between the places of historical interest in peace. He liked to be close to the ancient sites; it made him feel part of a great galloping history. Time was dispensed with; it was not possible to grow old among neolithic monuments. Maggie dropped stones into Rowton's Well near the old peat pit, small ones to fit through the holes of the safety grille. She lay over it and called down and heard her voice reaching back to her. Pop said there was a man buried in the old peat pit, at least one, must be two thousand years old. Sometimes he walked into Maggie's dreams on slimed feet and said, 'Hey, Maggie May. Hi honey,' lit a cigarette and winked a blackened bog eye. Once he threatened to rape and drown her in the pool on Penns Lane. 'Burn in hell,' he added cheerily and winked again.

The top of Lord Donegal's Ride sloped along the bottom of Rowton's Hill and you could roll down for a while before hitting the gorse bushes. If Pop was supine somewhere, licking smoke from his teeth and staring in a stupor up into the umbrella of a giant beech, Blowbroth and Maggie would lie in the butts in a little coppice off the Donegal's Ride. The concrete-lined trench was the butts for a thousand-yard rifle range used for training soldiers during the First World War. Sometimes Maggie walked with stabbing Nadia Comaneci toes and arching back along the high northern wall.

Pop enjoyed the old Roman road. It stretched across the western fringe of the park, straight as a flinthead arrow, through flat, parched heathland, an occasional solitary tree reflecting Africa in his drizzly eyes, an enormous pale sky rolling out above them. At the right time of year the heather and bracken would leak mauve, amber and khaki, but now everything was brittle and scorched the colour of sand. He could spot dull-looking little plants with wish-and-sigh names like harebell and bird's-foot trefoil. But mostly he lectured on all things Roman as he marched the one and a quarter miles, bombarding its length with information. Narrowing his eyes at the distant horizon he'd fart in short, sharp artillery bursts with his stride.

It ran from Bourton-on-the-Water to Templeborough in South Yorkshire. Several times along the Sutton Park section, Pop would throw a look over his shoulder as if he half expected to see Julius Caesar standing emperor-tall in his chariot, hair streaming and reins flapping, thundering towards them in a vortex of dust and hooves.

Due to an excitement at the Fox and Dogs one Wednesday, consisting of Tatty swaggering in with a freshly broken arm, and the introduction of a Hot Selection of Meat Pies at the north end of the bar, Pop misjudged his fag ration and ran out halfway along the Roman road.

He swung dramatically around in all four points of the compass like a man surrounded, gazing far into each horizon, calculating options, panicking. 'Bugger it. Blast. That's gobbed it. We're buggered now, mate. Damn. Nobody noticed the fags were down?' he asked, his face folded up, incredulous. 'Nobody saw I'd not picked 'em up?'

They glared at Blowbroth. He regarded them suspiciously,

his tail wagging faintly. Pop frisked himself again, sizzles of air escaping between his teeth. He flattened his hair. 'Christ, I always pick 'em up at lunchtime, bugger it.' He turned on Blowbroth. 'S'pose you're bloody blind now as well as flaming flatulent, useless pillock. Christ, there's dogs in bloody Russia can ride a horse and smell a loaded gun on a man at fifty paces. Fat chance you'd have on the steppes, mate, fat bloody chance.'

The dog found a spot in the middle distance and lowered his gaze there.

'Ones like you go straight in the goulash, ask questions later. You wouldn't last five minutes under the sickle, mate.' Pop was demon-eyed, desperate. 'You're supposed to be a ruddy trained dog, you are. Ye great gods and little fishes, trained to fart all bloody day, that's a fact. Vile, malodorous hound, I'd sooner have a bag of gizzards on a flaming leash, so I would. Jesus wept.' And he was off in a reel of jacket and white of eye. He flew like a bat down the ancient road, heading precise as a guided missile for the Parson and Clerk. Puffs of dust appeared at his heels as he walloped along and cries of, '*Juldee! Juldee! Haramkor!* Bugger it. Blastid hound.'

Girl and dog didn't catch him up until the Royal Oak gate, scuffing along his cordite trail. An enormous magpie watched them from a dying tree. Maggie didn't bow, spit or cross her fingers, but she returned its sentinel stare and in her mind took careful aim and blew it to pieces with a Winchester rifle.

Several yards on she could still feel it watching her back, so she turned and yelled, 'Blastid devil-worshipper bastard, bugger you!' A great charge of noise exploding across the park.

Blood fell in her head as the bird tore away, its black cape smacking around its shoulders, pulling it into the sky; the sound of a thin laugh where it used to be.

Spared the usual briefing that accompanied even the shortest journey, Maggie was able to hear the park's silent meditation for the first time and noticed how loud her steps were in the middle of a big nothing. Each scrunch of shoe in dirt was amplified in the stillness and was followed in a two-time beat by the rasp of denim against its opposite flare. Just like the grind and swish of the knives sharpened by the man who dragged his cart from door to door to ask if you had any needed doing; he'd turn them over in his greasy hands, creased with work, before stroking them over the wheel. Blowbroth padded lightly by comparison, tiny stones shifting. His breathing was his noise; he was always sighing, wheezing, clearing his throat, gagging and hiccuping and now, at last, panting like a proper dog. They shuffled on, scraping and gasping like a sword fight, until they caught sight of him at the Royal Oak gate, jumping up and down impatiently under a horse chestnut, jerking frantic shapes, a frenzy of semaphor.

He bought three packs of cigarettes at the Parson and Clerk and smoked all the way home. He quoted from the Rules and Regulations of Sutton Park and Promenade Gardens, written in 1869 and committed to his memory in Sutton reference library.

'All strange dogs found in the park will be destroyed,' he repeated, and let off his laugh on the railway bridge. They walked through long shadows, under cover of beech and oak where the light was green, through the clouds of midges and across the dual carriageway.

Near Grange Lane a mantilla of rooks trailed themselves across a yolk sun. Their spiteful laughter dropped jagged lines through the peace.

'*Corvus frugilegus*,' Pop murmured without looking up. 'Buggers, them. Ill wind. Like the bloke says, "Man that is born of woman hath but a short time to live." Someone'll cop it tonight, mate, mark me.'

Mere Green

Mere Green library was a small squat building, dashed with blue mosaic at the front, gloomy and brown within. Pop was working his way through it in preparation for the day he could call himself General Knowledge.

He returned his books to the desk with an attention-grabbing thump and a flashing wink for the horn-rimmed girl with the ink stamp. Maggie idled up and down the aisles of books, stumbling over her long feet, throwing her forelock from her eyes and burning her fingers on the backs of plastic chairs. She pulled out a tall, glossy book and sat down in a corner darkened by a dingy shadow. The pages were luscious with shine, silky with information. A series of photographs of a woman, pale and exhausted, drooping with sadness, weeping. On the following page, reminiscent of the before-and-after hairspray ad, the same woman smiling, animated, her hands flown up either side of her face to emphasise a hail of words. Maggie stared at the text in between. Cognitive/behavioural treatment of depression . . . dopamine . . . neuroleptics . . . hypomanic . . . cognitive therapy. She thought of her mother's face, the way it said Jesus Flaming Wept. In the middle of a paragraph, hooded and accusing, lay the word 'suicide'.

Maggie slipped the book inside her shirt and folded her arms over it. When they left she slid behind Pop as he nodded, winked and cheerioed, while she held the book's secrets against her ribs.

Omar Khayyám

He is semi-dressed with a wrung-out tea towel wrapped around his head to cool his brain. He is listing Catholic saints and Grand Prix winners. The newspaper reported one and a quarter million unemployed and also that some people had died in the heat, of dehydration. 'Cheers then,' said Pop.

Ninety-three degrees Fahrenheit, the hottest August day for half a century. Feverish temperatures, whole delirious weeks spent trying to breathe, to think. Nobody moves. Water has become a precious commodity, gold and silver out of the taps now and penalties for misuse. The water behaves badly of course, now that it is prized; it escapes unless it is carefully contained and covered over. Maggie sees it in the air, blurring the cars and houses, making whole afternoons jump up and down. The sun, bright metal in a hazy sky, pulls it up from the rivers and lakes just when people need it most. The heat roars down by day and rises into the black at night, warming the cool stars that weren't really there at all because they had done all their shining over the Roman road or the clear-eyed soldiers training in the butts.

The only effective response is to submit, so the old man and girl hang deadly still like photographs, in motionless dazed shapes, just daring to breathe. In Coventry they are having a freak storm, ninety-five-mile-an-hour winds, rain, snow, hailstones and a five-minute tornado.

'I don't believe a bloody word of it,' Ken says at lunchtime.

At dusk the clouds gathering over the sludge-treatment works turn a violent orange. A faint breath of air sighs through gaping doors and windows. People move about at last, they close their eyes and tip back their heads to receive the caresses of the frailest breeze. Maggie feels the air chilling her wet eyelids, laying a cold coin on each. The setting sun torches the front room until it blazes in shades of copper and garnet. She watches herself in the small speckled mirror on the mantelpiece, a stupefied stare, drunken. Damp dark eyebrows like scorches, hair all aflame in the inferno. Blowbroth has turned pink in the light; he pants and drools, bug-eyed with bad temper.

Pop is bewitched. He flits barefoot to and from the kitchen, shirtless, with his trousers rolled up, bearing dripping tankards of ale and R. White's lemonade, dunking and replacing his cooling tea towel turban.

'Gnat's piss!' he catcalls at the taste of the canned bitter before winking, coughing, igniting, and leaning into one of the stories that spread his arms wide with revelation. The heat transports him back in time, to Khumbirgram, Kalyan, Madhaiganj. He falls; arms out like a diver, through the years, squinting into the heat haze at the blur of names. Ahmadabad, Karachi, Hyderabad, Bangalore.

Maggie creeps upstairs, peels off her clothes and slides under the white sheet. She closes her eyes and lies like the newly dead, humming *Jerusalem* for her funeral dirge. When she opens one eye she sees the giant weave in the sheet and the glow of orange light pressing down. She pulls the library book out from under her feet. The pages flop, thickly varnished, pornographic with pictures, drawings of people howling with madness, cut and cauterised by dome-headed physicians to allow their demons out.

Seven o'clock. The dog refuses to make it to the pub in the heat. He is collapsed in the front garden a few feet from the door so that he is easily viewed from the street, for women to take pity on. His tongue is hanging in a horrible fleshy scroll on the path. Maggie is lead-footed down the stairs, the sheet knotted on her bony shoulder, heavy-lidded, humming, a foul-faced emperor. Pop complains heartily at the inconvenience caused by the dog, but the novelty of a revised schedule excites him and he has a freshly cooled tea towel on and is crouching like a dhobi, shirtless and barefoot, on the old armchair. He has reached verse thirteen of the *Rubáiyát of Omar Khayyám*, which he recites aloud with so much hissing pleasure it is hard to imagine he hasn't written it himself.

> Those, boy, who went before
> Have been laid in the dust of self-delusion;
> Go, drink wine and hear the truth from me,
> It was all hot air that they spoke.

Pop swipes up his can of ale and glugs.

'Gnat's piss!' he declares again, smacking his lips, chasing a dribble.

She begins to feel light-headed. She allows her face to fall over the side of the settee like the victim of a terrible accident and charts the path of an arrow of sweat zagging through her hair. The *Birmingham Post* has gone up to seven pence, it lies in sheaves across the floor. Pop burps neatly, sucks in a breath, sings out the first word like a prayer from a mosque.

> Those who dominated the circle of learning and culture –
> In the company of the perfect become lamps among
>   their peers,
> By daylight they could not escape from the darkness,
> So they told a fable, and went to sleep.

He hoists up the beer again, swigs, grimaces, slaps it down. He caresses the page tenderly between his fingers as though it were superb cloth, harbinger of some exquisite magic, as if he were considering it to buy. His voice, low and reverential, rattling with grit, falls out of him in long dusty rolls, like yards of prayer carpet.

> The cycle which includes our coming and going
> Has no discernible beginning nor end;
> Nobody has got this matter straight –
> Where we come from and where we go to.

The curtain of smoke rising from Pop's fingers doesn't mask his eyes, liquid marble, dazed with thought. It is so quiet she can hear the crackle and burn of his cigarette.

'Okay, mate?' he croaks.

'Yeah, not bad,' Maggie replies.

'Think I'll win?' he croaks again.

'Yeah, no hassle. Probably.'

'Malcolm Denton's brain is in his arse.'

'Yeah, I know.'

Just the crackle and burn again.

'You're my flesh and blood, mate.'

'Yep. I know.'

Far away there is the distant clang of a church bell like something falling down. She glances and sees he has the tea towel bundled against his eyes. He makes no sound.

108

Villa Park

He had a surprise he said, for her. A gift for life. He was going to fetch it, he said, and sprang up the stairs two at a time. Pop had always been an Aston Villa man, which meant little to Maggie the day she arrived at Clarendon Road, but a week later she knew that Keith Leonard and·Brian Little were strikers and that manager Ron Saunders was the man who put Villa back in the First Division with his relentless system of preparation and organisation. Ron Saunders. 'Two of the greatest names in football,' Pop murmured, his eyes cast up at the ceiling in the direction of miracles, like a martyr of the Reformation. The great man Saunders walked and talked in straight lines, short sharp sentences and unequivocal advice snapped through his gangland mouth like a clip round the ear. Ron Saunders. The words would for ever after suggest mystical dominion to Maggie, hanging whispery on her breath. In 1974 he came, he healed, and nine months later Villa won the League Cup . . . say it soft and it's almost like praying.

He glowered out from last season's programmes. Broad hoodlum nose, wide brow and quietly threatening eyes warning you not to argue with or underestimate him, in shades of glossy grey. His movie-star cheekbones were hollowed deeper by charcoal sideburns, the square-set jaw told you he would not be moved, ever.

'I prefer to let results speak for themselves,' he growled through the firm horizontal line of his mouth before turning up his collar, checking his watch and making off briskly for somewhere else, dapper in a sharp brown suit, single-breasted.

The paisley tie gave away the secretly romantic boy from Birkenhead, stargazing beneath the brawn.

Villa Park was just over five miles away on Witton Lane in Aston. Imposing Victorian redbrick buildings, with Dutch gables and Jacobean flourishes, rose high against the sky. Panels and window frames were decorated in the club colours, great gold letters spelt out its name in mosaic, lovingly constructed by Italian craftsmen beside a roaring golden lion.

Pop had sworn his allegiance as a boy. His own father detested football — 'Grown fellas traipsin' up and down' — fuelling Pop's commitment. The men on his father's side of the family were pigeon-fanciers. His great-uncle would position himself a mile or so from home and shoot any birds in front of his with a shotgun.

Aston Villa. Maggie liked the tall, glamorous letters and the drama of the claret and blue, blood and sky, death and salvation, colours of the bullring. She stared at the collection of programmes in Pop's room, assembled in towering stacks by his bed, all dashed inside with exclamation marks, declamatory capitals and men in mid-air. She'd heard the chanting on the radio, rising and falling like a mass prayer and the commentator choking over near misses. Grown men enraptured. The gymnastics of the old man on a Saturday away game — first to his knees in a blood-curdling cry, then down on his hands like the devout to Mecca when his team scored a radio goal — shocked and interested her, cheered her up. She liked the carry-on, the glory of the tournament, the male-dominated order, the serious business of belonging. She paid attention.

Then Villa played Leeds United at home on August 16th, the first home game of the new season.

Pop presented her with her gift for life standing stiffly at the foot of the stairs, feet together, jaw locked and eyes brimming.

'Surprise!' he cried and handed over her ticket. The lump in his throat was for him. To play professional football had been his cherished boyhood dream, him and all the rest. His childhood had rung with the sound of the Holte End goals he would score. In wilder fantasies he'd heard the wind snatch the flag of St George and the drumroll, stamp and cry for 'England . . . England'.

They took a train from Four Oaks station under a sky already flying one of the club's colours. Pop's watch was wrong and they were an hour early. He held it by the strap and thrashed it against his leg, mystified, inspected it and thrashed it again.

'Wrong with the bloody thing? It's going bloody backwards, mate, backwards for Christmas; all we flaming need.'

The platform was deserted, swaying in the heat that pushed them into the shadow of the pre-war wooden ticket office and waiting rooms. Peeling paint, green and white like a cricket pavilion. The cables hummed, the metal tracks turned to water under the glare and sang faint eerie notes like mermaids' warnings. The two of them were alone in the dusty blaze, anxious and impatient as gunfighters arrived early at the OK Corral.

The tension sent Pop pacing the length of the platform and back on a cable of smoke, his eyes narrowed suspiciously, spooked by the mystery of the missing hour, snapping his wrist around to check again. Then other feet echoed on the metal bridge that straddled the track with the high sides so you couldn't throw yourself off. Flashes of claret and blue, sloping lads, flinching and heckling, men and boys, mumbles and shouts, stalking the platform, squinting up the track into the sun.

'Time is it, mate?' Pop asked one and then another.

The train rushed past the Sheffield Road allotments, the broad green playing fields, empty save for two girls and a pram, and the crowd of silver birch that leant precariously out of the steep bank, waving on the carriages. Four Oaks, Sutton Coldfield, Wylde Green, Chester Road, Erdington, Gravelly Hill, Aston. 'Gravely ill,' Pop announced at Gravelly Hill. 'ANYBODY GRAVELY ILL?' he tried again when there was no response. The train filled up. Maggie stared out of the window. They floated past a discarded heap of pink and yellow foam squares on top of an old mattress and some tyres. Past the backs of redbrick terraces with their sheds and corrugated iron. Past the loaded washing lines and bonfires smoking. Between the giant cement pillars that held up junction six of the M6, a sudden temple of cool shade and dusty tangerine corners. And out again past the industrial warehouses and waste ground grown lush with weeds. The vast blue sky raced towards Villa Park, visible now from the train. A clatter of metal applause along the last piece of track into Aston while a flock of seagulls fell into the scrapyard opposite the flyover.

At Aston station they troop down the steps past the policemen and the dogs, under the bridge and on to Grosvenor Road. On up the Aston Hall Road, pulled along with the carrier bags towards the expressway where those on foot come from all directions trailing ribbons and banners. A denim army, footsoldiers with a stout song and hair on their shoulders like the Celts at Bannockburn for Robert the Bruce. Past the beefburger stands with their onion stink and bottles of lipsmackingthirstquenching Pepsi. Past the parish church of St Peter and St Paul where sometimes a bride trips out on a match day. Under the ancient beeches that sun-dapple the bubble-shaped words JESUS IS LORD, making them dance. Police dogs lean out on their leashes on Witton Lane where the wall declares 'Death to City + Utd'. On they march to the iron-gated entrance where the horses' hooves shatter and groups of lads start to run, scarves streaming from their wrists and heads. Wide-legged denim, cropped at the ankle, sprinting for the Witton, Holte and Trinity gates. Everybody hurries though nobody is late. Past the man selling rosettes, his cries skidding, shuffling through the pre-war turnstiles with their dungeon clang. Their feet flash up concrete steps, carried by those behind, almost running at the top of the last flight, shouts bursting out of the concrete. Level now with the earth bank, the terrace falling away beneath, already half full, barriers propping the leaners who lean their way from bar to terrace barrier and back to bar again. Cloth cap and sawn-off flares all thrown in, the retired and the jobless, our kid and our wench. 'Ob-La-Di, Ob-La-Da, life goes on, la la la la life goes on,' scratching through the public-address system in the Trinity Road stand, as though people might dance even though obviously nobody does.

Then the pitch, between bodies.

Just a flash and then all of it blazing.

Electric green, as though everything else were black and white. It floats up, exotic and flawless.

Crouching opposite is the Holte End, its floodlight pylons rearing twice as high as the Aston church steeple beyond. Pulling the sky down over the ground until nothing else exists in the world except the match, and today nothing else does because Villa are back in Division One. The song says so. It starts at the Holte End, travels in a horseshoe and rises up into the wider blue. Between the advertising for Dunlop, Bristol Street Motors, Davenports, Esso, Dormie Menswear and the Ansell's Bittermen, are rows and rows of Villa faces.

Pop tucks the both of them behind the railing at the top of the earth bank and a staircase of heads falls away beneath them down the rake of the Witton End terraces. Somewhere far below are the Leeds United fans and their lilting moan. From up here the whole world is green pitch and a swaying song. The Holte End answers the visiting fans, and the turmoil of noise brings more bodies behind Pop and Maggie on the bank. Another disco hit on the public-address. Pop's fingers shaking so his fag won't light. An ovation as Saunders takes the bench with granite jaw, and an ascension of claret and blue balloons lifting out of the Holte End as the players sprint out into a riot of noise. On the other side of the great green sea, deep inside the mouth of the Holte, a stew of denim bodies ripples and rolls. Here are the claret-and-blue army tipping in a storm. The tune is *Amazing Grace* but the only words are, 'Villa, Villa, Villa, Villa, Villa, Villa, Villa . . .', their arms stretched out in Vs, scarves trailing. They spill together, switching chants without command. A banner for Saunders, urgent clapping, the rumble of stamping. 'VILLA!' The noise rolling forwards and back and meeting itself again increased, the roar and thunder of stamp and clap. 'VILLA!'

Seven minutes and Leighton Phillips scores, running through the flop of his hair, chasing the long punt upfield from Cumbes, and Villa are one-nil up in the First Division. The men from Leeds, virtuous in white, do not look as perturbed as they might; they trot away on their hind legs while forty-six thousand voices split the air. Pop with his hands in the sky and tears in his eyes, surrendering, trying to shout but he's too choked. In the Holte End some are upside down, blue denimed legs scissored to make the V, swayed left and right by their mates, the cascading of coins ringing off the terraces.

'We all agree . . . Billy Bremner's a wanker . . .'

But the Aztec sun burns on and Villa's luck burns with it. Big-man Gidman with the longest hair on the pitch handles the ball and the penalty gives United an equaliser. Walk on. Then the Villa keeper, sandy-haired Cumbes, loses his grip and Lorimer for United strolls a second ball into the net. Walk on. Songs and chants still rising and falling around in a loop, battle-cry and prayer both. High above them a cloud slides past. Maggie imagines her mother clinging to its upper side, sees her white knuckles, catches the tail end of her scream.

'Oooohhh,' groans the crowd as Carrodus the roadrunner misses, followed by a sudden clatter of polite applause. Maggie watches as the cloud's final wisp is swallowed by the Trinity Road stand. Walk on, with hope in your heart. The final whistle hails a two-one defeat and a defiantly raucous cheer because worse things happen at sea than scoring a goal against Leeds United in the First Division.

Jesus Christ Superstar

She had a dream about her mother. Then another. Then she dreamt about her every night. Grotesque noisy fantasies, as she woke the familiar voice still speaking as if her mother were standing in the room.

Blessed Mary, ever a Virgin, blessed Michael the Archangel, blessed John the Baptist, pray to the Lord our God for me. Sometimes she scooped her mother up in a dream and tucked her into bed or propped her over a plate of food. Once she came flapping down like an archangel and blew smoke in her face. Holy Virgin pray for our sins. Then she woke to feel the length of her mother's breathing body tucked behind hers, the shock in her mouth, her heart falling over her ribs, another prayer of contrition, a last-ditch bid for salvation, a stab in the dark.

Sometimes her mother sang in dreams. The songs she used to sing, Burt Bacharach or Carole King, wispy songs in minor keys, tinged with wisdom and regret. She used to sing when she was driving. *Do You Know the Way to San Jose? en route* to

Tesco on the high street. Like Pop she smoked at the wheel, flinging the dog-ends out of the window and grabbing the gearstick afterwards to change up and roar away, as though the thing might explode behind them. She sang *Walk On By* with her eyes closed and it always made her cry. Maggie tucked herself behind a door to listen. She could hear the clamour of birdsong from the trees outside her mother's bedroom window, like the sound of heckling.

On reading a story in the newspaper one morning about a successful suicide from the top floor of an NCP car park, Maggie's mother remarked that if it were her she'd opt for pills or poisoning, or, in third place, walking into the sea like John Stonehouse. At Rottingdean perhaps, if it wasn't too cold. She was appalled at the idea of hitting concrete at sixty miles an hour, quite disgusted, and dismissed blood-letting in the bath and blowing one's brains out as inelegant and unseemly, a lousy bid for attention. She felt suicide was something to be got on with quietly by yourself, like Fuzzy Felt. Hanging didn't come into it. She added she would never choose a room with a decent carpet, or one that held fond memories for those left behind. She would choose, if it were her, somewhere innocuous yet familiar, that offered easy cleaning possibilities. Gas, carbon monoxide and fire constituted, she felt, a danger to others, both unnecessary and selfish. She would choose, if it were her, to cause the least trouble or offence. Something quiet and simple, perhaps involving water and violins, or an outbuilding on a summer evening. There. Then she lit a cigarette, took off her tights and put a Joni Mitchell record on, while the speech carved its slow alphabet into Maggie's memory.

Her mother liked Joni Mitchell singing about the last time she saw Richard, and Carly Simon with the clouds in her coffee. She read *Fear of Flying* by Erica Jong. She read for three days without looking up and had to smoke the stash of Sobranie cigarettes she was saving for Christmas. When she'd finished she fell into a depression and played her records a whole two numbers louder on the volume knob. The house was allowed to grow organic piles of mess in every room at which she would nod and smile icily, as though the disorder was evidence of some theory now demonstrating its cynical absoluteness. At Boots the chemist she asked the girl at the prescription counter questions in an American accent and retained the same drawl for the manager of Millward's Shoes, who asked her, with a muscle above his eyebrow bouncing with bewilderment, to repeat everything she said.

The book lay, crackling with radioactivity, on the hall table, black lettering on reflective yellow like a traffic warning. Her mother slunk about with the cat over her shoulder for comfort. A dark dusty familiar with long, bony hips that slept on the Potterton boiler until it reached blast-furnace temperatures. Maggie watched its Nefertiti face swaying behind her mother's back and the waving asp tail peeping around her waist.

The answer to all Carole's prayers came a few days later and was in the end heaven-sent. An audition, in London, for a touring production of *Jesus Christ Superstar*. 'Oh my God,' she said, 'it's a sign,' her eyes melting wider with awe as she explained how she'd bought the record of the show only two weeks earlier to replace her copy that got broken. A miracle. Carole decided she would stay overnight with her friend Trudi, a dancer, in Bayswater. For six days the house was filled with, *I Don't Know How to Love Him.* Maggie prayed for the foundations as Carole volcanoed through. '. . . *should I scream and shout, let my feelings out? I never felt this way before!*' Rugs, lamps and tables blew out through the shattered windows in Maggie's mind before the restful pause and quavering question '*What's it all about?*' replaced the roof gently.

Then on the seventh day Carole travelled to London in a trouser suit from the Trafford catalogue and a pair of high-heeled boots, with a clutch of miniature Martinis tinkling in her bag. Maggie went to stay overnight at Debra Turner's house. Debra had clear eyes, thick black eyebrows and a large brown mole on her shoulder. At school she was considered good at sport; if Debra Turner called your name for her team you were made. She rode her bike standing up, pumping it forward with her powerfully sculpted brown knees. Debra was a sexy bird; it said so on the wall of the dining hall. Maggie had been surprised by their friendship. A Bay City Rollers song had thrown them together because Maggie was the only other girl who knew all the words. They sang *Shangalang* at double speed during break-time through bursting mouths with graveside faces, eyes cast down.

Her house was older than Maggie's and surrounded by towering trees so that every room was dark and cool. When the sun shone it sent tall stripes up and down the hall and across the pale walls. Debra's mother wore green canvas gloves and dug with a trowel on her haunches in the garden. Indoors, strands of her long dark hair fell into her eyes, striping her face like the walls. Debra said all men and women cared about was having sex with one another and she showed Maggie her brother's *Playboy* magazines to prove it. When they were tucked up in bed in her cosily chaotic room, Debra read aloud from *The Exorcist*.

The next morning across the butter and jam and cornflake cockerel floated a jumble of breasts, buttocks, vomit and iron crucifixes. Maggie flinched with tiredness while Debra sprang up and down on her smooth cyclist's knees for another jar of something to swab on her toast. Outside, Maggie thought she saw the trees moving closer to the latticed window. At school, the intimacies they'd shared were forgotten and by the time the break-time bell clanged its death knell through the babble and panic of the yellow corridors, Maggie had already been dropped.

Carole returned in a new dress in a state of thrilled dismay. She wore the dress for two days for luck while she waited for the phone to ring. It was white cheesecloth with elasticated smocking across her bosom, making her look like a strumpet Miss Muffet. Too nervous to sit down on her tuffet, she smoked pack after pack of St Moritz menthol cigarettes, so that every time Maggie trailed into a room, she'd find her wreathed in white cloud like a fallen angel, billowy in the folds of her lucky dress. When the call eventually came, ripping open the hall like machine-gun fire, Maggie thought her mother must have got the job, because she heard her laugh. The guillotine crash of the phone and the prime and bang of the bedroom door told her otherwise. Her mother was not to be Mary Magdalene after all.

The Number 103 Bus

I Can't Give You Anything (But My Love), Stylistics, enters the chart at number thirty-five. It soars over the landing banister and waterfalls down the stairs. The doorbell throws everyone up in the air as usual. Pop is aghast from the shock. 'Why didn't you knock? Christ.'

Dolly rolls her painted eyes. 'Cos there's a bloody bell. Where's the kid? Feet are killing me. As if there aren't enough trouble in the world.'

Blowbroth is snapping, Dobermann-style, at her ankles. A wild card, a shot at seduction by fear, a bit of an experiment.

'What's got into you, you fool? Shut it! Now! Blastid hound.' And she slugs him with the Co-op carrier bag, pendulous with the weight of Pop's newly polished shoes.

'Saturday, Doll, I've got till. *Saturday*, mate!' He is half dressed, a fat tome swinging on the end of his smoking arm and his hair standing up at the back.

'Wrong in the head that dog is getting, Art. Where's the kid?'

'Follow the bleeding disco beat, Doll. Any shirts pressed?'

Maggie hears the gasping and wheezing on the stairs.

'You there, love? Watcha. Valhalla!' Maggie doesn't answer, she doesn't know why. A crocodile toe peeps and then a bulging knee and a green viscose skirt. Then the rest of Dolly in a sleeveless pink polyester-knit with bouncing beads and daisy earrings. She dances in on trembling spike heels, jiggling and grimacing, dragging round the phlegm in her lungs like gravel rolling in a drum.

'Hiya Doll.'

Maggie stares. There is something disquieting about her dancing this way, something comical but horrible, like a cat wearing doll's trousers.

'. . . *La la . . . is anything . . . but a love . . .*' Dolly sings.

'You look nice,' Maggie says.

'Not as young as I was, flippin' heck, damn stairs, make road,' and she heads for the bed while her lungs heave about their load of grit and tar. 'So help me Bob,' between wet barks. An attempt to spare Maggie a blasphemy, little did she know. She falls against the springs next to her and bounces there gently, which soothes her coughing and closes her frosted-blue eyelids. She sleeps for an hour and a half.

They go to the Plough and Harrow at lunchtime, pausing for Dolly to catch up, stopping every few minutes for her bad feet in their vicious crocodile-skin shoes. Eventually she takes them off and walks the final part up Slade Road barefoot.

'If it's good enough for Sandy Seashore, mate, it's good enough for me.' Her laugh sends the birds streaking from the trees, smears them across the sky.

Pop strides ahead. 'Daft wench, like some flaming hippy you look like.'

'Oi, be polite, you. Grumpy sod. I'll bloody streak I will, then you'll know about it.'

Dolly threads her arm through Maggie's and sticks her thumb out at an oncoming Hillman Minx. The moon-faced driver watches them with increasing alarm as he coasts nearer.

When they arrive at the pub Dolly falls through the shrieking door, instantly capturing seven men's undivided attention, and drives her damp and heaving bosom on a swaying journey to the bar. 'Hose me down with a bottle of your best stout, barman,' which rouses a weary but consenting cheer, while she peppers Ken with rounds of assault-gun laughter.

'Don't encourage her. Daft wench. Knock it off, Doll mate, you're making a fool of yourself.'

Dolly knocks them back. She's thirsty and flirtatious, a deadly combination. Her small hot feet are slung up on the ruby banquette where they arch and point and pounce at one another. She tells a joke which halfway through falls apart in her mind, leaving her completely baffled, so she delivers the punch-line without context and is left to cackle alone at whatever it is she cannot recall.

Pop leaves, stepping between the squeals of the door as if he has knifed it on the way out. Maggie is torn. So, momentarily, is

Blowbroth, and then he is trotting after, scorned one too many times that week.

Dolly is up to the bar with her empty glass, edging her bottom on to a stool and running her fingers through her yellow perm. From the giddy height of her new perch she begins to trill some more, wrapping her feet around underneath and hand on her hip too, as though this were Marseilles not Slade Road in Roughly. Maggie slips through the door, releasing it gently to silence its wail.

Outside the air is burned up with sun. She can feel the ground rising and falling under her feet. The scrape and scratch of grasshoppers makes her sleepy, the empty roads look ethereally strange. Pop and Blowbroth are nowhere to be seen. Her shoes graze the tarmac. The whole world has died again. She squints up and down. Nothing. She puts her hands in her pockets and drags along, stinging with self-pity. Then on Grange Lane she brightens at the sight of the post office, having hauled up twenty-three and a half pence from the gritty hollow of her pocket.

The 103 bus goes from Slade Road to Lower parade in the town centre. Maggie sits in the front seat on the top deck and bites the top off a long, scrolling wand of Curly Wurly, wishing her radio were on her knees blaring, keeping folk away.

She gets off at High Street, before the parade, and walks along Railway Road to the park's Town Gate. She can hear the other kids' screams before she sees them and hurries the last bit until she is bobbing in the queue at the Mr Softee ice-cream hatch.

Kids spin, tumble and fly up on metal swings against cotton clouds, open mouths crowded with yelling. They storm from slide to roundabout, ransacking and pillaging, dispatching opponents and removing objectors, hurrying nowhere, spoiling the view. Maggie dives for a vacant swing; her height leaves the smaller ones hesitating so she never has to wait long. Her long legs hang in the grit; she lets her feet rake up dust. She forces her mouth, tartan with frozen flavours, wide to catch the drips, then swings high on sinewy forearms until her big feet tip at last into the blue. Flashing by next to her is a heavy boy set like a pit pony with a Walsall scarf tied round his head, a raspberry spatter of acne down his cheek. He lets out a banshee cry that fills every inch of the broad sky, sending her higher into space, towards Stanley Kubrick's silent black, where no one can hear you scream, even for a First Division team.

She asks someone the time and stands in the queue at the bus shelter next to a pregnant woman in flip-flops. The top deck is almost full and the woman next to her chats in friendly Brummie tilts. Maggie leans her forehead against the window and hums a Frankie Valli song so she can't tell what she is on about. She feels her blood chilling and rolling down her legs. She notes the woman smells faintly of sweat and wears a wedding ring. Trapped now, have to make the best of it. Poor, better, much better, best. Best. George, striker, Manchester United (137 goals), genius, likes a drink. That's the third zebra crossing on this journey, counting crossings now, red cars, orange cars. She begins to relax again. The bus swings slowly on its route, heaving and growling, lunging around obstacles. She remembers travelling this way with her mother before the first Cortina stood glinting like Memphis sequins in the driveway, waiting for her father to slide into the shining blue seat, park his elbow and croon the first line of a country ballad. As they lurch off the Mere Green roundabout in Four Oaks and rumble towards Maggie's stop, the woman next to her lights a cigarette and says, 'I wouldn't mind, but it's not as though I'm here very often, least they could do is get us a day return.' Maggie feels the weight of the bus quaking through her temple, focuses on the houses floating past. Bugger off, bugger off, bugger off, bugger off . . . She sees her stop coming but she cannot move at all now. The woman's smoke rolls against the window, greying the sunlight, a creeping doom-laden fog. Maggie watches as her stop arrives and departs and disintegrates into blurred fragments in the trembling glass panels. Another two stops come and go while she sits humming in the smog, until at the third the horror of the Birmingham depot sends her bolting down the steps.

The light turns blue as she reaches Turf Pits Lane and a blaze of pink streaks the sky as she rounds the bend by Roughly Farm, stepping out at a pioneer's pace, the shelf of hair bouncing over her eyes, her mouth swung open, a look of composed astonishment slapped across her face.

St James's Churchyard

Pop had spent his precious last few brain-sharpening days making a bird table to present to Iris. 'Just a trifle to wet her palate,' he said and Maggie rolled her eyes in disgust.

'Psychology,' he hissed with a whistle in his teeth while they ate Maggie's toad-in-the-hole, more hole than toad but he was wolfing it, smacking his lips between greasy forkloads. 'The way to a woman's heart, matey, is use your brain.' He was using teak for now, which was expensive and difficult to work with, but there was method in the carpentry madness. More than just a courtship token built to woo and waylay, it was also an artful display of casual confidence for Malc's benefit. Psychology again. He sanded and shaved on the front path, so Malc would understand he was ready and fearless and had time for a spot of woodwork.

He was a talented carpenter. Once upon a time he had made

cabinets and doors for the first home he shared with Eve. He made the bed she died in. He carved little seahorses with his knife for Carole when she was a child.

At the RAF station in Yelahanka in 1944 he was chosen to present a model of a Mosquito aircraft, suitably inscribed, to His Highness the Prince of Berar, on behalf of his father HEH the Nizam of Hyderabad. As squadron chippie he'd been commissioned to craft a painted model and had taken painstaking care. The accuracy of the detail was remarked upon and it was fitting, the CO said, that he present it himself. The Prince took the salute as the squadron paraded, Present Arms was given as the bugler sounded, the RAF standard was hoisted behind the dais and Pop stepped stiffly forward with the little aeroplane he'd made, in his full service blue with his matching eyes and a sharp salute. Afterwards aircraft shot up the aerodrome, flying line abreast in grand Mosquito style while a ballot was drawn to select a number of men to join His Highness and his party at luncheon in the station Chinese restaurant.

Once the tools were in his hands Pop was a happy dog, full of swaggering charm and warbled verses. Tossing hammers and chisels in the air, catching them behind his back, grinning, whistling and shrugging through the drilling and sanding like some woodworking Tony Bennett routine.

When the work on the bird table was going well he sawed, planed and bevelled in a mini tornado of sawdust. Smoking and winking at the spectators: Maggie, a black pipe of liquorice between her teeth; the dog with an eyebrow raised.

> *You are my sunshine, my double Woodbine,*
> *My box of matches, my bottle of gin,*
> *My bottle of brandy from Tommy Handley,*
> *Yours sincerely Vera Lynn.*

And a burst of drilling at the end. When the teak refused to obey, the show was adapted accordingly. If he lost his temper the bird table suffered the occasional violent attack. Gone were the winking, singing, joking and grinning, in their place a slow persecution. He threatened it with a saw, a drawknife, a hammer; he wrestled it to the ground and circled slowly, a chisel at his shoulder, like a matador, considering punishments.

When they returned from the pub at lunchtime, his spirits greatly improved, he joined the spectators amid the wreckage of tools on the dead lawn. 'Well, if that doesn't soften her, I don't know what will,' he commented eventually, grinding a dog-end underfoot while the other two neither agreed nor disagreed and the bird table leant defiantly at its slight but discernible angle.

'When I've trimmed the feet,' he added, 'obviously.

'Oh ar,' he agreed with himself, 'you can carve your way into a woman's heart if you've a mind and tools to.' And he strolled towards it, moved by his metaphor, and knelt poetically beside it, as though he might try seduction.

They delivered it on foot, carrying it as if it were a sedan chair, one at each end, with matching stately steps. They stopped off for a rest at St James's churchyard, which lay around them in a sort of wistful chaos. Tall cotton grass and cat's-tail hung in fraying bunches, ancient lichened headstones leant left and right like crumbling members of a gentlemen's club, random scatterings of columbine and early forget-me-not turned their frail heads when a breeze passed by. The overall effect was informally poetic with a hint of romance.

Out of this graceful disarray grew a Gothic-revival church,

blushing a warm shade of rose sandstone, some of it the same blackening pink slabs that built the awe-inspiring Lichfield Cathedral with its flying buttresses, octagonal spires, crocket-covered pinnacles and elaborate towers. Pop's grandfather had carved the bishop's throne there, more than a hundred years ago. The campanile was decorated at the top of the turret with four black, Bavarian-style pinnacles straight out of *Sleeping Beauty*. Maggie imagined a tousled maiden calling from the top, pale from the shadow of the Black Forest, gold hair flying against the telephone cables, while below, waiting to prick your finger, were creeping thorny roses, stretching up to the tracery that ran over the lancet windows.

A wild cherry tree stood over Eve's headstone. Pop had planted it himself with the gravedigger's shovel. In the spring it wept ivory flower tears. She lay deep below, several fathoms under, a family grave. Pop would join her one day. 'Budge up then, matey,' Maggie thought, and turned to look at his long cheek that would one day be locked in the dark beneath them, reunited with his bride under a falling confetti of white blossom.

Maggie carried violets, cool from the shadow spread by the dark yew, for Eve's grave. She followed the path towards the spire of smoke rising out of the stone beneath the cherry, now lush with leaf. Pop lay on his plot, flat on his back with his arms folded, face to face with his creator, tobacco in his teeth.

'Due south-west. Can't complain. Poor buggers over there've got the north wind cutting through 'em all year.' His long shoes were splayed in a V at the end of the oblong, unlike the noble knights buried in their armour, their feet neatly appointed, toes together, supported by the stone likeness of their faithful dog. Then he grew still. Maggie felt the sky watching him back. For a moment he almost was, feet notwithstanding, cast in stone. A raven leapt from the giant horse chestnut, breaking the spell. He turned his head. 'You can see the boozer from here actually.' Which was true. Even with all the trees in leaf, the foaming golden jug and gleaming bold lettering of the Pint Pot shone clearly between the breaks in the foliage. He coughed and rolled his eyes. 'I tell you what,' he said, smoke siphoning out of his nostrils, 'eternity looks like a ruddy long time from here, mate.'

They picked up their ends and stepped a mindful rhythm along Tower Road until they got to thirty-one. They stood the bird table in the porch and lined up to look. It was magnificent, tall and proud with a pitched roof and turned feet, built to last from durable weather-resistant wood and an indefatigable passion. Pop was pleased, he sprang on to the step, smoothed his hair and leant down to the letter-box, pushing it open and taking a breath.

'Just to let you know,' he announced in his most reasonable rising and falling test-match tones, 'in case you were not in fact aware, I shall be taking part as an official contestant in tomorrow's annual general-knowledge quiz at the Fox and Dogs. Thank you.'

That night the sun slid behind the South Staffordshire Waterworks earlier than usual and the gathering reef of clouds bled pink and burgundy. For a small breath of time the day's flat sky hung broad and blue, providing a celestial celebration in the Villa colours over North Warwickshire. Maggie listened to the roar of the home crowd rising in her head and stared without blinking at the claret-and-blue banner flung randomly in the sky so that it would stay in her memory. Villa Villa Villa Villa Villa. Like the pulsing sweep of a lighthouse beam, scooping up the word and throwing it into a chanted spell meant to beguile the gods into offering a ten-point advantage in the First Division. Even as the clouds darkened and cooled to ash, their pink optimism remained warm and precise in her heart. An accident of weather had unfurled a Division One promise in the West Midlands sky.

Wendy King

While he tossed and turned in the other room she dreamt of a girl she'd known at school who, in reference to Maggie's boniness, addressed her – both in cursory conversation and when issuing earsplitting commands across the playground – as the Biafran.

The girl stood proud and big as a buffalo and roamed every break-time with the self-conscious certainty of the herd bully, weaving through groups and around skipping ropes, signalling her approach by the giveaway tinkle of her chemist's jewellery like a tom cat among sparrows. Her name was Wendy King and she suggested with folded arms and dogfish eyes that Maggie carry a tin around her neck for collections like the ones organised for the Biafran children. During class-time Wendy would sit frozen in a near paralysis, staring sightlessly into space with her damp little squid mouth hanging open and a hot finger drilled up her nose. In her more charitable moments she referred to Maggie as Skel, affectionately short for skeleton, but mostly the insults were designed to devastate and Maggie kept a wary distance. Despite all this she couldn't persuade herself to dislike Wendy. There was something mournful in the huge Hallowe'en face and the deep-sea predator eyes, made menacing by gravity, and anyway she was hooked.

'What are you looking at, Skeloid?' meant Maggie had to study her from behind if she wanted to stare for long periods, and she did, trailing like a zombie behind her, pretending not to, stride for stride with her speckled bull calves, strangled at each ankle by a grey sock. She swung easily in her wake, pulled by her force and mesmerised by her marbled skin, her fluffy gobs of spit, the callousness of her insults and the atomic blast of her power.

Older ones watched spellbound while Wendy tormented the little kids with an accomplished sadist's meticulous rigour, demoralising them with softly spoken insults before including the standard physical assault, complete with bondage, devastation of personal property and incarceration in cupboards and PE lockers. Maggie's height saved her from these but could not deflect the verbal attacks, especially when the henchmen were in tow. Deaf and Sue had adopted the same rolling stroll and menacing glamour, listing on their big shoes, chewing like cattle. A teacher had enquired of the former on her first day at the school, 'Are you deaf?' and it had stuck. Sue had a round waxy face and a long straight nose like a sharp knife in a cheeseboard, Deaf had olive skin and a pudge nose with soft curling nostrils. They walked behind Wendy, one at each shoulder.

They liked to re-establish their command at the start of each term and on the first day back at school in April they stopped Maggie in the corridor.

'Your mum's been on telly,' Wendy accused. Behind her Deaf and Sue swayed like triffids. Maggie waited for a reply to form in her head.

'So?' she replied eventually.

'So,' Wendy prepared to explain, mouth widening, shark eyes flattening, tilting, ready for the kill, 'she's a dirty randy slut.'

Maggie joined the dots between the freckles mapped across Wendy's face, a thousand pinpricks led to her mouth, little jabs at the serpent words, running up her neck and stippling over her lips, stopping only when they reached her wagging tongue, turned purple from aniseed gobstoppers.

'You're a Biafran freak, Skeloid. You think you're Mike Yarwood. Well you're not. You don't know any funny jokes. Geddit? Yours make me wanna cry. Boo-hoo.'

'Boo-hoo, boo-hoo,' echoed Deaf and Sue with wobbling heads and rubbery downturned mouths.

'You give me the bloody creeps,' Wendy continued enthusiastically, 'and,' she warned, snot-drilling finger raised, 'there's a petition to send you back to Biafra. Don't say you weren't warned.'

They turned and clattered away up the glossy corridor as the sunlight crashed up its walls. As a parting shot Deaf yelled, 'Mike Yarwood!' back over her shoulder when she was at a safe distance. Into the dazzle went the barracuda, tails flashing.

Boldmere Road

Mother of God, quiz day. Maggie lay deadly still for a moment, only her feet flapping and whirling, panicking at the bottom of the bed. Then the rest of her panicking with them, swallowing air as she dressed. Mother of God. How could he whistle at a time like this? Loud and clear, shaving in the bathroom, calm as you like. Typical. She couldn't eat, she stirred his tea for him and he slurped it with a big fat wink and a crackling cigarette.

'I'm ready, mate,' he muttered, goosebumping her skin,

making her light-headed so she dropped the teaspoon and tripped over the dog.

Dolly had an appointment with Martin the hairdresser. Pop had promised to pick her up on Boldmere Road at the appointed time.

Maggie liked to trail up and down Boldmere Road looking in the shop windows. Vogue of Boldmere, JOY Couture, Avalon Hair Design with its brown and cream bubble lettering and its buxom employees clodhopping on their platform shoes. There was the Washeteria launderette, whirling with revelation and hot gossip, and Brian Hill Fine Menswear with the slouching youths in their first job and a packet of ten Rothman's in their top pocket. She read *Pink* and *Jackie* in J&S News & Convenience. She gawped at the explosion of gowns in the window of Singular Sensation – Fine Bridal Wear, and vowed never to wear one. She hung against the window of Cinderella's Continental Shoes, releasing her hands so that her forehead took all the weight. A longing lunge at a pair of tan and chocolate wedge shoes with thick edible straps on a hessian-wrapped platform. There was another pair higher up in the display on a crisp volcanic mount of red tissue paper, silver with deadly stiletto heels and a strangling mesh of straps meant to lace over a foot and lattice upwards. Shoes to beg for your life in. Their glaring aluminium sheen made her think of Neil Armstrong, of the film her mother had taken her to see one afternoon, the one where the spaceman was cut loose from his moorings to float silently away into the black. His eyes under the visor, *2001: A Space Odyssey*, a tiny dot eventually, sinking to his death. When the lights came up they were still in their orange seats among the rows of empty ones. Her mother, Maggie realised, would have looked good in the silver shoes; they could have been crafted especially for her. The colour would have created the right metallic chill against

132

the platinum gleam of her hair. The binding of the straps would have served to remind everyone that she was only a slave child after all, a helpless victim. Her tentative sway on the skyscraper heels would have urged them to rescue her, the men with the approving glances. '*This girl's in love with you*,' she could have sung in a drowsy Bacharach voice. As it was she never did get to wear these ideal shoes that lay here dreaming of her. She had, it turned out, been lolling around all those years in the wrong shoes and now she had upped and gone with the spaceman to float in the black for eternity. Maggie could see her mother's clogged, navy lashes resting on the freckles that ran high on her cheek, gauzy under face powder and disappearing into a quick fan of creases when she laughed. Haa haa haa, long and low, full of elegantly tinted alcohol and spearmint-flavoured smoke. She saw the pale lips closing over her teeth after her mother had said something she didn't believe and the squirm of sorrow in her laughter lines.

Sutton Coldfield boasted a glut of hairdressing shops; there was one on every street. On Boldmere Road alone there were three competing salons with windows stuffed with images of gleaming, snake-eyed people, photographs of George Best or Britt Ekland garnishing the windows, as though these were regulars of a Saturday morning with milk and two sugars and the rollers in. Some, like Marion's Hair and Beauty, offered beauty treatments. Dolly liked Martin's Hair Design Centre and Beauty Emporium on Maney Hill. She took pictures cut out of magazines.

Liz Taylor as Cleopatra is the challenge she sets Martin on quiz day.

Framed in the mirror behind Dolly's chair poor Martin gropes through the smoke while she cackles, 'Go on duck, I know you can do it. Don't be shy.'

Martin moves quickly like a pickpocket, talks in breathless gasps, rolls his eyes, stamps his foot and tosses his fringe out of his eyes like a pony. When he stands back to survey his work he hangs on one hip and throws the other leg out at an angle with his hands on his hips, a pair of human scissors.

Dolly ransacks her brain for something to amuse him. She settles for a torrent of *double entendres* that sends her rocking with hysterics, shrieking and slapping the table, the chair, Martin's thigh.

Pop was supposed to collect her in the car so that her new head wouldn't get blown off in a breeze, but he is twenty minutes late so Dolly has two more cups of tea and a battery of fags while she waits. By the time he arrives her bladder is bursting for the second time. Pop watches her walk stiffly towards the car. On the back seat lies a small bag in the sober colours of Brian Hill Fine Menswear. The towering bouffant of hair, held down by an enormous red headscarf tied under her chin, is dyed a dark mocha brown. She takes ginger steps, wide-eyed as though the whole thing might collapse, her newly painted fingernails fanned out either side of her head as if to catch it when it does.

'About bloody time and make haste 'cos I'm busting.'

Pop cranes lower to catch a clue to the hairdo.

'Well why the 'ell didn't you go in there?' he asks.

Dolly wrenches open the passenger door, her heels scraping around in a circle as she considers the best mode of entry. She eases the hair carefully into the car and removes the headscarf with a half-hearted 'Ta-da.'

The bouffant springs to its full height, grazing the ceiling and releasing choking fumes. Pop stares in disbelief. 'Christ,' he manages, before the hairspray pierces his eyes and glues his tongue to the roof of his mouth.

'It stinks a bit, Doll.'

He steals incredulous glances at it all the way home, turning away again before Dolly notices and clouts him. By the time they lurch to a halt on Worcester Lane, Dolly's towering bouffant is full of smoke. Tiny wisps of it escape through the gaps as though she's dropped her fag in there.

Carl spills his tea when he sees her. Dolly sticks a scarlet fingernail under his nose. 'Not a peep out of you till I've done a face to go with it, right? It don't work without the face, you don't get the full effect.'

'Righto, Doll,' Carl says, transfixed by its size. 'What's that smell?'

Dolly swings out with her head high but her face has fallen. As she wheels by she flashes Pop a rancid glare and he sees a glassy tear arriving in her eye.

The Fox and Dogs Annual General Knowledge Quiz

Pop shaves for a second time, 'a close shave' he calls it, which is about right because he has nicked himself in more than one place. The wounds are festooned with florets of toilet paper and a paisley silk cravat is knotted loosely and implausibly at his throat. He looks like a suave turkey. It is part of the psychological pressure on Malc, he reveals, and anyhow people respect a cravat. It doesn't suit him. Underneath, his neck panics red and the knot keeps slipping around the back so he looks like a sort of cocktail cowboy.

Maggie wears her mother's crimson velvet waistcoat with the diamanté fir trees on the back and the favourite floppy hat with the bunch of cherries falling off the side.

They can hear Dolly's laugh from the bottom of Grange Lane. Pop walks with long purposeful strides and Maggie and the dog have to hurry to keep up. His eyes are fixed to the front and his face is determined and glowingly smooth, the ruts of congealed blood now serving to remind that he's ready for war if need be. Only his fists clenched at his sides give away the tension.

The cravat turned bandana makes her think of the wild west and a picture of her father falls into her mind, of him in an American bar with a beer, knowing no one.

They step from the hazy stillness into a carnival of voices and colour. Through the smoke, a smear of faces are yapping, calling out, shrieks, taunts, bolts of laughter. The landlord with his shoulder towel is struggling to serve quickly enough, even with the extra help (Sheila, a man with sweating black hair and a girl with a neck like an emu and two big front teeth). The women all wear lipstick and have spun-sugar hair, and gold flashes off their fingers and cleavages. The men are pointing at each other, guaranteeing one another, kidding each other not. Dolly is leaning on some bloke, she is all blood-red mouth and Tutankhamun eyes, explaining something to him with a jackdaw's cry and cackle. She ooh-hoos to Pop and Maggie and waves a windscreen-wiper arm. There is no sign of Iris, Maggie notes.

Eight o'clock sharp and the six men are perched in a row on tall bar stools like so many green bottles hanging on the wall. Some fella is singing it '. . . *should accident'ly fall, there'll be five green bottles . . .*' a couple of others are chorusing with him and some more are laughing.

'Right, simmer down, simmer down. Thank you Charles Aznavour, yes.'

The landlord spreads his hands for quiet, sweat streaking his forehead. Pop is grinning from the singing, unable to resist, even at a time like this. Malc blows his nose; he fills his oak bar stool to the edges. Below, his legs dangle like Humpty Dumpty's. Maggie's hand is hotly gripped in Dolly's. They were late up the stairs to the function room – an oblong of flock wall and gaudy carpet where the contest is taking place – due to her tittle-tattling downstairs, and now there are no seats left. Carl stands between the folds of a thick curtain and Maggie sees him mop his brow against it.

'Ladies and gentlemen,' the landlord begins grandly after a slurp of his pint. 'Welcome to this year's Fox and Dogs General Knowledge Quiz Night, held annually at this veritable establishment for going on, ooh, five years now. As is my privilege in my capacity as landlord, I should like to share a couple of quick funnies with you to kick off proceedings. Starting with: Doctor, doctor, I keep thinking I'm a pair of curtains . . .'

Heaven's sake, woman, pull yourself together, thinks Maggie.

'For heaven's sake, woman, pull yourself together,' says the landlord. He ha, says the crowd. 'Get on with it,' says a voice at the back.

'One more, just one more,' the landlord assures them. 'Doctor, doctor, I can't stop singing *The Green Green Grass of Home*. Ah, that's what we doctors call Tom Jones syndrome. Oh really? Is it common?'

It's not unusual, thinks Maggie.

'*It's not unusual*,' says the landlord. Ha ha ha ha, replies the crowd, shifting in their seats. 'Right, that's your lot,' he says and a cheer goes up.

'And with no further ado I shall introduce this year's contestants, many of whom will be a familiar face to you around these parts.'

137

'Nothing familiar about *his* parts,' a bloke shouts out, setting off another clatter of laughter.

The landlord points at him, 'I'll see you after. There's always one.'

He starts reeling off the men's names. Maggie hangs her head so that the cherries bang against her nose and stares at all the shoes squeezed around hers.

'And of course our reigning champion three years running, always dainty on his toes, Malcolm Denton.' She peeks up through the clapping. Malc raises a fist like this is a revolution they are having at the Fox and Dogs. Pop is expressionless, eyes front.

'And last but not least, the Duke of Clarendon, from Clarendon Road of course, one man and his dog, Arthur Landywood.' Clapping. Dolly whistles then cackles at the noise she's made. Blowbroth, curled under Pop's bar stool, taps his truncheon tail softly. Pop, blinking, licks his teeth.

'An easy one to kick off.' A sipping of pints, a forest fire of smoke rising.

'Your question first, Arthur. What is a spittoon?'

A groan at such an elementary start, but Pop is unabashed.

'A bowl or similar receptacle for the receiving of spittle,' he enunciates carefully, spitting only a little.

'Correct. Malcolm? The Milky Way – what is it? And don't say the snack you can eat between meals, mate.'

'Our galaxy. The distant stars in the night sky,' he says, raising his pint as though he'll drink to it.

'Correct. Des?' Des, local Lothario, Burt Reynolds lookalike, glances up in alarm. 'Name if you can the two famous movie stars from the film *Gone With the Wind*?'

Maggie hopes Pop doesn't get a film question. He has seen very few films. Those he has seen were for the most part about the Second World War. He sat between Dolly and Carl and watched *The Dam Busters* and *The Bridge on the River Kwai* on their black–and–white television set while he filled three ashtrays and emptied four ale bottles. The only film he could remember seeing in a cinema was *Zorba the Greek*. Dolly had taken him in 1964 because she had her eye on Anthony Quinn.

'Waster money,' Carl had said.

'All be in bloody Greek anyhow,' Pop concurred at the time and the two men laughed up at the ceiling and down at their shoes together.

It was on at the Odeon on Maney Hill. Dolly and Arthur sat under a cloud of smoke at the matinee, with a bag of toffees in luxurious velvet seats that creaked when they leant forward to the ashtray. Pop never went to the cinema again but remained deeply impressed by the film he had seen.

'Bloody good film in fact, not bad at all. Greek bloke and an English bloke in Crete, renovating an old tin mine. Decent fleapit too. Deco, original lamps. He dances a bit, the Greek fella. Not poofy, none of your top-hat-and-tails rubbish. Quite good actually. Fascinating civilisation, the Greeks.'

At a pub called the Barley Mow in Mere Green, Pop tried to smash a saucer in homage to Zorba. It was shortly after they'd bought the spell for the quiz from Lob o' Lob. It was not a pub he liked; they were there on account of Dolly temporarily joining the picket line outside the Yote factory on the Mere Green Road.

'S'pose you're a bloody feminist now are you?' Pop teased, whining through a delighted grin.

'Might be. Mind yer own,' she replied nervously.

''Sup with you? I got some lighter fuel for your bra, mate.'

'What the 'ell d'you know about it? It's workers' rights. It's industrial action.'

'Unionist eh, Doll? Stone the flaming crows, to think that under that sweet, feminine exterior you were Che bloody Guevara all along.'

He tittered and hissed. 'If we'd known earlier, love, I could've gone via the smithie's and chained you to the railings.'

'Belt up and give it a rest!' And she landed him one on his arm that stayed black as newsprint for days. 'You're miles behind the bloody times, you mouldy old fool. It's a laugh, anyhow,' she insisted.

Later on outside the factory gates she clobbered him with her placard. '½ A SAY IS NO GOOD TO DECENT WOMEN' it said. Pop threw his arms up in mock alarm. 'Knock it off, you daft bat, I was only kidding.'

Maggie had fancied holding a placard, so the women sat her down among the garden chairs under the umbrellas to keep the sun off and shared egg sandwiches. Dolly's friends were Gwen, Maureen and Shar. Gwen wore a tank top with big sunglasses like Jackie Onassis, and Maureen had a short mac on and beads. Maggie's placard said 'AUEW LOCK OUT!' She hadn't chosen it. She wanted the one that said 'OFFICIAL UNION DISPUTE' because it sounded grave and sanctioned. She held hers up proudly anyway. She marched fiercely up and down in front of the others with a grim expression while they chatted and unscrewed flasks. She glared at puzzled passers-by with revolutionary rage and moaned the chant with them when they shouted, 'ALL WE WANT IS A FAIR DEAL!'

Maggie had found it hard to keep her mind focused on the facts when they were explained to her by Shar. Some women had been unfairly dismissed after complaining about incorrect holiday pay. Their original query had resulted in the complete removal of all their holiday pay and when they queried that as well they were fired. Dolly was not one of those directly involved but workers must stick together, Shar said. The Associated Union of Engineering Workers said the dispute had official union backing and that it was regarded as a lock-out because the women had been verbally dismissed. Whatever it was, Maggie decided, it was a diabolical disgrace and she wished her placard said so.

That evening at opening time, Pop appeared by the factory gates with his fist over his head, clenched in a salute.

'Flaming heck,' Dolly muttered and steered Maggie and the others away under the cover of a Rothman's umbrella graffitied AUEW all over in felt-tip pen. Pop followed their legs to the Barley Mow, a short distance away at the busy crossroads in Mere Green. He grinned and waved at them from a table in the corner while Dolly rolled her eyes and clinked her Dubonnet and lemonade against the reassuring alliance of other glasses, all stuffed with a wedge of lemon like a party-political emblem. Giddy with the novelty and *esprit de corps*, the women toasted themselves and raised a cheer, to which Pop responded with his own glass raised and something Maggie couldn't hear. 'Ignore 'im,' Dolly said and passed her fags round. It was fun with the women, they were energised and redefined and full of jokes. There were names and dates, unfair dismissal, industrial tribunal, manning the picket lines, union rules, government policy and official union backing, all of it to discuss. They would succeed and things would be better, they would not be trodden on or stand idly by, they said so, they were determined and gasping with words. Maggie felt included, infected by their enthusiasm, the good-humoured sense of outrage. She was comforted by their husky voices, hoarse from shouting, and their strong, curving arms, grabbing her, squeezing her. She had no words to add so she dropped crisps into her lemonade and watched them float with intense concentration to contain her excitement.

Pop bought himself another pint at the bar. 'Drink girls?' he enquired, beaming wolfishly through a keyboard grin, with his feet planted wide apart as though an earthquake had split the ground between them.

'No ta.' Dolly responded before anyone else had the chance.

The evening sun, loitering low in the sky, striped gold epaulettes across their shoulders, lit up their perms, skidded off the empty glasses. Maggie heard Pop clearing his throat. Dolly looked up.

'Up the workers!' he called out from his corner, and crowed with laughter as he raised his glass again. Nobody paid any attention. Dolly was listening to Shar, but blinked whenever she caught the sound of him.

In a corner at one end of the bar stood a jukebox, something Pop heartily disapproved of in pubs, along with fruit machines, and one of the reasons he was a stranger there. After *Amazing Grace* by the Royal Scots Dragoon Guards Band came the theme from *Zorba the Greek* by Mikis Theodorakis, lightly plucked and hardly noticeable at first, but gradually gathering more string parts and speed until it couldn't fail to catch his attention. They heard him squawk from his corner. Maggie could see him straighten up and look from them to the jukebox and back again.

'Ignore 'im,' Dolly repeated, pretending to. Out of the corner of her eye Maggie saw his arms rising slowly to a snapping finger-click. The words she'd been hanging on to continued though she no longer heard them. Instead she heard her own blood in her ears followed by a Holte End cheer and a wave of distant applause. Dolly said it was time to go before he got any worse. They all stood up around the same time he did. He'd started the gliding part with dipping hip bends as bags were lifted and chairs scraped. Gwen, Maureen and Shar laughed and Dolly clouted him as she flew past. He said Maggie's name as she moved off, so she stopped and smiled a tense nod of support with her hands in her pockets and her heart in her feet, until Dolly fetched her away by the sleeve.

It was ten o'clock before Pop rapped the knocker at Dolly's.

He was drunk. Strangely, Maggie had never seen him drunk before. His arms were still out wide for Crete, fingers snapping and feet swinging underneath. From his throat came the mewing whine of the melody while his skin ran streaky with sweat.

'A plate,' he said in Anthony Quinn's voice. 'For celebrating.'

'I'll give you a flaming plate in a minute, you great daft bastard. Get inside.' Dolly pulled him in by a piece of his shirt, so that his head and arms swam backwards and followed the rest of him a fraction later, like a genie into his bottle. She cuffed him anywhere she could reach, she pushed and pulled him and he bobbed obediently left and right, grinning like it was a game. She pointed at Carl, who cringed and blinked, she pointed at Pop, she pointed at the state of his shoes, she pointed at the clock and she pointed at Maggie – 'Time you thought about this kid, Arthur' – and lastly she pointed at herself, whom she referred to as 'muggins 'ere meanwhile'. Anger shot out of her pointing arms like tracer bullets; everyone got hit.

Pop pulled a small white saucer from his pocket and narrowed his eyes.

'Thing won't break,' he complained, frowning.

'What d'you want to break it for? What's it doing in your pocket? Where's it from?' Missiles out of Dolly's mortar mouth.

'The pub,' Pop replied loudly.

'No need to shout. I can hear you,' Dolly shrieked.

'Bloody Spanish Inquisition, woman,' his eyes reeling in temper.

'S'pose you've nicked it, that's all we need, a copper on the doorstep this time of night. Bugger off home, Art, before you upset the kid. Doing wonders for my flaming blood pressure, you are.'

'Eh? Am I? BOO!' Dolly shrieked and clasped her bosom while he cackled and winked at Maggie. 'Okay, Maggie mate?'

Carl pulled on his cap and peered nervously from under it. 'Come on, Arthur. I'll walk you home.' He strolled between them, objective and reasonable, a tweedy referee. Maggie crept to the upstairs window and stuck her head out while Dolly folded a sheet on to the camp bed. She watched Pop and Carl on the road below, bathed in orange street light, Pop tossing the saucer into the air.

'"Tain't plastic,' Pop murmured, examining it. 'Bloody strange.'

'It's that reinforced stuff they use in canteen catering. It's got a substance in it,' Carl explained quietly.

'Eh? Has it? Substance?' Pop tossed it again. The two men stood demurely by in bowling-green fashion while it bounced across the road and rolled for a while along the gutter. They followed it the length of Worcester Lane, one light and frothy on his Cretan toes, the other hunched with careful steps, wandering through the flame-coloured landscape like the first men on Mars. At the bottom of Worcester Lane Maggie saw Pop spread his arms in the middle of the road and begin creeping delicately to the side on bent knees and swivelling feet, the distant whine of the tune following. She could see a plume of smoke floating out of the top of his head. Carl stood on the pavement with his arms folded, waiting patiently. Pop danced from side to side and forwards and backwards while his tongue plucked the bouzouki's part in double four time. His head appeared oddly still, compared to the whirling and shuffling of the rest of him. He swam with serpent arms through the orange phosphorescence like an ale-soaked version of Shiva the Hindu god, who ruled all life and death in the world, who created life when he danced. Seven pints of bitter had rendered him immortal. Maggie could hear the scrape of his shoe as his dance turned him matador-slow through one hundred and eighty degrees, king of all Peloponnesia, his extended arms in all four directions of the compass as he rotated, dancing as he lived, self-absorbed and belligerently alone. It was easy to imagine, watching him swivel and stamp in the breezeless air, that he danced in celebration or appreciation of some blessed fact. Maggie watched as his eyes closed and his head fell back. The light burnished his skin until it shone gold. A slick smile, a quick crescent of teeth, the grin of a horse thief.

'No, don't tell me! Oh hang on, not him, the other bloke wannit? Jesus, don't tell me, don't tell me!' Poor Eddie, contorting on his bar stool, sweating into his bitter.

'It's gotta go for a bonus, mate. Anybody?'

'Archimedes,' Pop shouts, waking the dog.

'Archimedes hmm,' follows Malc but Pop has it.

'Okay, Malc, your question. The last letter of the old Greek alphabet is what?'

Malc nods. 'Origa, omagon,' he tuts, shakes his head, 'oregon, onega, bloody 'ell.' He shakes his head again, wipes his eyes. 'Oma-thing, bugger it.'

''Fraid it'll have to go for a bonus, mate.'

'Omega!' Pop crows. 'Omega,' he repeats to Malc. 'Omega, mate.'

Malc mumbles something back, mops himself with a handkerchief. Maggie thinks of Lob o' Lob and is amazed.

The crowd can smell a fight; they are louder now, taking sides. Dolly is enjoying herself. 'Never mind, Malc, you can always go on a diet, duck.' And, 'Get after him, Arthur,' as if they should do away with the stools and get their fists out. Maggie can feel the sweat on her back, in her hair, darting around her ear. The room is a carousel of colours, it pitches as if they are afloat and the smoke rolls. 'Oooh,' say the crowd, then 'ahh . . . ha ha,' and a cheer as the room tips back again. She closes her eyes, just for a moment, to clear them of the smoke and din, and feels the earth turning on its axis as somebody shouts, 'The Ivory Coast!' Then the scrape of carpet on her cheek, a perfect Kojak homicide, down like a ninepin, and the strange comfort of the bruising contact.

She comes round downstairs. She sees the nicotined ceiling first and then Dolly, Egyptian-eyed, wafting her with a brewery towel like an acolyte.

'Hallo, duck, how d'you feel? Bit pale round the gills you've gone. Eh, you'll never believe it,' she says, slapping Maggie's leg. 'Go on, guess what?'

Upstairs Pop is standing with his fists in the air, blinking through the fog and footlights of his achievement, flashing the keyboard grin. Arthur Landywood, this year's winner, a gallon of beer and five pounds. He spends most of it there and then, downstairs in the bar.

Sutton Coldfield

She breathed hot swallows of air through the doughy mattress. It smelled of old paper and skin and death. There was a mournful twang deep inside the bed as if to warn her a tragedy lay ahead like on TV films. She lay still, delaying definite action until

146

she was able properly to form a thought. She could hear the loutish call of a magpie outside her window and the slam of a cupboard downstairs. She sat up as Pop's ragged baritone rumbled up through the floorboards.

When Satan stood on Brierley Hill and far around him
    gazed;
He said, 'I never shall again at Hell's flames be amazed.'

This detonated his cough as effectively as the removal of a grenade pin and off he was carried on a sea of choking until he managed finally to slam a door with belting force. This never failed, he always insisted, as a remedy to silence a coughing fit by surprising the lungs and thereby arresting the spasms. It didn't have to be a door, a shotgun or firework worked just as well. The odd thing was it never failed. Something to hand down through the generations, Maggie considered. Her mother too had adapted it and employed it to therapeutic effect.

Downstairs a proper breakfast lay in wait, neatly arranged on the table with a triangle of napkin and everything. 'I did it, mate,' he breathed, beheading her egg and standing back with the teaspoon dripping. 'I beat him, didn't I eh?' as if he wasn't sure now, though he spoke it like a brag.

Pop wanted to share himself with Sutton Coldfield. A sort of victory tour, a lap of honour, starting with Four Oaks. He'd already been to the phone box to enlighten the local paper and offer himself for a photograph. They said they'd get back to him. Wearing his cravat, which let off a bonfire-booze stink, he tore along Grange Lane, propelled by success, so that Maggie and the dog had to trot to keep up. They called in at all three pubs and he was honoured at each with handshakes, congratulations and a rusty cheer with a pelting of back-slapping at the Fox and

Dogs. 'The champion returneth,' croaked the landlord, fresh towel on his shoulder, the previous night's smoke still hung up in the corners. At the Pint Pot the yeti spoke, first time on record; and at the Plough and Harrow, Ken, who had to believe a bloody word of it whether he liked it or not, said, 'Oh look out, bloody brain of Britain's about, I'll have that fiver you owe me now then, mate,' and filled him with free beer all morning. The post office, the newsagent's and the Baptist church all got a look-in, and when finally he was ready to present himself to the town even the Anglia obliged by starting first time.

They called in at the garage, then the library, where the girl with the ink stamp blushed when she heard. He told all the women on the cash tills at Tesco who raised a tittering little hurray, the man at Brian Hill Fine Menswear and the fella he sometimes sat with in the Gracechurch shopping precinct. He mentioned it to the roadsweeper as they crossed the high street to get to the town hall in King Edward Square, where he stood with his hands in his pockets gazing up at the windows. And then with his head bowed at the war memorial, Maggie thought she heard him murmuring to the dead.

When he grew tired they sat on a bench in the Vesey Memorial Garden near the pansy-covered roundabout and watched the cars going round. On the high street beyond, Maggie saw people with packed lunches pointing cameras at them, taking photographs of the fourteenth-century Holy Trinity Church that stood behind. She doubted they would even notice the Four Oaks Fox and Dogs General Knowledge Champion reclining in the corner of their snaps when they got them back.

The Sutton Park Blaze

They had still not heard a whisper from Iris about the bird table. His new status as quiz champion did not help; on the contrary it made him feel worse. He became despondent and read out another Kipling poem called 'The Female of the Species'. Maggie ran upstairs and slipped under her sheet while he reviewed his campaign in the kitchen. She pulled out the library book and looked with interest at drawings of brains, mid-section, and pictures of people being electrocuted. Below, she could hear him accusing himself of ineffective action, of time-wasting and shilly-shallying, berating himself out loud on all counts. She wondered if next door could hear. He took a dim view of his record so far, deplored the lack of originality, lack of flair, his voice rising. 'Action not words, mate,' he railed. He had serious misgivings at this stage, a boom of warning; it would take an entire rearrangement of strategy really, to stand a bloody chance now. Only himself to blame, he concluded, and put the kettle on. As it boiled he consoled himself in more reasonable tones. After all, he was still the bloke who'd thrashed Malcolm Denton; all was not lost, surely. Then he had a brainwave. The heat had generated some small bush fires in Sutton Park; some blamed boys with matches, the *Sutton News* reported. He decided he would join the volunteers fighting the park blazes alongside the fire brigade. He wore his old goalkeeper's gloves. He went alone because it was men's work, dangerous perhaps, life-threatening he hoped. Maggie waited up for a while, then fell asleep with the dog on the sighing settee.

At dawn the next day he strode purposefully with only the

slightest limp along Tower Road. Behind him the sun threw pink and gold ribbons across a dimly marbled sky. His face and clothes were smeared and blackened, his wisps of hair stood out from his head at angles, for all the world a survivor at Gallipoli. He put out his cigarette before ringing at number thirty-one. There was a long pause during which Pop felt like lighting another and then the sun poured molten metal around the rim of the horizon, turning him into a charred silhouette. Her face appeared in a blur through the door's frosted glass, rising up to him as if she were surfacing through water. They looked at one another, distorted through the rippling. Iris hesitated, alarmed by the sooty face.

Eventually she opened the letter-box flap. 'Go away, Arthur.'

Pop stooped a little and whispered. 'Iris?'

'It's five thirty in the morning, Arthur Landywood.'

Pop moved nearer to the door. 'It is done,' he said.

'Bugger off,' she said. Then, 'What is done?'

'A man who's spent the night in battle could use a brew, Iris.'

He could hear her exasperated breaths.

'Not now, Arthur, for crying out loud, it's half-past five in the morning.'

The flap snapped shut and Iris's watery face swam away.

Pop pulled out his fags and lit one. He exhaled a plume and gazed up at the bedroom window. He turned around, hands in pockets, and looked at the street. This was fine, he reassured himself, she was playing the game. It was a dance after all, like Indian peafowl and so on, like those South American birds that mate for life. Eventually he swung back, bent forward, slipped his fingers into the letter flap and roared out a whisper.

'The fires are out, Iris. All of them. It was not too taxing. Only cost us our time, Iris dear.' He straightened again to think.

Be brief, he reminded himself, romantic perhaps but not soppy, be lofty, include nuggets of interest. He bowed once more and drew a breath.

'"Time's glory is to calm contending kings, To unmask falsehood and bring truth to light." Shakespeare, that is. Well, order is restored, mate, the park and its utilities are safe, I am not hurt. Final score was conclusive by the way, quite a winning margin. Malcolm Denton's brain is in his posterior, it would seem. Thank you. Good morning. Over and out.'

As he straightened again Pop noticed that it would be a beautiful day. The milkman saw him black as a chimney sweep, swinging along Clarendon Road in a pillow of smoke, as though he'd exploded.

Manchester City

This is an important season for us. It's now or never, as Elvis says. The tension is etched into Ron Saunders's lightly tanned brow, but there is a radiance in the eyes too, a low burn. Impending victory perhaps, or burgeoning madness. 'All your bona fide geniuses, stark raving mad the lot,' Pop says, pulling a hair from his nose. 'Flaming fact, mate. Name me a visionary, any century, who wasn't right round the ruddy twist.'

He pauses while Maggie and Blowbroth blink in different directions.

'See? Not one of them knew what bloody day of the week it was, but any one of those blokes will rustle up the theory of relativity soon as look at you, so they will.'

Pop figured out that Ron Saunders had come up with a similar theory to solve Aston Villa's problems. A theory of irrelativity.

If it don't work, dump it. Start at the end of the equation and work backwards, if it don't add up, it has to go. So one by one outmoded tactics, positions and players fell. Neil Rioch, Tony Betts and Bobby Campbell were subtracted. Frank Carrodus, Leighton Phillips and Steve Hunt were added. 'Everything in the universe is mathematical,' Maggie's father had said. Ron Saunders's arithmetic worked. On the first day of the third month of 1975 Aston Villa beat Norwich City to win the League Cup Final one-nil. Fair-skinned Ray Graydon, with his long preacher's face and his miracle-worker's right foot behind a penalty, sent it twice into goal until it stayed there. Ray Graydon, the Grader, with his supernatural right foot, in his lucky number-seven shirt.

This season of course they are playing football in Division One. Pop is smoking more fags over it. Ron Saunders and his quantum calculations produced last season's four-nil victory at Sheffield Wednesday that guaranteed their place in the top flight. Now they have played Leeds United without disgrace. 'Ye great Gods and little fishes,' Pop had yelled when it was announced. 'Bugger, that's gone and gobbed it, damn. Not at all, mate!' he argued back at himself. 'Don Revie can kiss my *kulha* so he can. Take more than a couple of shortarses like Bremner and Lorimer to frighten us, mate, and that's a fact,' he had reminded himself, looking for a match.

Only a year ago they were struggling halfway down the Second Division table, losing games to teams like West Brom, Notts County and Bristol Rovers, sending their fans shuffling home, silenced and stooping. Now they had faced a side who, while Villa were cart-horsing in the Second and Third Divisions, had been champions in the First not once but twice, and runners-up three times.

'This club is near to an explosion,' smouldered Saunders at

the reporters, before striding a straight line to an exit, bursting through swing doors and out the other side like a Martin Scorcese hero. The fans were ready, their banners and flags unravelled, pint jars raised, the claret and blue flew on washing lines again, their numbers swelled, their voice about to become a vale of noise once more.

The sun crouching low in the west has laid vast shadows across the pitch, blocks of megalithic grey. The sun leaks through a gap, spills in two directions and spreads up towards Trinity Road, leaving the shapes that welcome the summer solstice, and like the tourists at Stonehenge some in the crowd stand hushed at Villa Park this evening. This is the second home game of the season and Villa have yet to win a match in the First Division. Manchester City, the club who sacked Saunders the previous year, leaving him free to rescue Villa at the eleventh hour, are in the visitors' dressing room. The City players' revolt against his tough methods and harsh discipline sent him out, a gun for hire. Ron's pride sits tall with him on the bench this evening, tonight is all about Ron Saunders. The match result will declare him fool or genius, likewise the boards of both clubs, one for hiring, the other for firing, one way or the other the defeated side will be forced to concede that mistakes may have been made at all levels off the pitch. Tonight is about campaign, about brinkmanship. For Ron it offers the opportunity to lay to rest his past defeats and hint at his future glory; he sits poker-faced on the bench.

Maggie can feel her scalp creeping in the heat, Pop is drenched as a dray-horse, it is over eighty degrees. Columns of dust and midges swing in the late sun and the air is tangy with the rusty stink of beer. *Land of Hope and Glory* goes up from the Holte End with new words.

We hate Nottingham Forest,
We hate Liverpool too,
We hate Tottenham Hotspur,
But mostly we hate you.

A synchronised roar from the first word as though the Red Army Choir are in residence on the Holte with a conductor leading them from the pitch. Pop and Maggie sway slightly at their barrier, tipped by Britannia's waves. He shouts something unintelligible through a mouthful of smoke. Behind them sour-faced lads with wet fringes scramble up and bodies press around. The sweat, smoke and ale close in with the sweet, dry clay smell of the earth bank. The Holte End is awash with claret and blue, flags, pennants, streamers. The clap, rumble and roar of the full-voiced denim army rolling. From somewhere the faint thudding of a drum and in the Trinity Road stand the golden lion rears up on a banner. The linesmen and referee are striding across the shadows, grave with the weight of judgement, clerical and impartial in their black. Then the manager, coach and trainers, with their snap glances and urgent steps. And the players with a rush of noise at their backs, bright in their battledress, shining like fresh paint in the leaning sun. One and then another starts to run; easy falling steps, then a burst of speed on gleaming minotaur legs, grinning through the wind that shifts their fringes and curls. Manchester City in green and black stripes, chasing the matching colours of their sloping shadows.

For an hour both teams run up and down between the goals while the crowd falls forward and back on the terraces. Cat and mouse, Pop calls it.

'BOLLOCKS!' the big man next to Maggie calls it. 'COME ON!' The heat is fierce, Maggie watches the stadium pylons swaying like cobras in the haze. The sky, reddening in the west from the scorch of the day, is strewn with jet-fuel streamers

154

and along with all the hue and cry makes for a carnival above and below.

'Go on, you fucking wanker!' City's deep defence continues to present a problem. 'WHAT NUMBER'S THE FUCKING REFEREE?' Oakes is playing sweeper for City. 'WANKER!' Thirty-five thousand bawling experts, every single one. 'CHICO! CHICO! CHICO!' For the flash feet and gliding tricks of blond midfield bombshell Ian Hamilton. City have the ball at the wrong end again. 'THIS IS DANGEROUS, THIS IS BLOODY DANGEROUS!' The big man can't look. 'BLOODY, BLOODY DANGEROUS. SHIT.' The big man peeps and puts his head in his hands again. Pop makes suggestions through a clamped fag. 'To Little, son, to Little! Go on, son, alright, to Aitken then.'

'Men only use the left side of their brain if you really want to know,' Maggie's mother mentioned once, while they waited to pay their way out of the supermarket car park. 'It happens to be a fact of life. Sometimes the other side just shrivels up.'

Maggie didn't dare look at Saunders on the bench. She couldn't stand to see his grimly locked jaw, his carefully positioned knees, no body language for the commentators, nothing poofy with the hands either and no eye-rubbing to be misconstrued as despair.

'Go on, son, go on, son!'

'YES! GO ON!' A colossal roaring, a ton of it pushing up.

Then she does glance at Ron. His hands are clasped . . . say it soft and it's almost like praying. It can work. If they play to the system it will work.

'Ooooooooooooooooooohhhhhhhhhhhhhhhh.'

Applause like shingle stones as the Holte End wave washes back again.

Brian Little walks on water,
Tra-la-la-la-la la la-la la . . .

Striker Keith Leonard, tall in his number-nine shirt and *Gone with the Wind* moustache, has almost scored twice and keeper Cumbes has flung himself out of his box to save a shot from Rodney Marsh. Suddenly after sixty-five minutes there's drama at both ends. Little Brian Little makes a dash and shoots into a lunging Joe Corrigan in the City goal. Keith Leonard and City's Dave Watson battle it out up and down, until Villa are awarded a free kick at last, taken by Phillips down at the Holte End.

He floats the ball across the penalty box.

Together they go up.

Leonard and Watson.

And hang there for a moment.

While the numbers spin and wheels of fortune turn.

Then Leonard for Villa, higher in the air, heads it into the roof of the net. One-nil. For a millisecond nobody moves, just blood gathering. Then the first bodies go up like water against a rock, their voices after, the boom then the roar and other bodies following. The din launches, spreads and shatters like an atom split. The Holte End is liquid, wave after wave of bodies falling. The noise lifts Maggie off the ground, knocks her into the clouds. Beside her the big man throws back his head and bellows at the sky, his arms, huge and burnt by the sun, fly heavenwards like Jesus at the Mount. Maggie shouts with him, the same howl, yards of it in her, the wind of twenty men. She and the big man yelling while her arms fly up the same. Walk on.

Pop has turned gold in the last of the melting sun; it fills his mouth, turns his teeth into bullion. His arms are an almighty

V for Villa, like he's swinging on the hinges of heaven's gate.

> Aston VILLA, Aston VILLA,
> We'll support you evermore,
> We'll support you EVERMORE . . .

First win in Division One. Maggie's sleep is full of claret-and-blue men shouting at the sun. Battalions roaring, mouths stretching wide until they are jackals with long tongues, dragging a combat hymn up through the ground. Rearing up from the terraces until they are tall and blue as a tidal wave, a wall of denim standard bearers, rushing with deafening song.

In her dream Maggie is wrapped around with yards of shining sari, claret and blue, barnacled with gold. Villa have won the FA Cup and Maggie must drop off Pop's washing at Dolly's before Indira Gandhi gets there, otherwise it would look like the whole FA thing was fixed and the entire team, board and Ron Saunders could likely be excommunicated by the Pope, leaving Birmingham City as FA Cup winners lining up to meet the Queen.

Croydon

'You can make out every single word Shirley Bassey is singing.'

It was true, she never mumbled. *For All We Know* was one of Carole's favourite anthems. Every verse and key change had been carefully committed to her memory and sung with slugging sentimentality; the same fierce allegiance she saved for

I Vow to Thee My Country. Through tiny radio holes, a gale of contemplation and regret. Her mother used to call her to the settee when Shirley was on the telly and together they would sit respectfully, with feet off the furniture. Shirley, monument of sinew and spangle. 'Look at that,' her mother sighed. 'From the back streets of Cardiff, don't forget. Tiger Bay. No shoes on her feet, never knew her father. Coal miner, I think. Or West Indian. Christ, from nothing,' she cried, louder now, up a key along with Shirley's chorus. 'My God, not a roof over her head, nothing. Just a golden throat, just that voice to call her own. Go on, Shirley, bloody show the lot of 'em how it's done, girl.' And her eyes would glitter with pride at the shining mother of musical variety entertainment. Goddess of costume. Mistress of the epic song. Carole's pale brow sank until it was level with Maggie's and her voice was lowered to the respectful murmur they used for the catechism. 'Name me one really big name from Tiger Bay. Go on. No one, see? You name me one, go on.'

Silenced, Maggie visioned the infant Shirley practising her scales on a pearly rock while the sea reared up all around her and tigers strolled loose-hipped at her back. On the TV flashes of light ricocheted off the bead and sequin dress and exploded in brilliant flares until Miss Bassey was burned, halo and all, like a sizzling brand on to the back of Maggie's memory for ever.

The Stylistics crooning *Betcha By Golly Wow* reminded her of the marathon shopping expeditions with her mother to the Whitgift Centre in Croydon. The long hours in search of some unremarkable thing, a ribbed cardy or Indian bangles, anything that altered Carole's perception of herself for an hour or two. She would clack like a packhorse over miles of grey pavement in heels so high they made her gasp, until they reached the hot, swirly

158

interiors of Etam, Chelsea Girl, Snob and Dorothy Perkins, all sweet with the reek of perfumed sweat and jungle-sexy with the sounds of soul. To Allders department store and the perfumery floor which could choke a healthy person to death. The stench of Charlie, hanging in great nimbostratus sheets like a chemical weapon, clinging to every surface, person and textile within its considerable range. The cosmetic counter girls nudging and nodding in groups behind racks of little pots and jars, all present and correct in regimental rainbow rows, leaning over them like medieval hags with cure-alls, anointing her mother's wrist with multicoloured smears, courting her with shimmering pastel eyes, long chinchilla lashes and small wet-look mouths that shushed promises into her face on warm citrus breath. Mary Quant's entire new range, colours the shades of terrible injuries, lying gloomily in shiny coffin-black packaging, branded with the enigmatic white Q, waiting for Maggie's mother to point and claim them.

When they'd hampered their progress with enough bags, they would float up the escalator to the fifth-floor cafeteria. Maggie was table-bagger, while her mother made signals with her eyebrows from the self-service queue. Once a table became free, Maggie would rush at it, like musical chairs, coshing seated heads with the shopping, and park her bottom defiantly in front of the scowling losers. While Carole paid for their tray of lunch it was Maggie's job to build a fortress of shopping bags around herself to officially claim it before she peeped out with giddy eyes.

She remembered them in matching leopard print cardigans leaning into the gale that blew permanently around every corner of the grey, multistorey precinct, snatching their store bags to shoulder height and blowing her mother's dress up into her face.

'Marilyn Monroe did this,' Carole yelled through the flapping fabric as it wrapped itself around her in a slamming gust. Maggie watched the hollow of her mouth making shapes under it, binding her like an ancient Egyptian. Mummification, she thought coolly, and wondered why she didn't move to help her.

She kept her mother's photo album in a drawer by the bed at Clarendon Road. Spongy white plastic, turning ivory already, with fine gold lines running horizontally across as though it contained a wedding. Inside, preserved under transparent sheets, were her parents in happier days, wind-blown and laughing, smoking and pointing like a Peter Stuyvesant advertisement. Then the grandparents and great-aunts, and faces that were strangers to Maggie. There was a pressed flower, dry and thin as a Communion wafer, and a cutting from the *Radio Times* featuring a picture of Carole in hot-pants with a toffee apple in each hand, laughing so hard her face had goblin corners. There were pictures of Pop, young and clean-shaven, thick dark hair slicked glossily back, a contained cocky amusement, self-conscious, impish. Another photograph, later, a few years maybe. A strange blankness in the waterfall eyes. Heavier lids as though he were tired or disappointed, a flicker of shame in spite of the cocked eyebrow, eyes from a newspaper story. All done up in this one, kippers and curtains, stiff collar, handkerchief, an air of controlled fear hanging about his sloping shoulders. Next to him, distant and mild, as though she'd been collaged on afterwards, his wife Eve, perching timid and soft as a songbird. Each looking off in diagonally opposite directions, their gazes crossing a foot or so in front of their faces. This invisible point of contact in the air that you could almost draw a circle around, held the only clue to their intimacy.

And him in 1939, in RAF uniform, alert and brimming with humour. Buttons shining and forage cap perkily askew, as though he might perform an impersonation or sing a light-hearted song.

Madhaiganj

She had spun lists, chants and rhymes out of Pop's World War II. She repeated them at night in long whispered chains like the chant of the Litany.

> *Vultee Vengeance,*
> *Vera*
> *Lynn,*
> *khana, kidder,*
> *ginger and*
> > *gin,*
> *jaldi, kitna, Orderly Dog,*
> *malum,*
> > *mespot,*
> *tea kai,*
> > *wog.*
> *Binding nuisance,*
> *Peelo,*
> > *erk,*
> *charpoy . . . dhobi . . . dimwit . . . berk . . .*
> *peachy,*
> *asti,*
> *one . . . two . . . six . . .*
> *What's*

the
gen?
Tell
   the
men.
Wingco at the flicks.
Spawny
      sprog,
kite
    a
wreck,
Jap in pieces,
        hit the deck.

She stood the two tall Vs from Vultee Vengeance, the American-built aircraft that 110 Squadron flew for a time in India, at the foot of her bed at night like sentries, like both pairs of Churchill's victory fingers. She balanced the words across her tongue until they rolled out satiny, like French cigarette smoke. Wings and talons in the name, and an unequivocal intention too; deadly and double-barrelled, it would punish and avenge on its first mission in the skies over the Bay of Accra.

110 were known as the Hyderabad Squadron. They had flown long-distance bombing missions while the unit were based in France during the First World War and the DH9A aircraft they flew then were the gift of His Serene Highness the Nizam of Hyderabad. Each one bore an inscription and the Nizam's demi-tiger leaping from an astral crown, and at the outbreak of World War II the Nizam's contribution continued. Pop would explain to anyone who would listen that they carried out the first bombing raid of the war in September 1939, when five of their Blenheims attacked German warships near Wilhelmshaven. In

August 1945 eight Mosquitoes, which they flew in the final six months of the war, attacked Japanese troops east of the Sittang River, so the claim went that 110 Squadron carried out the first and last bombing raids of World War II. A boast not lost on Pop.

Maggie couldn't picture the vast quantities of bombs. During World War I, 110 dropped ten and a half tons, and a ton she knew was approximately the weight of a young elephant, and so it was these she saw floating out of squawking Vultee Vengeances as they flapped over Japanese targets during her first bombing-raid dream.

Then she dreamt monsoons. They followed the drought, as they had done in 1943, lashing through her sleep until her brain swelled heavy and sodden with imagery, the slap and drip of water still tapping in her head the next morning. In the moment before the click and roll up to the grey order of consciousness, the light scorched white and hot behind her lids, refracting shining swords off the wild banana trees and palms and igniting the bamboos and basha roofs with a radioactive glare. Her feet dashed over dead leaves, the debris of bamboo cane and blackened palm fronds, cracking and splitting under her sprinting steps like gunfire, giving away her location, allowing the enemy to lock on co-ordinates. Red dust turning to red mud licking round her ankles like geckos' tongues.

The rain fell in steel spears, driving steeply into the ground through the crust, releasing a noise like leaking gas, while gauze skirts of steam twirled. Just a few seconds and the earth rushed left and right in rivers of mud. Jagged lines, loaded with dashing mercury, spilled out of the rainclouds till a tributary hit the earth and flashed wildly on and off, dancing at the point of contact. The sky filled with fluorescent white light, off and on again like a laughing child was at the switch, and then the rolling boom and crash, shouting through bone, tearing up time.

When the skies were pale blue again – fathomless, bleaching white on the horizon – the red dust was gone and in its place lay a mire of mud. Outside the air was hot and slow, slopping against their shins. An uproar of crickets and bullfrogs, hell broken loose, a *coup d'état* on the ground. Voices broke in to Maggie's dreams, fractured like radio messages, in and out of range. 'Bastards shot him after he baled out. Got him as he was coming down, poor sod, nice fella, American, Judy Garland fan. Our lot itching to have a go next day, bagged six Japs. Not bad; lads were chuffed with that.'

The pilot floated into her sleep, she could hear Judy Garland belting out *Somewhere Over the Rainbow*, luscious painted lips making careful shapes for the words. She saw the pilot jerking on his strings, a ruined marionette, and his hollow sound like 'oh'.

Erdington High Road

Pop, Blowbroth and Maggie turned left instead of right along Clarendon Road because Pop hoped to alarm Iris with his absence; an expedition, a dangerous quest. It was arranged that she should hear about it from Carl. Arthur has taken off, bound for goodness knows where – something like that. He had been hiding for days now and imagined that quite soon she would be making general enquiries as to his whereabouts. He was enjoying the subterfuge, limp at the thought of raising her fear, chain-smoking. His excitement made him exceptionally alert and he flinched at doors slamming and birds launching out of trees. He had taken to wearing a pair of dark sunglasses he'd bought at Frost's the chemist to go with the deception.

When he turned to face them, Maggie and Blowbroth saw their expressionless faces reflected in each dark lens, multiplied, so that they were no longer three but five.

Pop made sure they did not visit the usual pubs, which meant long mysterious journeys through uncharted territory to undiscovered ones. He imagined the head-scratching and head-shaking in his locals and at the post office. He imagined Iris saying his name. He informed Maggie they were on walkabout like the Aborigines, and explained that research had indicated this was likely to increase their mental agility, possibly render them more vigilant and heedful. It was also common, he warned, for native Antipodeans at least, to hear the voices of ancestors and find themselves possessed by ancient spirits. The sun flared in his dark lenses while he spoke. Maggie watched a sparrowhawk fall into the fields beyond the Dugdale estate.

Pop stepped on his fag butt and resolved to find an exquisite object on their travels to present to Iris on his return.

Striding into strange pubs with a new husky voice, glowing and watchful behind his sunglasses, he told strangers his name was Albert, and in one or two others, George. The Aborigine thing pressed down on Maggie. She closed her eyes under the veil of hair and hummed while he talked.

In a pub called the White Horse in an area near the M6 called Erdington, Pop introduced himself as the reigning Four Oaks Fox and Dogs General Knowledge Champion and selected an audience. It was the birthday of Lord Krishna, Janmashtami, he pointed out with his hands on his hips, and bought everyone a drink. This leased their attention long enough for Pop to describe the bombing raids over Arakan and the Mayu Peninsula.

Afterwards, he explained the point of window displays to Maggie. He revealed the devious tactics employed by shops to seduce their customers into buying things they didn't need, and spent an hour judging the temptation factor of shop windows on the Erdington High Road with points out of ten. He faced each shop squarely on, with legs splayed and arms folded like a Crufts judge, while she pointed half-heartedly at items she felt unreasonably lured by. During the judging Pop forgot himself and bought a broom, three tins of pea and ham soup, some red-cherry shoe polish, some partly damaged cut-price Christmas decorations and an enormous black onyx coffee-table lighter, like the one used by James Bond with Pussy Galore in *Goldfinger*. Maggie imagined it on Iris's coffee table. 'An out and out bargain is a different matter entirely,' he clarified.

They walked past the electrical shops, the Indian restaurants, the yellow boards for Wall's ice cream and the signs for the motorway. As they trudged home, the scalded flesh of the passers-by began to fall in Maggie's mind like the slices of fatty bacon the butcher cut for Dolly to put in her butties. Slabs of soft white and red lardiness plodding over pelican crossings and hauling on to buses bound for Castle Bromwich and Walmley Ash.

Ahead, Maggie saw Pop watching his strolling reflection in the windows of Woolworths; he straightened and lengthened his stride to a brisk march and she imagined if his hands weren't full he might have saluted. Perish that thought. For distraction she placed her mother by a dazzling swimming pool with a cocktail in a typhoon of rainbow colours. When she was little her mother had sung in a big hotel in the Canary Islands for a whole season. Maggie and her father had flown out to see her. She performed

166

in a white dress, shimmering like sea foam against her bronzed shoulders, next to a matching white piano, and sang *Walk On By* and *Goin' out of My Head* in a room called the Flamingo Moon. Everyone clapped and her mother said, 'Thanks a lot. Okay, thanks a lot.' There was a man who was not tall, with an even darker tan and ebony sideburns who sang *Oh Carol* every night. He was her mother's friend. 'We're just friends,' she would say, as though friendship were a very trivial thing. He used to catch her eye and stamp while he sang it; just before '. . . *darling there will never be another*' down came his foot. His name was Tony Valentine and pretty women made him stamp.

Pop sang *O Little Town of Bethlehem*, brought on by the Christmas decorations. He swung ahead with the broom rearing up over his shoulder and his pate burning at the centre of his crown of hair. Blowbroth slunk behind, wheezing and tripping over his tongue.

'*Que sera sera*, Geoff,' Maggie had heard her mother say to her father while they were there. She learnt a lot of Spanish words in Gran Canaria.

They traipsed along Witton Road. Pop liked the redbrick streets in Aston, made soft with the billow of sari silk. Witton, Trinity and Whitehead Roads were among those that reminded him of the East. He ranged through them with long, bountiful strides, as though he'd triumphed in an election, his face split in two by a swag of smile, his eyes full of 1943. They paused on street corners so he could step back and gaze, hands on hips, fag in teeth, as though he'd painted it all himself from memory. When he got sentimental he tried his mispronounced RAF Hindi on the uncomprehending shopkeepers.

'Pretending they don't bloody speak it!' he reassured himself back on the street when none responded, shaking his head in disbelief. 'You don't have to prove your sovereignty to me, mate, I was there.'

Dusty cats baked on hot walls, net curtains hung at every redbrick window, milk crates lay in the road, and bright saris and shalwar kameez came floating through flapping groups of pigeons.

On a match day he liked rolling with the crowd past the pubs, doors flung open so the sun could burn across the mildewing carpets, all of them crammed with people and raining sun-spangled hailstorms of dust and the sound of Gladys Knight and The Pips. Under the railway bridge, past the mossy canal, through the blurred smiles of Indian children dashing like a welcoming committee.

After the post office on Witton Road there was a string of small hairdressing shops with red and white striped poles in each window. A. Khaliq gents hair salon, Mehrban Khaliq gents hairdressing and the Bismilah barber shop. Then a hill of fruit and vegetables, waxy reds, yellows and greens shining in the sun, a whiff of spices from inside where a group of men talked under a blue shadow. The halal butcher next, then Khadim & Sons the jewellers, and a shop called New Rangdhanu, 'electrical goods, music centre, arts, craft and wedding decoration', with a huge net of orange footballs hanging over the door next to a gobstopper machine. Trays and baskets of shoes next to that, sandals and flip-flops, golds, pinks, reds, more gobstoppers and Noddy's car, two pence a ride. A veil of black smog settled over the baskets from the number 103 as it grumbled away from the bus stop, and through its grimy filter Maggie could see the sunlight setting fire to the windows of the tower block next to the flyover.

Across the road the pavement is filled with fridges, settees, veneer sideboards, and a couple of washing machines. Second-hand bargains are to be had from Suite Life and Witton Furniture

Grotto. Pop sits down next to a rubber plant, in a smart oatmeal and brown armchair with matching settee, and lights a fag. He crosses his legs both ways to see. 'How much d'you want for this then?' he asks lightly in English and the old Hindustani woman tells him a price almost half his weekly pension. The matching settee is extra. He gives no reaction other than a suspicious squint at a patchwork pouffe. Then he bounces up and down in it a few times, spilling ash on his knees, wallops the armrests with both hands and nods.

'Okay. I'll think about it, mate,' he informs her, springing up and pointing at it with his cigarette while she smiles graciously. He gives it a last fleeting look as they walk away. Words all strung together seem to moan out through his nose while he bites down on his ropy fag.

The 'eathen in 'is blindness bows down to wood an' stone;
'E don't obey no orders unless they is 'is own;
'E keeps 'is side-arms awful: 'e leaves 'em all about,
An' then comes up the regiment an' pokes the 'eathen out.

They stroll with the sun at their backs towards the Salma Saree Centre on the corner of Trinity Road, its large windows bursting with banners of silk in red, gold, turquoise, indigo, black and silver, and set ablaze by the sun as it falls behind the football ground. They watch their reflections growing larger in the glass, walking stride for stride, and the ragged shape of Blowbroth paddling between, all of them ringed in fire. Pop stops to stare. The colours roar in the window, violet next to saffron and pink, gold, jade and ultramarine, beautiful and logical like Pop's Bengali sunsets, drifting layers burnished in the last copper rays. As the glass darkens his dog-end drops and he grinds it underfoot, lost in the window.

They pass the bearded men in white shalwar kameez, walking sticks tapping, all talking and pausing on corners, neat turbans and watchful glances, and they skirt their way round an enormous pale-pink mattress propped against a wall on the Trinity Road, which Blowbroth sniffs carefully with lecherous, half-closed eyes. The pub on Trinity Road promises Good Honest Beer in gold, sloping letters. The doors are fastened open, creating a black hole on the street, dark and sleepy inside. Just the gentle ringing of coins. It swallows them up.

When they got home Pop peeped through the lounge curtains at the street. He pulled them tightly around his eyes so he could scan incognito. According to Carl nobody so far had enquired after him. He was disappointed but pretended he was enjoying himself. The room was dim with the curtains drawn and Maggie lay on the settee, cooling in the grey shadows.

'Foxed 'em, ha! Fooled the lot of them, mate. Not a single one, if you asked, would have a bloody clue where I was.' His head, snugly wrapped in curtain, rotated left and right checking for signs of anything at all, like Red Riding Hood's wolf in Grandma's clothes.

'Dozy bastards wouldn't notice if the flaming Martians landed.' He flung open the curtains finally in disgust, filling the room like a newly discovered tomb with blinding light and waterfalls of glittering dust. Maggie closed her eyes and he looked at her. The glare bleached her skin whiter still, her wrist cocked high and her face turned away on a fragile neck, like a boy king. He saw how like her mother she was at certain angles, staring at her freely while she dozed, the thin arms thrown like snooker cues. Her shoulders were straight not cringing as his had been at the same age, her chin was fallen to the side, not confident

170

enough to challenge but smart enough to doubt. Pop waited for a feeling to form itself in him and when it did it rushed up, taking him by surprise, sending him out of the room before he could make a fool of himself.

That evening, just before opening time, everything fell silent. Like a story out of the Bible, like some sinister calm before an apocalyptic judgement. There was no birdsong or hammering, no cars or distant voices, no breeze. The sky was empty, wiped of clouds and planes, the streets deserted, the trees motionless as though everything had been murdered. Pop was disturbed by it, he loped from room to room and slunk nervously into the garden where he stood with his hands on his hips looking up at the blank sky as if the pilot light had gone out.

Maggie tried to read the paper. 'If only Mr Cutler had known about patio doors, life would have been much easier,' a double-glazing ad pointed out.

Pop was distracted for a while by the dying rhododendron bushes, all toasted due to the hosepipe ban. He kicked at the scorched lawn; the drought had turned it golden and had crackle-glazed the crust with splits and cracks running like horizontal lightning in all directions. He bent over it, fascinated, and followed a crack to the edge of the garden where it had tunnelled under the fence and away. He swung around suddenly and threw an impatient face up at the sky again as though he might demand an answer, like in a film. Instead he turned himself into a fire hazard and sent trembling haloes of smoke Indian-file over the fence. He returned at breakneck pace, slamming the door, jolting Blowbroth's head out of his cooling water bowl, the wet side of his face all smudged away as though it were being repainted. Maggie stiffened at the thought of another shambling journey to an unfamiliar place.

'Ready, mate?' Pop called as he blurred past. Blowbroth fled after him with his new blunt head and concave cheek, drizzling a trail across the Sahara of brown and tan carpet. Maggie followed eventually, the gate's cry deafening in the silence. Ahead she could see Pop step inside the red phone box on the corner of Grange Lane and Blowbroth whipping in around his feet, his tail waving demented as a coronation flag, the only movement of air in the West Midlands.

The scarlet box, matchless blue sky and the hushed heat reminded her of school sports days, and the business of winning, the flutter of red ribbons pinned during cold-hearted little ceremonies on the chests of those who had triumphed. The indifferent clap clap clap of the losers, the endless green running track smacking like steel underfoot, the hot, bony elbows of the other runners, bursting for breath, blood curdling and falling away, the shouts of the excitable cheese and ham crowd, turning to a gale by the finishing line. Jolly red ribbons, jolly red injuries, and the jolly red shame of the losers, always under a perfect hip-hip hooray sky and a big bashing sun.

He was shouting into the phone; Maggie could hear every word halfway up Clarendon Road. Blowbroth was barking a shrill assault that ricocheted off the glass, and sprang up repeatedly like a kangaroo, snapping at the mouthpiece. 'Knock it off!' he yelled at the dog. Maggie checked the windows for curtain-twitching but everything was still. They could probably hear it in Wolverhampton, they could probably hear it in Tennessee. 'Can't hear myself think, Christ!' And her mother slammed a door in her head. Blowbroth was ejected from the phone box, pausing in the air like a cartoon dog, while a struggle to effect dignity reduced the astonishment on his face to an expression of mild curiosity. He sniffed the spot where he landed as though he'd intended to arrive there all along.

Pop was shouting goodbye. 'Good enough, ta-ra a bit each. Eh? Hello?' He slammed the receiver down and peered out at Maggie through one of the glass oblongs. For a brief moment he seemed exotic, faintly elegant in his dark glasses, like Dr Who, then he shuffled out.

'Flaming dozy hound! There's a penalty, mate, for terrorising phone boxes.'

He lit a cigarette and looked up at the sky again. 'Right, I've made enquiries and ascertained that the coast is clear. Suggest we dispense with the undercover element for now. Might as well go to the Dogs.'

Maggie wondered what life would have been like if Pop had never come out of the phone box, if he'd dematerialised and stepped out into another century like the real Dr Who, left to smoke and brag his way through the French Revolution or into a welcoming party of Druids – Right mate, I've had it with your lip and them flaming horns.

Iris had gone away of course. She and a friend had gone to the Lake District the previous week, Carl had found out at the post office. The Aboriginal expedition to Erdington had been pointless.

'What does she want to go there for?' Pop demanded. 'Got bloody lakes here, six of 'em in Sutton Park. Bloody choking with the things, we are. Crammed them lakes'll be up there. If she wants lakes I could've given her lakes, never so much as mentioned them before.'

The return to his own pubs transformed him like a midsummer spell. He was gleeful at being back and weaved around the bar like a sprite. He bought rounds as fast as everyone could drink them and slapped all the shoulders and arms as he spun past. A fanatical grin peeled back his face until it was possible to see the boy he had been, quite clearly, shining out of his air-force blue eyes and cackling through his jeered greetings and yelps of laughter. Three times he was asked where he'd been putting himself about lately and three times he shone with pride at the success of his subterfuge and the attention it had created. By the third enquiry he had formulated a response and adopted a quietly measured philosophical voice, with narrowed eyes, lowered chin, pointing finger, and gravelly monotone descending to a whisper. 'Ask not where, my friend, but how. The highway of my heart goes to many destinations, some far, some not so far, and all can traverse this highway.' He'd rushed it at the end but it still brought a wary silence around the bar and beyond, leaving them with the ominous ticking of the pub clock that had stood over the back door, counting down people's lives, for thirty years. Then he hooted: 'Hindu proverb, mate! Had you all going there for a minute anyhow.'

Someone mumbled a joke about a big-game hunter who couldn't speak Swahili and Maggie watched Pop craning forward, straining to hear, trying his left ear then his right. At the end, without having heard the punch-line, he let off a shout of laughter, then he bought another round, and another, until he ran out of money.

Jack Spence

Instrument basher AC Meadows was afraid of dying. The cholera, dysentery and malaria frightened him as much as the air raids, but it was the thought of snakes that really got to him, more than disease or the Japanese. The slit trenches terrified him, his eyes were milky with fear under his tin helmet.

'What'll I do if there's a bloody bastard cobra in there?' he demanded to know on a cannonball of spit.

'Tell the bugger to budge up a bit and make room for you!' Pop's story went.

Pop hated the ones who moaned, dripping they called it, made him nervous. He said he'd rather be in a trench with a madman than a moaner. 'Funny thing,' he mused, 'a moaner'll never offer a smoke or buy a round neither, too busy dripping. Selfish lot they are, but they'll soon smoke yours, always on the scrounge moaners are.'

He had a pal who had no trouble offering his smokes around. Jack Spence from Tyneside liked a tab and a chat and a popular song. He built houses made from playing cards and never minded if some fella knocked them down, accidentally or otherwise. He was a cheerful optimist with big tragic eyes who prayed every night, wore a St Christopher around his neck and always looked on the bright side. He was a good listener with an easy laugh, very light on his toes, an excellent ballroom dancer, always went to sleep at night, he said, with a song on his mind. Could cure any sadness, he said, a good song. *I'll Think of You* was one of his favourites, 'Beautiful melody that, dear me, near break your heart that will, mind.' Then he'd laugh as though this was something dead funny really. Pop liked him. They talked continuously like women at their laundry; not even the Japanese could interrupt their chelping, always one of them yacking in the trench or over the scramble horn.

The long wet summer of 1943 brought flooding. They had moved base from Madhaiganj to Dohazari, a few miles south-east of Chittagong. The monsoons were bad that year, making their bombing missions to the Japanese military targets in Burma difficult. The floods brought disease and conditions grew worse, casualties, aircraft and air-crew losses were high.

Pop thought he had caught the flu when he woke drenched in sweat and shivering in his charpoy. Later the chills shook his muscles until they were slush and chased icy canals, looping like dread, up and down his body. There were rules about long sleeves and mozzie nets down by dusk, but no one took much notice, there were more pressing worries. A female mosquito had slipped inside the netting one night and delivered the parasite. As it flowered in Pop's blood his malarial symptoms developed, holding him sodden in his charpoy for days. His aching bones swelled heavy as railway sleepers and swam as if freed from their sockets and joints, buoyed in a soup of poisoned blood. The dry dome of his skull throbbed and split slowly open, making him groan like an old man. In soaring tropical temperatures he shivered until he was exhausted. His skin prickled and burned with cold, a frantic stippling, peculiar, like anxious fingers searching for something. He felt his hands growing leaden and huge, inflating. Eventually he hallucinated them adrift from his arms, waving and pointing in a corner of the sick bay. Then the cough arrived, reassuringly familiar. Jerking spasms that snatched him up and winded him, dry barks on his hands and knees like a prairie dog. A few days later it was all gone. It would return sporadically, unannounced, for the rest of his life, surprising him

176

on grimy English mornings with the flopping sound of his blood rolling thick against his bones.

After he had recovered from the initial bout, he strolled out into the glare on straw legs and lit a trembling cigarette. He laughed loudly at jokes he'd heard before and passed his fags around.

'Got a light there, mate?'

'What's the gen anyway?'

'Bags of new blokes.'

'Hutchison stopped a couple of bullets before he got to the trench.'

Talking washed up in her sleep, voices bending through and fading again. Sometimes the dreams turned bad. There had been a story about Dohazari, people were dying in a cholera epidemic. In her dream Maggie walked along a dusty road lined with corpses; Pop had seen them dropping on the street as he passed. Some had been detailed by the RAF to burn bodies in an attempt to control the outbreak. In her dream Maggie saw the corpses struggling to free themselves from the pile, blinking at the splashes of petrol, attempting to stand in the flames.

She dreamt of the Japanese plane Pop had seen crashed in the jungle, the numbers and scroll on the tail fin, sun rising on the fuselage, pilot still in the cockpit, cut almost in half. Deep in the bamboos the sharp leaves and thin shadows formed the face of a Gurkha in a low-slung hat. She thought she saw the curve of a kukri blade but when she looked back she saw only the waving shadow of a palm, wiping him clean away. She glimpsed the same Gurkha from behind, his kukri hanging at his back, and she was afraid. Then he turned around and she saw that he was Ron Saunders and he was singing. '*Oh Carol, I am but a fool. Darling I love you, though you treat me cruel.*'

Until Pop had switched off the engine that first time outside 99 Clarendon Road, Maggie had never seen a man cry. The closest she'd got had been her father's gloomy episodes with a tumbler of brandy and Coke pressed like a field dressing to his forehead while George Jones sang *How Do We Get There From Here?* Now she knew that Flight Sergeant Johnny 'Fred' Roberts, who could sing through his nose, had cried for his mother as he lay dying in his sick bed, half of him rotted away from the gangrene, what was left already carrion.

The sounds fell into her sleep, the incessant crickets and belching frogs through the hours of darkness, the girlish cry of a jackal from the Chin Hills, the creak and rustle of wind in the palm tops and bamboos, the chug of the electrician's chore-horse, the rip of the Browning gunfire and the distant hum of enemy bombers after the klaxon's blare.

Maggie could smell the boiled potatoes, beans and gravy and the corned beef pretending to be something else. She knew the sodden bush shirt and the skin burnt angry and red across the collarbone, the stink of petrol and oil, and the loose talk turned stale by the endless char. The chat aired over and over in the smoke-filled crew room known as the scrounge room: prices, going home, wogs and women, the latest exploit of the squadron buffoon. She knew about the long nights on duty that started with the laying out of the flare path along the runway at dusk when the fireflies gathered and floated through the trees. And the dying pilot, fallen back to earth, his skin grated and frayed, revealing bones burnt black while the marrow dripped out. His amazed heart still beating, head lolling, and his Crucifixion eyes flung up at the sky with the same old question: Lord, Lord, why hast thou forsaken me? While the first-aid crew, smart in their armbands, failed to mend him with their box of lint bandages.

The Drain Man

From the tangled copse of wilderness came the riotous echoing shrieks of kids, like parakeets' cries rising in the rainforest. Feral screams, death and destruction now in the woods.

Spring of '75, a warm April day, just nine weeks before the heatwave, thirteen weeks, unlucky for some, before her mother died.

Maggie knelt in the stream to scoop up frogspawn with a net. She wore her mother's flop-brim sunhat so she could see fish under its shadow. The water was running with galeweed and tiny stickleback hid among the stones. Her fingers swept through the cold moss while the water bubbled, always hurrying towards the Swale at Sheppey. Minnow grass, sellet and frose grew along the banks, and water grasses spread themselves to stream in the current.

She pillaged them all to make a home for frogs. She filled a tin bucket brimming with whatever she could tear up and carry, struggling the last few yards, dragging the bucket, spilling water, sweating under the hat. The frogspawn plopped in hesitant and then dashing lumps from net to bucket and from there into more bowls and basins. She tipped and poured, delighted at its slimy vulnerability, the awful miracle of it. Wincing at the thought of its wet touch, solemn and scientific in the grip of her power. She squeezed four buckets and five assorted bowls all bobbing and quivering with frogspawn into the garden shed, enough to choke the estate with frogs. It all lay fermenting in the stale dinginess, still and silent under the spring moon as Frankenstein's lab.

Her reflection shimmered back morning and evening as she peered into the buckets for signs of life. The scrape of her shoe at dawn and creak of the door sent chills through her, short breaths, loud as a stallion's in the cool motionless air, flowers cold and clenched before the first graze of sun peeled them open. Inside the shed the air became gassy with the smell of yeast and fish and rotting weed. The stench heralded the beginning of Maggie's private miracle as the buckets and basins turned black with tadpoles.

For days she gazed, transfixed by their prehistoric whipping tails, their swollen cystic heads, black and menacing as tumours. She watched them flashing about in pointless circles, racing through the minutes to reach the moment when unseen magic transformed them into frogs. She hung her hands in the algaed water until they turned khaki and stinking, while dozens of tadpoles panicked between her fingers. She lifted one out to see it thrash and jump, like an electrocution, a game of execution, and dropped it back in again before it gave out, except usually they didn't swim again. She sprinkled some on the floor and watched until their gills stopped flapping. Not all the eggs hatched and some died mysteriously, their black corpses floating until the others ate them. A few were monstrous mutations with two heads or no tail, their movements either peculiar or non-existent, signalling the others to attack and destroy. It was Armageddon in the shed.

Maggie's mother complained about the smell. No matter where she positioned her sun lounger it curled under her nostrils, a fishy-foul sewage stink. She had to soak a handkerchief in Joy by Patou and clamp it under her nose whenever she became overwhelmed. The stench made her angry, then depressed. Eventually the drain man came to check the drains, front and back. He found nothing untoward but he came back the next day to check again. Maggie's mother leant against the house in cat-eyed sunglasses and a yellow blouse, loosely tied at the waist over a leopard-print bikini top. The drain man blinked away the sweat in his eyes and prostrated himself beside a hole in the ground into which he lowered various rods. Every time he gazed up at her he cleared his throat and brushed at his nose. He prefaced every sentence with 'I'd hazard a guess . . .'

After a while she was tottering in and out of the kitchen in clacking mules, bearing clinking drinks choked with fruit. He abandoned his hole and they finished their drinks in the garden, she reclining on the sun lounger, he leaning awkwardly against the rotating washing-line pole. He swiped at it, sending it into wild rocking whirls on its pole so that it released a scornful whine each time it flew round. As the ice smacked back into their empty glasses they began to laugh at each other's remarks. He hung his arms high in the aluminium spokes with the washing, like a drip-dry version of James Dean's rifle pose. She opened the French doors so that *Windmills of Your Mind* rolled out into the garden and off across the estate. As she made more drinks her body began to melt; she sang while she metamorphosed and by the time she carried the quivering little tray outside, ice cubes ringing like Pentecostal bells, she walked with a new pigeon-toed sway, chin tucked low and eyes blaring and saucy over the top of her sunglasses. Maggie went to the wood and blew loud screams through blades of grass between her thumbs, emptying the trees of birds, until she noticed that the drain van had gone. The stench remained. Her mother barricaded herself against it with a battery of door-slamming, perfume, appeals to the Saviour, menthol cigarettes and Martini Bianco.

The tadpoles grew legs and then their tails fell off. Maggie carried rocks to the basins so they could climb out of the water. Her father had built the garden shed from a kit and was proud of it, so her mother wouldn't acknowledge it. Nothing could tempt her inside, not even an opportunity to solve the stench mystery. The shed did not exist for her; as far as she was concerned its four creosoted walls and little pitched roof were not there. The frog laboratory remained undiscovered.

The morning it rained – contrary to the forecast – Maggie was later than usual to the shed. Her mother was in the kitchen reading a magazine in a gloom of smoke. Outside, the air was spiky with hydrogen, everything was ionised, crackling, and thick with water. From inside the house Maggie heard the crashing slam of a door and the rain stopped abruptly as if her mother had carelessly shot the rainmaker. She opened the shed door and a frog leapt out. Maggie's sandals jumped and skidded in a panicking dance. The frog paused, then leapt again. The sandals danced again. It was small, muddy green in colour with a spattering of splodges. It had bulbous, fluidy eyes, gaping and insane. Splayed at each corner was a set of long satanic fingers. At intervals it launched itself into the air with a slow spongy jump and landed with a faint slap. She realised with horrified delight that inside the shed dozens more were jumping and landing. Inside Maggie a thousand people cheered. A judgement, a plague of frogs, a curse of toads; a sign, they would say, an omen. They hopped with blank eyes over the scuffed sandals of their caretaker, down the front path towards the stream. Maggie ran ahead of them laughing, doubled up like a drunk. She would escort them across the road like a lollipop lady, salute her green amphibian army as they scrambled to the water. She turned back and there was the first one, jump, slap, and another behind and then three. She skidded and staggered, ha ha bloody ha, a ton of frogs. She sat all day in the middle of the road in her mother's Biba hat, wide as a goldigger's pan, waving on the occasional car, while the frogs went in all directions. Mostly into people's gardens for the cats to catch.

Chittagong

There was one who went mad. A wireless mechanic from Shropshire, Hannan. Weeks of Japanese raids in Burma had loosened his grip. He developed a slack-jawed stare in Madhaiganj, then he stopped talking. He shat in the bamboos, he hid in the empty oil drums on the dispersal. Once, during a raid, while Pop and the other airmen were taking cover in a slit trench, they saw him peeping out of an oil drum near the runway, while behind him a formation of Kawasaki bombers began to drop their loads. There was no question of him surviving. The bombs burst all around while he lay in his drum with the ants, deafened and battered by falling debris. But some miracle spared him.

They had to tip the drum upside down to get him out and when they did he rolled, still curled tightly, his chin in his chest, half naked and covered in a thick layer of red dust as though he'd been born of some long-dead mother.

Pop did his best with the coffins, it was the only piece of carpentry he didn't whistle over. The wood was poor quality, rough and unplaned, but he was proud of his skills and didn't like to see them sent down like so many packing crates. It was always someone he knew, however vaguely, and sometimes it was a pal. The malaria served to remind him he'd be lying in one of his own boxes if he copped it himself.

He made beading for the edges and carved the name and

date on the lid if there was time; he was big on pomp and dignity. The forty or so little board and peg grave markers in the RAF cemetery with their hurriedly stencilled information weren't much of a bloody send-off, he reckoned. He would have liked to have carved the squadron's motto, *nec timeo nec sperno*, I Neither Fear Nor Despise. A morally enlightened slogan compared to The First of the Legion, or Swift to Vengeance. One composed of self-knowledge and ethical wisdom that appealed to Pop in its superior tone. He quoted it with a chaplain's rise and fall on fear and despise.

When he watched them go, bumping their way down the clay roads across the paddy fields to the cemetery for burial, he felt that in a small way he'd done right by them. Sometimes it was his duty to bump towards the paddy fields with them, a long mahogany hand steadying the coffin as it slid, the same long fingers smoothing the blue silk ensign over the lid to dignify the short ceremony, the removal of it after the words 'rest in peace' had hung themselves high in the hot air, so that it could be folded away for the next one. Another RAF pettiness Pop felt bad about. 'Poor bastard can't even go under with his own force's flag, tatty old scrap from wear and tear anyhow.' He distracted himself by concentrating on the ants trooping along the edges of the graves and the giant dragonflies halting in mid-air, flashing oily shades of amethyst and jade. He watched the dwarf trees squatting low on the perimeter, as though they too were sinking into the dust where the forgotten now slept.

He removed his bush hat and squinted under the dazzle. 'Cheerio then, mate,' before following the others to the rumbling wagon. Always the same words, spoken carefully but with real optimism, as though when this was all over there was still a chance of a pint in somebody's local, a chance to shoot a line, spin a few for the flat-footers and asthmatics in warm oak chairs under a dome of smoke.

She dreamt one of Pop's eastern sunsets. The best of them would bleed the sky a dozen hot shades of magenta before cooling to pink and violet. Shelves of pale light filled with colours that drifted through the spectrum, turning green, primrose, watery blue. The sun, yawning full of blood and slipping further on the smoky horizon, sent out flares of orange across curls of darkening cloud while higher, the colour turned pale lemon and formed a massive bruise with the grey. The edges of the larger inky rainclouds were trimmed with silver. In her dream it turned the whole sky claret and blue as far as Bhutan.

The din from the warm jungle on a Bengal night, a comfort and a warning both. Maggie ran though the clinging black, sprinting between the parallel lines of softly twinkling glim-lamps that made up the runway's flare path, her hard feet shattering the dust, little mushroom clouds of it rising under each contact, atomic steps. Above her a crescent moon was collapsed on its back, behind her the red glow of cigarettes on a bamboo verandah, waiting. She'd dreamt the blue and gold flames swimming out of the bomber's exhaust vents, heating her face, chucking sparks in her hair. The roar of the engine pushing her heart against her ribs, the duststorm biting through skin as it tore away and sprang up to the moon, light as a seabird in spite of its bomb load. She dreamt the bottle-nosed Vengeances in thunderous formation, towing the lazy moon like a chariot, dripping strings of violet lights across the black, shaking the enemy out of the sky.

'Hirohito's little yellow customers,' a speckle-lipped pilot called them in an official tone, before he roared down the strip fully loaded, and arced a wing over the sun, turning the day inside out and dragging its deadly secrets with him to the operation in Razabil.

She dreamt herself eye-deep in a slit trench between the airmen, fag in teeth the same. Instead of the tin hat she wore a Villa hat with matching scarf. Together they murmured carefully through:

> And it's Aston Villa,
> Aston Villa FC.
> We're by far the greatest team
> The world has ever seen.

Each thud shook the ground, dull thumps displacing subcutaneous layers so that Maggie felt the earth rolling like a restless bedfellow; sleeping hips and shoulders shifting, bursting an elbow into the trench. Mud walls swaying, needing sea legs now, while above them the sky groaned open and metal fire rained down.

The relief of the silence then, pure and beneficent like a blessing. The gabble of talk washed along by quicksilver adrenalin, the ceremonial lighting of the fags. The comforting communion of shared disappointment if one of the planes on the dispersal was smouldering from a hit, and the raucous joy if it was one of the dummy kites, the decoy ducks, that Pop and others built on a ton of fags, char and natter.

The time was broken up by counting down to the next blare of the scramble horn that sent men running all over again. Pilots jumping off the verandah, tea still hot in their mouths, an erk on every wing-tip, chewed thumbnails squeezing white against the contact button to throw the blades in the airscrew. The relentless repetition, refuelling, rearming, reboring, dulled even the keenest fear eventually.

The Indian children darkened under an acid-pink sky. They stood about awkwardly on stick legs, thin string around their curved bellies, luscious eyes, huge enough to take in Maggie's dream, set wide apart in heads too large for their tiny bird chests, a slick of ebony hair, shiny as oil. The beggar on his grasshopper legs, blue-black skin, hanging at the creases, dug-out cheeks, eyes glassy and yellow as turmeric, seeing nothing or everything depending on who was judging. She saw the bloody smiles, '*Thīk hA sāhab?*' Teeth stained red from betel-nuts. She knew about the slums and brothels and the rickshaw boys who got a kicking when they raised their price.

Men running like the clappers or sprawling in the crew room, panicking or bragging, scrounging or cheesed. The RAF 'Wakey, wakey' as if they were at scout camp not war and 'Come on! Two-six', 'good show', 'bad show.' A pilot going down like a comet, screaming for his mother.

Pop wept not just for the pals that were lost but for the days that were gone. Even mid-rant through a tale of RAF incompetence, one of his 'right flaming balls-up' anecdotes, he could drop 'best damn days of my life' next to 'ruddy disgrace' without so much as a drag on his fag in between.

His long tortoiseshell fingers trembled infinitesimally, a tiny blur in the air, a hummingbird's flight. They swiped across his eyes, down his long cheeks and split sideways to flatten his uneven moustache, as though he were checking he was still there, lingering over the Braille of stubble along his chin to be sure.

His first day out of sick bay, catching up with the gen on wobbly legs, they told Pop that Jack Spence had been killed.

They'd got him as he ran for cover during the previous day's strafing, shot him in the back. He never was much of a runner; dancing yes, and building houses made from cards. He would go to the cemetery in one of Arthur Landywood's boxes. Pop would accompany him, with his new quivering hands laid long over the lid, his face Hallowe'en-hollow, a twist of grief trembling boyishly in his chin. First night back in the billets Pop noted the new bloke in Jack's charpoy, but it was the old tunes he could hear at night just the same.

Airmen   ·

Pop denied that he shouted at night. He said nightmares were for children, sleepwalking was for women and shouting for madmen. His dreams were so raucous that Maggie often woke from her own and wondered whether they might have been dreaming the same one.

'*Asti! Kidder Jaiga?*' In his RAF Hindi and worse Urdu. She had found herself in a muddled India too, wandering under a blinding Bengal sky, accompanied by an enormous dog with a long yellow tongue dragging after it like a fireman's hose. She watched the dazzle over the baked paddy fields, the withered arms of the dwarf trees stretching with a beggar's pleading for a drop of water. Hotch-potch facts and pieces of fiction borrowed from the spinning tales. The English heatwave had melted his cargo of memories and they drained out of him as easily as the ale splashed in. The drought inspired yet more yarns and Maggie had lain on the floor, the defeated opponent, while Pop breathed out enough Bengali air from under a tin helmet for Maggie to taste the warm biscuits and stale cheese from the bottom of his regulation kitbag.

She knew they visited him at night. She wondered if dead souls could enter peoples' dreams. She wondered whether they could rest in peace, the ones who were never found. Pop shouted suddenly from the other room and Maggie felt her skin chill. Could a person die in a dream? She couldn't remember. She felt a shelf of cool air slice through the warm. She allowed herself a quick glance around the room. The shadows watched her back, grey and alive, and as they did Maggie realised there were RAF personnel in every corner, crouching, sitting, standing, looking at her. She fell with no sound, dropping through her panic; her blood sprang, then drained away. When she looked again one of them was opening his mouth to speak, his jaw dislocating until his mouth opened a full hundred and eighty degrees, like an anaconda; his voice was a soft hammer hitting musical notes: 'Help me.' A smell of gasoline. The din of her heart and blood and rush of air, the burn of sweat turning to acid on her arms and legs, a scramble of wings in her ears. 'Please,' a single note, diminished, speech made from piano keys. Another airman on the ceiling. High in the corner, tucked up, his arms become frilled wings, black and gold. 'My mother will come,' he said, a child's voice, a girl's, his teeth falling in broken pieces as he spoke.

'My mother will come for me.'

Pop wondered about her. About how it would turn out. About what he'd said to the woman carrying a file with their names on. The stuff about family, about blood ties, all that thicker-than-water speech. The prohibitive wave of his hand to knock the alternatives into a cocked hat. The rise of blood in his temples as he moved himself to trembling, and the final whispered declaration of love for her, that he didn't feel then but was saddled with now. He'd listened, incredulous, while he spouted this stuff, convincing the woman. It was the right thing, he'd expected it of himself, but afterwards he felt ill. Then the sight of her on the platform, great big stringy lass, hair all hung in her face, dragging her suitcase, a disaster she looked, walking the wrong way. And he thought, Bloody hell. Here we go again.

He thought of them, the women in his life, their unnerving predilection for seeing themselves out without so much as a by-your-leave. And his brief emancipation, the raucous freedom of the RAF, the sweet liberation of his World War II.

Her radio was playing in her room; he could hear the song tipping down the stairs. *King of the Road*. Fat chance. Trouble with his flaming road was too many women'd thrown themselves like bags of nails across it, impeding his progress, blowing his chances, breaking his heart, one after another, like teamwork. Minute you feel for them, that's gobbed it straight away. And he felt for her now alright. He laid his chin in the cradle of his free hand and closed his eyes. Buggered it again, you fool.

The Plough and Harrow

Pop is dressed up in his best suit, as if he is getting married. Maggie and Blowbroth stare, waiting for an explanation to fall from the sky.

'I have decided to take the bull by the horns,' he says. 'This afternoon after closing time I plan to pledge my troth.'

The air feels cooler, it moves in soft, luxurious breezes and sways the treetops, sending the leaves into rapturous papery applause. Some low-lying cloud clots around steeples and chimneys. 'Malaria weather,' Pop mumbles, peering suspiciously around with a jaundiced eye, says it makes his lungs play up. The pub is warm and sweet with the smell of booze and furniture polish. Maggie's legs stick to the padded red banquette and a dazzling white light presses at all the windows. Blowbroth spreads himself across the cool lino floor and his yellow eyes roll back in his skull.

'Arthur.'

'Morning, Ken.'

'Turned a bit.'

'Malarial conditions, mate.'

'If you say so.'

Pop counts out his coins on the bar. A man in the corner with long ears and a thick head of oiled hair calls out:

'I see your motor could do with a bloody wash, Arthur.'

'It'll rain soon enough, don't you worry.'

'Full of muck, rainwater. Worst thing of all, that is.'

'Oh ar. Bag of them scratchings, Ken, for the kid, ta.'

'Make it all streaky, rain will.'

'You've got the job, mate. Ken'll fetch you a bucket and sponge.'

That shuts him up. Pop sits down. The door squeals open, the glass panels strobing light explosions.

'Oh. Didn't see me there, Arthur.'

It's Tatty, always in black with a dusting of dandruff, like ermine across the shoulders.

'Tat!' Pop barks and sips.

'Nice motor the Ford Anglia actually.' The long-eared one, making amends.

'Inconsistent, I find,' Pop replies. 'I'm considering the Austin Accord for reliability. I'm going to enquire at the garage about part-exchange.'

More arrivals. Maggie slips her slice of lemon over her front teeth and tries out a welcoming smile. Pop contorts over the bag of pork scratchings.

'Can't open the bloody thing.'

Men idle towards tables with their drinks; each has his own spot; few sit together.

'*I write the songs that make the whole world sing,*' Ken warbles as he pulls taps and squeezes shots from upturned bottles. The clock counts down the seconds, matches hiss.

'I've laid my bathroom and toilet carpet out on the front lawn.'

Pork scratchings burst over the banquette and on to the floor.

'I can't cut it indoors, I've got no bloody room now, where am I going to lay it out to cut it?'

'How big is it, Jim?'

'Just my luck if it bloody rains.'

Blowbroth crunches loudly, like splitting bones.

'Coventry on Saturday, Arthur,' Ken calls out with a tease in his eye. 'You wanna watch out for that Dennis Mortimer,' he adds.

'Oh, ar,' Pop replies, as if he doesn't believe a bloody word of it.

'And who's the other one?' Ken asks. 'What's his name? Can't remember his name now.'

'Wouldn't worry about it, mate,' says Pop through a mouthful of scratchings.

'Damn, it's gone.'

'I know who you mean. Couldn't kick a door if he was holding on to the handle.'

A wiry man with sunken cheeks and a trembling whippet drops his cigarette into the ashtray.

'Navigator of mine died last week,' he says.

'Who?' Pop, quick as a flash.

'Hamilton. You don't know him. Young bloke, only sixty.'

'Blimey. A few starting to join the choir invisible now, mate.'

'There's a pilot not far from here, Tamworth way.'

'Campbell, I know him,' Pop says. 'He was with Seventy-Nine doing the damage in Burma.'

'Asia. It's a funny place. My son goes to Taiwan tomorrow,' says Woody with the jerking hands.

'Oh ar, that'll be nice for him.'

'He's a university lecturer, but you wouldn't think so to look at him, scruffy bugger. You can't tell these days by looking whether one's more cleverer than the next.'

'Never mind that. You can't tell which are the fellas and which bloody aren't.'

'You can't say "more cleverer than the next", can you? That's an adverb.'

'No, well, it's a dialect actually. That's different.'

'Those pocket calculator things come from Taiwan.'

'Pocket calculator, fat lot of use if you're naked.'

A pause for thought. The whippet snatches demented glances at Blowbroth. The lemon rind drops out of Maggie's mouth.

'Daft bugger, what the bloody hell d'you wanna calculate when you're naked?'

A rumble of laughter that becomes a group coughing fit. Pop coughs longest; it doesn't sound good. It creates another silence.

'It isn't the cough that'll carry you off, it's the coffin they'll carry you off in,' he reels off at the end, but it doesn't pull the laughter back.

'They play a lot of rugby in places like Western Samoa, strange that.' Woody on his second pint. 'It's all they really play, they don't bother with cricket or golf.'

In the pause there are voices and a shriek from outside. Then Ken bursts back behind the bar. 'Right, we need some able-bodied men outside now please, quick as you like, tie up the dogs.' Everyone rises, lifts their pint and files out quickly. A sunburnt woman is standing in the car park holding a carrot, while in the corner a small donkey eats cow parsley.

'Tractor frightened him,' she cries. 'Can't get hold of him now, silly bugger. I've got to get him up to a field on Weeford Road.' Ken orders everybody to stand back, takes the carrot and approaches the donkey with casual confidence, strolling on the back of his heels with his chin up as though he's going to arrest it. The men stand in a crowd to watch, hands in pockets, holding pints. Ken gets close. It looks at him, then at the crowd. He moves in more slowly, right up so he's in reaching distance. He presents the carrot like a crucifix and it jerks back its head. He makes a dive for it, misses, and it skids away on scrabbling hooves. The crowd lets off a heartfelt 'ooohhh', same as they would for a missed penalty, and 'Hard luck, Ken'. Ken strolls back to the others swinging his carrot. The donkey gives a honking bray, which rouses a cheer from the crowd. Ken is offered cigarettes, condolences, advice. He eats the carrot.

'Bugger in't he?'

'No easy beast, the ass,' Pop explains.

'You could try a hosepipe, mate.'

'A hosepipe?'

'Don't be daft.'

'How the bleeding hell does that work?'

'Just spray 'em, they don't like it.'

'What about the flaming ban?'

'Don't be daft, bloody daft idea.'

'Works. I've seen it.'

'What about a tranquilliser dart?'

'What about it?'

'What's she trying to do now?'

The woman is approaching it again with her arms out like an aeroplane.

'That'll never work. What's she doing that for?'

'Dozy cow can't have had much of a grip on him. Where's she taking him anyhow, the Fray Bentos factory?'

The donkey flattens its ears and trots away again.

'Bugger in't he?'

'Nervous animal, tractor spooked him.'

'Castration, that always calms them down.'

'You could hood him like they do racehorses. I've seen it done.'

'Haven't got a flaming hood.'

'You can use a shopping bag, I've seen it done, works just the same, or a pillowcase.'

'Okay, here's the plan. We'll surround him,' Ken says, holding his hands in a circle to represent a surrounded donkey, 'corner him first.'

'What about the fire brigade?'

'They'll never come out for a donkey, mate.'

'They come out for bloody cats, don't they?'

'True.'

'Cos cats is ladders and all that, in't it, contraptions and so forth.'

'They will not, I can categorically assure you, matey, come out for a damn donkey. You'll have to light him with a match first.'

Pop walks away. He turns to face the group with narrow eyes to indicate that he is concentrating. 'It's perfectly simple,' he says quietly, feet apart, instantly capturing their attention with melodrama. He continues in a low, unnaturally relaxed voice, like an actor in a film. 'We'll have to outwit him, that's all. I suggest we surround him like Ken said, drive him into a corner, then two of us grab on to his headcollar, one either side, perfectly bloody simple, a child could do it.' The sound of a woodsaw floats by on the breeze from somewhere. No one can think of a reply.

Pop has coins for the phone. Carl is instructed to deliver the information to Dor at the post office for Iris to hear.

'Arthur is leading a team of men in the task of capturing a large beast currently running loose on the Slade Road. Thank you very much.'

The donkey watches the men form an uncertain semi-circle. In spite of its big cuddly head and pantomime ears it is obviously making calculations. Maggie sits on the bonnet of the Anglia to watch, a length of cat's-tail grass between her teeth. As the self-appointed architect of the plan, Pop busies himself tutting, hissing and waving them left a bit, right a bit, until he considers their positions appropriate, as if the donkey were about to take a free kick. When he is satisfied he starts to creep forward with his knees together. The others do the same until Pop motions for them to stop. Tat takes a glug of his ale in the pause, so Woody does too. The donkey turns a glossy long-lashed eye on them. Nothing happens for a moment while they all consider each other. Then the donkey, sensing a trap, flees suddenly through the gap between Tat and Jim, leaving them in a straggly, pointless formation. Glasses are drained, Pop lights a fag and flattens his moustache. 'Intelligent beast, the humble ass,' he says.

It is decided that they will dispense with formation and concentrate on taking it by surprise. Ken starts with a riot-control-style dash that shakes his belly up and down. The donkey ducks away and the chase is on.

'Quick, before it's had time to think!' Pop yells, sprinting at it, ale slopping over his shoes.

'Go in on his blind spot!' someone shouts. 'Get behind his

frame of vision.' Woody dances backwards alongside it in the hope he'll become invisible. Each man makes a run at it, Jim even catches hold of its tail, but no one gets anywhere near its head and morale begins to run low. Sweating profusely now and bending double to breathe, members of the team are beginning to sit and lean and curse.

'Where the bloody hell's she buggered off to anyhow?'

The donkey's sunburnt owner is in the lounge bar with a gin and orange, which reduces their resolve further. Pop lights a fag, narrows his eyes again. 'Pity there isn't a Mongolian among us. Masters of the equine art they are.'

'Oh ar. Flaming Nora, Arthur, where are we going to find a ruddy Mongolian this side of Lichfield?'

'Bloody twelve bore'd do the trick, I reckon.'

'Right, one of us'll have to try to mount the thing,' Pop suggests. There are groans of disbelief and murmurings of dissent and more than half the men take themselves back inside the bar.

Pop watches the donkey chewing daisies on the verge while he finishes his fag. 'Pity that, we were wearing him down. We'd have had him if we'd kept at it.' He winks at Maggie. 'Ah well,' and tosses away his fag, before he too strolls back to the bar. 'Come on then, mate.'

When he pokes his head around the door some ten minutes later to check where she's got to, he discovers Maggie rubbing the animal's nose, stroking his ears and feeding him Fox's glacier mints from her pocket.

Leading Aircraftman 848509

It is decided that the troth-pledging is best postponed. Pop's suit is spoiled with ale, ash and grass seed from the donkey drive and anyway he is no longer convinced of its suitability for the task.

'Touch funereal,' he admits suspiciously, brushing off the jacket, 'Doesn't really do the job.' He wants to look heroic but dependable, in a colour that lifts the spirit without alarming gentler sensibilities.

He has no full-length mirror in the house so he has to check his next choice in bits. He is pleasantly surprised. The jacket and trousers are a little tight around the waist, but otherwise not bad. Maggie discovers him standing on a chair in the hall. He is dressed in full service blue. If he bends his knees in a *plié* like a ballerina he can see the jacket in the mirror. Buttons a little dull, he thinks, hair a little long, other than that, pretty good. He straightens up and salutes.

'What are you doing?' she interrupts.

He wobbles and gasps, 'Stone the crows, creeping up like that, I'll have a bloody heart attack.'

'Sorry.'

Pop hurries upstairs to find some shoes. The uniform carries him taller, quickens his steps, the smell coming off it makes him pause. He lights a fag, the exact combination in his memory, smoke and serge.

They'd buried Jack Spence deep in red clay, dry and dusty, with the cruel sun hanging over him. Pop had stood with his hat off, pale and sickly, reeling under the dazzle as the words were read out. The others waited in the truck while he spent a moment alone. He dropped some dust in, tried to think of something meaningful. Finally he said, 'Cheerio then, mate.' He said it twice. Then he thought of the Vera Lynn song. He sang all the verses, none too loudly, but as tunefully as he could, holding the final note on a wispy breath, because that's what Jack had loved, a good tune.

He thinks about the cemetery now, thirty-one years on, of Jack in the dust by the paddy fields, and the song. *I'll think of you, no matter where you are.*

Pop notices the grass has been cut. I could have done that for her, he thinks, she only had to ask. The whole place looks neatly trimmed and ordered. The sun is washing the sky pastel now and the insects are swinging around in droves. Phase two, better late than never. He takes a breath, soft and gold the air. The first line wavers a bit and then he finds his way and his voice carries up to the windows.

> *I'll think of you, more than you'll ever know,*
> *Because I love you so*
> *I'll think of you.*

His voice improves as he sings. He holds himself well, feet slightly apart and his arms against his sides to prevent them waving about in an unnecessarily theatrical way.

Inside the house Iris's phone rings. She picks it up hesitantly. 'Hello?'

'Iris, there's a man in Royal Air Force uniform in your garden, singing.'

It was Eileen from across the road. They edge their telephones nearer the windows to look.

'I know,' Iris murmurs, craning to see. 'It's Arthur Landywood. Should I call the police?'

Pop finishes the song. He blows his nose and stoops to look at her dahlias. He lights a fag, reminds himself it would be bad manners to pick one of her own Bourbon roses to present to her. Wishes he'd picked someone else's earlier. Admonishes himself for this oversight. He looks up to see the moon is out as well as the sun and he stands marvelling at this.

'Arthur?' It's Carl at the gate, surprising Pop.

'Oh hallo, mate. These marigolds are doing well.'

'Very nice, yes.' Carl joins him, walking on his toes, hands in his pockets. 'Thrive on a bit of sunshine, they do,' Carl agrees.

They stand for a while, admiring the beds.

'Fancy a pint?'

They check their watches. 'Stone the crows, is that the time?'

They stroll to the Pint Pot, in step, heads down, watching their shoes.

The Doctor

Blowbroth followed Maggie as she climbed the stairs the following day to hunt down Pop's malaria tablets. He had complained of feeling queer on the way home from the Fox and Dogs and now he was lying face-down on the settee with his legs over the end, shoes pointing at the floor. He let off shuddering sighs into the foam cushions with the splitting sides as though it were all one big laugh a minute. He shouted out something but the words were smothered and Maggie was glad not to catch them.

Pop's room was a spectacular still-life of debris. Ashtrays piled high and overflowing, balls of socks, a collection of tall sticks found in Sutton Park strewn about like an abandoned crazy-golf course, a leaning tower of vests, skyscrapers of newspapers, collapsing blocks of brainteaser books, encyclopedias, quiz and crossword bumper editions. All divided north and south by a river of trousers and shirts whose arms and legs made a rushing tributary east and west between the mahogany wardrobe and the iron bed. Across the tangle of white sheet and green blanket, tilting at all angles over the folds, lay a rockery of books on random subjects. *The FA Yearbook*, *Epiphytic and Parasitic Plants*, *Sitar for Students*, *Indoor Cricket*, *The I Spy Guide to British Birds*, Bronowski's *The Ascent of Man*, *Competitive Alpine Skiing*, most of them overdue library books.

Eve's photograph watched from a dusty frame on the rosewood chest made by Pop's grandfather in the Black Country. Her sleepy sepia gaze held the room perfectly still. Around her like sacred stones in the dust landscape were a large hairbrush standing on its bristles, a bottle of hair tonic, two enormous tarnished keys weighing down some Villa programmes, a coiled metal cobra table lighter whose tongue was a flame when you squeezed the back of its head, and a ball of string.

Blowbroth lay across the doorway and watched her with a gimlet eye. He raised one eyebrow, sniffing and smirking as she searched. Maggie opened the drawer in the small bedside table: a cook's box of matches, a tin of salmon, buttons, coins, a nail clipper, an old photograph of herself, stick-thin in her school uniform, and a menu from the Aberdeen Angus Steakhouse in Wolverhampton.

Her foot sent something rattling like a child's toy across the carpet. She crouched low and lower still until her chin grazed the old rug, with its smell of moths and the stuff used to prevent them. She snatched a breath to sneeze and relaxed again as the itch subsided. Blowbroth thudded some impatient blows against the door with his tail and a spider illuminated in a fork of light shivered at the vibration. As her eyes grew accustomed to the murk beneath the bed, she spotted the little bottle of pills that her foot had disturbed.

She could reach it if she lay completely flat with one side of her face pressed against the floor and her arm stretched out in the correct position for dancing the Argentinian tango. The thin scraping of carpet grazed her ear as she pushed her shoulder further. As her fingers made contact with the bottle and she heard the clattering applause of the pills, she caught sight of a brass handle glowing soft as a martyr's candle in the gloom. She swept the pills towards her while she stared, and slowly the oak wood around the handle revealed itself. She felt a vague prick of fear and then the weightlessness of dread as she realised the length of the object which lay above and below her eye line and became aware of the folds of cloth that hung over it. She counted her breathing, in, one, out, two, in, one. The fibres in the carpet were scraping in her ear, amplified, like the ground splitting open. Her thoughts ran left and right in her head in the panic, she felt blood rushing to her brain and then draining away as quickly on discovering no one in charge and rippling down her legs. An image of Kenny Rogers flashed unhelpfully in her mind. *Ruby, are you contemplating going out somewhere?* She heard the roll and crash of a jukebox coin through an aluminium slot in her head. Maggie closed her eyes; she could hear Pop moving around downstairs. *The shadow on the wall tells me the sun is going down. Oh Ruby, don't take your love to town.* She looked again and it was still there, but clearer now, unmistakable. A coffin with brass handles covered in a moth-eaten blanket and a faded bath towel with what looked like Sootys and Sweeps all over it.

'Oh Christ, don't tell me,' her mother clattered past.

Hail Mary, full of grace, the Lord is with thee.

Blessed art thou amongst women.

Think, think, think.

Maggie stuffed her fingers in her ears, held her breath and rolled away until her head hit the door. She struggled to her feet, hurdled over Blowbroth's zig-zag eyebrows and flew down the stairs before even considering that she should move at all, falling down them in twos and threes, pedalling the air for contact.

'There'sacoffinunderyourbed!'

Her heart was beating in deep water, the waves making her wobble where she stood. Pop was sitting upright under a halo of smoke, he looked pale and overwrought like a saint, his hands shaking.

'Eh?' he shouted.

'There Is A Coffin,' Maggie said grandly like in the theatre, 'Under Your Bed Up There.'

He stared at her. His eyes were creamy and strange, whipped up like two eggs. Ash fell from his cigarette to the floor making a silent crash.

'Oh ar,' he said without moving his lips. She felt sweat tattooing the soles of her feet.

'Might be,' he said, one eye narrowing in the smoke.

'No, there is, there is one there now, I just saw it, it *is* there, it's under your bed, I saw it with my eyes, why's it there?'

He looked away and back at her again.

'Why not?'

She tucked the pills in her back pocket and wondered how long the malaria would take to kill him.

'What's it flaming doing here?' she shrieked, a tin can bouncing off the walls. Pop looked as though he might laugh. Then he did laugh. Several rockets up through the roof and then he fell forward, slapping his knees. A tall ache rose up in

Maggie's throat and divided behind her eyes. He spoke through gasps.

'There's no bleeding bugger in it, you daft kid. It's mine, I made it for meself. I like oak.'

Blowbroth entered hurriedly with the Aberdeen Angus Steakhouse menu in his mouth, sped officiously past them and into the kitchen. Maggie swayed between the caramel stripes of sun on the carpet, the fear broken up now into floating fragments.

'For you?' Maggie said flatly. It sounded like phew.

'I bloody hate pine,' he explained. 'Can't stand it. It's vile, isn't it?' An arrangement of sweat beads glistened across his head, another boulder of ash shattered across the floor.

'Anyhow, some pillock'd make a codge of it. No good a chippie going down in a tatty old box, looks terrible that does. Waster money anyhow.' He reclined, sinking gradually to a concerto of pings and twangs. The settee had almost completely swallowed him, just his sprinter's legs and nicotined smile left.

'What d'you want to make yourself an oak coffin for?' she asked.

'I like oak,' Pop insisted, spreading his quivering hands wide as if to indicate how much. 'Actually I love it, I love oak. Time is it, mate?'

She tapped out two pills and filled a glass with water from the tap. Blowbroth slept across the grilled rib-eye and sirloin section of the steakhouse menu in a puddle of drool. By the time Pop swung his legs into bed to the boom and thud of library books across the floor Maggie had raised the alarm. Dolly arrived in a purple turban heralded by the fire-drill doorbell, which electrocuted Pop even in his sweating delirium. She tripped up the stairs, sat on his feet, lit his cigarette and her own and shook her head sadly at the photograph of Eve.

'Nothing changes, eh duck?'

Pop blew a line of smoke over Dolly's turban and thundered, 'Spare us the blastid quack, Doll, he's no cop at all.'

'You'll do as you're told, else Dolly'll punch your ear'ole.' She kissed him tenderly on the forehead, bending dangerously low so that her knees and hips fired cracking shots. Pop rummaged for her hand too late as she straightened, the plump tapered fingers had already hurried to the hem of her dress, a size too small, to haul it over her thighs.

His eyelids closed and his body jerked as he gave in to sleep, a tow of liquid lead, wave after wave dragging him over the hushed frontier. Dolly creaked across the room, glancing around for secrets. 'They 'aven't half got a lot to answer for, flaming British Parlimint,' she commented cryptically, followed by a phlegmy sigh that wafted her out for a rib-splitting cough on the landing. She gripped the banister with both hands as she sidled down the stairs in lethal heels. 'I'd've washed my hair last night if I'd known there was going to be an emergency.'

Downstairs, while the kettle wailed on the gas ring, she plucked off the turban and tousled some bedraggled strands in the mirror. She watched herself with a long Sister Bernadette face, sucking her tongue like a lozenge. The turban was dragged back on and draped with a hiss, crackle and puff in white fog. When Blowbroth woke and saw Dolly swathed in a purple head-dress towering over him in a pillar of smoke, he had to wonder whether he had crossed over in his sleep. He lifted his head in an attitude he hoped suggested Labrador puppy. Attached to his lower lip was the Angus menu, glued snugly on with dried drool at a casualty-room angle.

'That dog needs a bath,' was all Dolly offered by way of a response and lowered her pink lips into the scalding tea. 'You're a daft hound, you are. Eh? What are you?' between slurps. Blowbroth dissolved in ecstasy and the menu dropped to the floor. She straightened her turban, poker-backed suddenly. She didn't mind a bit of fun, a game of mistress and hairy slave. She crossed her legs, slicing the air above Blowbroth's ear with a spike heel, while he goggled golf balls and dribbled a bouncing strand of drool from his curly jaw.

'Roll over then, you dozy pillock,' Dolly cooed. Blowbroth collapsed obediently. 'Catch,' she sang, flicking a sugar lump high into the air with her thumbnail and in a blur of gums he captured it with a little snap. 'Play dead,' she instructed sternly with a wicked smile and he expired with his eyes still open. 'And don't wake up till I say so,' stepping over his body with a sly wink at Maggie. 'Mangy mutt.'

The doorbell threw everyone in the air as usual. 'Oh Christ. Coming!' she shouted.

Filling the door as high as the frame stood the doctor, with a hurried smile. Blowbroth exploded from nowhere at Dolly's feet, exposing his fangs and the whites of his eyes. She lifted him away on her shoe, spooning him into the air. 'He's a hybrid, Doctor,' she explained. The doctor climbed the stairs two at a time. He was unusually tall and had to duck as he plunged across the threshold, startling Pop, who yelled, 'Touch of malaria, mate,' at the top of his voice, repeated several times during the medical examination in different styles of tone, including one on a laugh. 'Don't want to miss the game on Saturday, mate, we're playing Coventry, don't want to miss it, just a touch of malaria anyhow.'

At the end, after the doctor had taken a blood sample and was snapping things closed, Pop said, 'Chance for Villa this season, Doc?' in a fraying voice, his head heavy on the pillow.

'Couldn't comment, I'm afraid,' the elongated doctor chimed in some other accent. 'I'm a rugby man myself.'

'Oh ar.' Pop turned his head as he croaked. 'Fine prop forward that David Evans for Wigan, head like a brontosaurus.'

'Ah excellent, yes, isn't he? I'm a Gloucestershire man myself,' standing now with his feet together and nodding like an umpire.

'Oh ar, rugby union.' Pop's eyes, unfocused and unblinking, shone hard as marbles above a watery grin. 'Funny game, rugby,' he grunted, in someone else's voice. The doctor lunged out sideways with his head bowed and his black bag trailing after at the end of his javelin arm. In the hall he released a quick cheer of laughter and a flash of dry teeth before the door slapped shut. The letter-box trembled while Dolly squinted at the prescription.

He missed the Coventry game. Villa won one-nil. Graydon with his miraculous right foot again; they heard the match on the radio. Pop was adrift in his sickness, only one eye open and secrets whispering on his lips. For three days he thrashed and shouted and slept under the square of white sheet draped across his chest like a flag. He sang out names and curses in thick feverish voices, he shone glossy with sweat, drenched, as though he'd swum up through some deep pool in the floor. The day his nose bled Maggie discovered him knotted in the sheet stained bright with blood. A large damp blot of red had crept outwards at an equal rate forming an almost perfect circle, soaking the emblem of his old enemy across his back. She stood transfixed for a while, peaceful in the loop of inaction, swallowing his shame for him. His breathing chased whining rattles through his chest, ragged inhalations and exhalations, hoisting and lowering the Japanese rising sun at his shoulder while he slept a dead man's rest.

Dolly dropped in every day after work at the Yote to change sheets, collect washing and check on his progress. She clanked in with a chip pan one afternoon and made chips, bubbling in

207

fat, for Maggie's tea. Huge oily ones with brittle gold corners and shining sardines lifted dripping from their tin, soft and salty and crocheted with fine bones. Afterwards Dolly drew pink bows across her lips and helped herself to brandy. Soothed by its spicy heat, she reclined in a hammock of smoke and cooed at the prostrate Blowbroth.

'Ahh,' she said, 'you're a good kid, Mag,' creasing up her face in a grin so wide her eyes disappeared, like an oriental cat. 'Come to your aunty Dolly for a love,' bouncing on to her feet again to pull Maggie under her arm, squeezing her in a scrum hold. 'Eh?' she enquired softly, so Maggie could smell the pink sweetness of her lipstick and the hot rust of the brandy. She wrapped her arms around her waist and rested her cheek against the soft upholstery padding her hips and Dolly grabbed her tightly again.

'Ahhh, course you are, love. You're a blummin' great kid, Mag. Eh? That's what I say anyhow.' Maggie felt the steel ring of the embrace squeezing away her doubts and a heavy warmth creeping, like sleep.

'Bugger the rest of 'em,' she added oddly. And they swayed in their clasp, so that their feet had to shuffle like slow dancers to prevent them keeling over.

The Convalescent

On the fourth day Pop sat upright in bed, licked his dry lips and requested egg and bacon. An ashtray already nestled between hillocks of sheet and was filling with grey powder, charcoal smears swerving across the white cotton around his calves.

He grinned, showing the dull ivory of fragile teeth against the snowiness of the bed folds. His skin stretched sleepily to make the smile, pleating his cheeks and tilting the bristles of his new explorer's beard, a survivor's grin, surprised. Above his limp strings of hair cigarette clouds floated; only the harp was missing. He ate three meals from his bed, reclining like a Bedouin in the tent of smoke. He told Darjeeling stories. He'd recovered from the first malarial attack there, in the hills by a tea plantation, shortly after they buried Jack Spence. The shivering and weight loss made an immediate return to duty impossible, so he sat beside a hillside of tea, spilling cup after cup, waiting for it to stop.

That evening, after boiled ham, potato, and pickles the size of doorknobs, he craved beer. He swung his long feet into a pair of ravaged torpedo-shaped slippers and whistled loudly while he combed his hair down with hair tonic.

> *This is my story,*
> *This is my song,*
> *I've been in this air force*
> *Too blooming long,*
> *So roll out the Nelson,*
> *The Rodney, Renown,*
> *You can't say the Hood*
> *'Cause the bugger's gone down.*

He put on a clean shirt, almost white, and delivered a shortish lecture to Dolly about hypochondria and types of foot fungus, accompanied by some exaggerated hand gestures he was trying out. He was pleased with the gestures, he enjoyed watching them flowering in the air and descending like fireworks. Intrigued, he reviewed them in the mirror, until the sight of his fallen-in face and omelette eyes pulled him in close to the glass to study the bleak terrain of himself, just for a moment as though he might step through. Dolly went home to 'do' Carl. 'I can't sit here all night,' she hollered, cuffing him across the head.

'Ta-ra a bit, Doll.' The words spun through the middle of a wobbling smoke ring while her metal heels scraped down the path.

When she'd gone, Maggie was dispatched to Tower Road with a folded note. A leaning scrawl of words: 'I appear to be dying from a tropical illness contracted while defending the realm in '43. Ah well. Yours ever, Arthur Landywood. P.S. Not contagious.'

She pushed it through the letter-box and thought she caught a drift of movement beyond the nets. She hurried stiffly down the path and away, not daring to look back.

Pop sank two bottles of beer, announced he'd never felt better in his life, then got up too quickly, bringing on another wave of malaria that sent him collapsing on to the settee again, stirring the string quartet within. He burped and fell asleep. He snored, shattering the air in the room, bending the walls, loud as an industrial digger. In the distance Maggie heard the jingle of an ice-cream van tinkling dementedly. A hurtling version of *You Are My Sunshine*, its electronic notes punching sharp holes through the hot air until all sense drained out. She thought of the way Pop shouted 'Chocks away, mate!' before he stamped on the accelerator and they shot like Apollo 13 down Worcester Lane, their heads trailing over the backs of the seats with the G force.

She closed her eyes and tried to recall how many weeks she'd been there. Then she remembered her father saying, 'My life is a joke,' as though everyone had forgotten to laugh.

The following morning, just before noon, Pop and Maggie ate the cold remains of the chicken curry Dolly had made.

Apparently fully recovered, Pop slung giant dollops of chutney on to his plate and glanced around the kitchen in mild reflective amazement while he ate. Blowbroth watched them from under a wiry eyebrow, one amber bauble glinting. The mouthfuls were deliciously chilled and sticky in the heat, sharpened with spices in swollen creamy rice. Maggie kicked her feet under the blue Formica table. Pop had taken a bath that morning to celebrate his victory over malaria. For almost an hour the crashes of water and bellows of song had carried out of the window and under the door, filtering like a public address down Clarendon Road.

> Gentlemen will please refrain
> From using the toilet when the train
> Is standing in the station
> I love you.

The room was drenched and slippery with steam and male sweat, as if a whole platoon had bathed, a strong orange tang of carbolic soap spicing the corners. Maggie had crept curiously across the chessboard of black and white lino squares, amazed at the shipwreck of towels, suds and droplets, the room still stiff with surprise. Afterwards he'd smoked a luxuriously damp cigarette, collapsed across a chair in an ancient rope-belted dressing gown like a grizzled Noël Coward.

When he'd scraped up the last of his curry, Pop dashed his fork against the plate and dropped it into the sink. The tap sang the high note, 'i', from the final beseeching 'Maria' from West Side Story. He strangled it before it added the 'a'. Maggie watched his Adam's apple bouncing up and down as he glugged a whole cup of the musical water. Blowbroth walloped his tail against the floor a few times like he was counting everyone in

211

for an a cappella song while Pop gasped and blew a blast into his handkerchief.

'Right, mate,' he announced as Maggie pulled a fragrant boulder of chutney from the jar. 'Fox and Dogs?' He threw his arm up to check his watch. 'Christ! Come on, mate, *juldee karo*. It's only a couple of hours till closing time.'

The Fox and Dogs

He carried a brimming pint of ginger beer with both hands, like the third king with the myrrh.

'Cheers, mate,' he said to Maggie and they crashed glasses. 'Celebrate my recovery,' he mumbled and tipped his ale back.

'Alright, mate? Hamilton looked fit,' Pop called to a big man called Lop whom he didn't know very well. Lop wasn't his real name. He'd suffered with a malformed leg when he was a boy, the story went, and had developed a strange lolloping gait to get around. They'd fixed his leg at the hospital when he was in his twenties, but he'd retained the pitch and roll of his previous style. He would always be Lop now. He never said much, sometimes he opened his mouth as if he were about to, but no words actually made it out.

'Phillips don't look bad either,' Pop called to Lop again, who nodded once slowly in response.

The pub filled up as lunchtime arrived. Pop's eyes widened and brightened; he flinched left and right like a grass–court commentator. He wore a sloping welcome grin as though he had been appointed host, nodding and raising his cigarette. A group of men at the bar laughed at something inaudible and Pop chuckled too, beaming at their broad backs. Another heavy smoker Pop knew called George came in trailing white wreaths.

'Hallo, Arthur, congratulations on your victory. You've been a bit scarce.'

'Touch of malaria, mate,' Pop responded cheerfully. 'I was just saying, Hamilton looks a bit useful, doesn't he?'

'Oh ar, so he does,' George replied. 'Gave Coventry a lot of trouble so he did, mate. Set it up nicely for the Grader.'

'So I heard,' Pop said.

Old Leonard Brierley appeared, squinting behind his box-shaped specs through the fog. He'd had quite a good job once at the town hall.

'See the game on Saturday?' Pop called out to him. Leonard closed his left eye as he tried to locate the speaker.

'Over here, Len! Were you at the Coventry game at all?' Pop shouting now as though he was deaf as well. Leonard nodding as he finds Pop.

'No, Arthur, saving meself. Too much on anyhow this time of year.'

'I missed it,' Pop yelled. 'Damn good game. Had to listen on the wireless, touch of malaria.' His eyes rolled around the room to check the reaction to this, snapping double takes at glances in his direction.

'Take tablets for that, do you?'

'Oh ar, bloody tablets. The quack hands out the same little white ones for everything, mate. It's all in the mind.'

'I thought it was quinine you took for malaria.'

'Oh I'll have a large gin then, ta mate,' cackling like a parrot at himself.

'Killed Oliver Cromwell you know.'

Pop looked appalled. How a fact relating so closely to his own personal experience had escaped him of all people, this year's flaming champion, he couldn't imagine. 'You're pulling my leg.'

'I ain't kidding you, Arthur. The ague they called it.'

'No mate, that's in the Netherlands.'

They all laughed together. Ha ha ha. One–all.

'Len,' Pop yelped, brimming again, defender of the jokes, 'you're not as green as you're cabbage-looking, mate.'

'You're s'posed to know it all, Arthur, you being champion when all's said and done.'

'No one likes a know-it-all, Len.'

'True. Fella I worked with came back from abroad with the smallpox.'

'That's right, I remember him, civic-committee bloke.' Pop pointed his cigarette at Leonard as though it were a tiny smouldering sword. 'What the hell was his name, Len? You'll have to remind me.'

Leonard plunged his hands into his pockets and looked away, blinking, waiting patiently for the answer to come. Pop fidgeted and slapped his beer-mat about. 'Oh I don't bloody believe it, on the tip of my tongue, ye great Gods and tiny little fishes.' He squirmed and groaned and dropped his head in his hands.

'Robert,' Leonard said, bending his knees on the word.

'Eh?' Pop was incredulous. 'Are you sure, Len?'

'Robert Barr, the chess bloke, drank Riddlingtons, halves, very interested in the Tour de France, nice fella.'

'That's him, Robert Barr. Thank Christ for that.'

Leonard leant forward as if he were bowing a courtly compliment and sent a shy smile towards Maggie. 'Nice lad,' he commented. 'Pint, Arthur?'

Pop twisted around, rearing back until his chin disappeared into his neck like a pelican, to check whether Maggie had metamorphosed quietly into a member of his own sex while he'd been talking. She felt her blood tingling over her face. She fixed her attention on the Ansell's beer-mat, making quick anagrams of the word in her mind, starting with LASS LEN.

'Bloody hard to tell these days, sorry mate,' Leonard mumbled in his own defence with his hands up as though it were an arrestable offence.

'You want to get those glasses changed, Len,' Pop said. 'Not up to much at all, those. You can't see a damn thing, you'll have a bloody accident. Pint if you're up, mate, ta.'

They walk up Maney Hill, under the shivering copper beech, past the Odeon cinema that had screened *Zorba*, now showing *The Land That Time Forgot* and *Doctor in the Nude*.

At the newsagent's Pop buys his Player's Navy Cut and matches, lets off a remark about unemployment and John, leaning on the till, Bic biro behind his ear, agrees and together they warble and screw up their faces at the disgrace of it all. The worst jobless total for thirty years, bloody shambles, one and a quarter million, just over, dear God, how many? No wages at the Norton Villiers Triumph factory in Wolverhampton, two million in debt they are, and another thing . . . blah blah, right bloody cods of it, so they have, mate. During the head-shaking and sighing Maggie holds out her shirtful of blackjacks, fizzers, spaceships and liquorice pipes for John to add up.

Afterwards Blowbroth charges at a mad-eyed raven picking its feet high on Dugdale Green; its clothes are ragged and gleaming, its coffin beak heavy and blunted. The bird has time to stare with a polished purple eye before it flaps away, turning a slow black circle around the top of the solitary sycamore. They traipse home. Villa have lost away to Newcastle, Arsenal are next at Villa Park and then the UEFA Cup in Belgium.

215

The great Ron Saunders would become manager of the year in 1975.

'We all know about Villa's vast potential, it's been talked about for years, but now we are doing something about it,' he warned with his collar up under a blustery sky. 'This club is going places, believe you me,' his face turning ominous with conviction. He was not wrong, Ron didn't make idle promises. If Ron said it would happen then it would, and it did. Aston Villa were on their way. The League Cup, the Football League Championship and the European Cup awaited them.

Anglia Television

Pop has a letter in his pocket. It's been there almost two days. On the envelope it says Anglia Television with a big A and then it says Mr A. Landywood and the rest. He is mystified. He rarely gets post and when he does it comes in brown envelopes. He takes it out and looks at it again. He has handled it so much the envelope is developing creases; he is trying to guess but cannot. Now he has delayed this long the thought of actually opening it and unveiling the mystery makes him feel ill.

'Anglia Television. Norwich,' he murmurs again, studying the postmark.

'It might be important,' Maggie mentions.

'Important,' he repeats in a tiny voice while he examines the seal.

'I'll open it,' Maggie tries.

'Addressed to me,' he retorts, tucking it back into his pocket.

'Bugger it then. I'll get the sheets off Dolly,' she counters and gets up to leave. Before she has reached the door he has torn

216

it open and she turns in time to see the long white sheet of paper spring out of the envelope in neat concertina folds. He looks down at the page and then up at Maggie, his face raised in an attitude of vaudevillean surprise, his teeth drying in his gaping mouth.

'I shall be appearing on the television,' he says eventually. There is a moment of complete incomprehension between them and then the room shatters with his wailing cries of laughter.

Carl burned a deep flaring crimson the moment Pop produced it like a warrant from his pocket. 'Flaming Nora,' Dolly gasped and punched Carl hard on the arm. Pop read it through once again with gobstopper eyes and then it was off round the Fox and Dogs, flapping in and out of all the other hands.

'It was me,' Carl confessed, his face darkening mauve, glittering tears wobbling in his eyes while he quaked with a combination of fear and excitement, holding his own hand through the panic, patting it, comforting himself. 'I wrote in about your general knowledge,' he admitted. 'Told 'em you were our new local champ, explained it was official, the contest and so on.'

The letter was passed around at the Fox and Dogs and afterwards at the Plough and Harrow like a kind of parlour game. As it circulated, Maggie caught a glimpse.

Dear Mr Arthur Landywood,

Congratulations! We are delighted to inform you that you have been selected to appear as a contestant on our new series of *Sale of the Century*, broadcast live from Norwich. If you would like to accept this invitation to take part, please be good enough to telephone our production assistant, Sandra Henson, who will arrange your

217

travel and accommodation and assist with any queries you may have.

With best wishes from your host, Nicholas Parsons, and all of us here at *Sale of the Century*!

Pop leant back on his elbows as the fringe benefits of the situation began to dawn on him. He imagined Iris dabbing away tears of laughter as he and Mr Parsons sparred with witty asides, pictured her wide-eyed amazement as he chose a piece of priceless ladies' jewellery.

The whole pub was full of it; he was pointed out to people who didn't know him well. Dolly talked him up like an agent; she pinched his cheeks and ruffled his hair; she propped herself against the bar, one hip thrown out, while she described his great gift for general knowledge, his various idiosyncrasies, his long, narrow feet that made buying shoes difficult. She winked at him and creased up her cat's eyes to laugh, clap and heckle over people's questions, applauding the thought of the excitement to come.

The regime to sharpen up his brain began again in earnest. Everyone was instructed to surprise him once more with obscure questions. This time not only were the questions to be demanding, but he requested that they be posed at unexpected moments, like Cato from the *Pink Panther* films, to encourage lightning responses. This had to be reviewed a day or two later, after he'd been frightened so badly he hyperventilated.

En route to the Pint Pot he danced backwards on his toes in the style of Muhammad Ali so that Maggie had to trot to keep up, calling out the questions she'd been working on all evening.

Carl was at the bar as Pop flew in the door without breaking his stride.

'Christ, I'm on form tonight, mate.'

'Evening Arthur.' Carl counted his change without looking up. 'Duke of Clarendon's in,' he said to the yeti to signal Pop's pint, then he winked at Maggie. '*Who takes care of the caretaker's daughter when the caretaker's busy taking care?*' he sang and then, 'What d'you want, Maggie love, fizzy pop?'

Blowbroth licked his teeth in an effort to remember when he'd last eaten. Pop swung himself into a chair and lit up. 'Right, Doll, any subject you like, go on then, hit me. Go on.'

She clobbered him before anyone could blink. Her shriek of laughter had the yeti covering her ears. It should have shattered every glass in the place. He got a good sherrakin', lacquered fingernail jabbing about under his nose, bracelets rattling.

'Don't you go taking the fork, daft bugger, you asked for it, so there!' She slapped his leg and another firework of laughter split the air.

'Oh, hallo, Jim, didn't see you.' Pop craned forward to speak to bony-faced Jim, tucked away in the corner with his stout. 'You're early tonight, mate.'

'Been finishing that bathroom tiling job on the Hartopp Road,' Jim explained.

'Ooh, big houses them,' Dolly cooed.

'Decent size, ar,' agreed Pop.

'Buckingham Palace,' Jim corrected. 'Lose yourself, just like that.'

'Oh I bet,' said Dolly.

'They've got a bloody jewelled toilet-roll holder, I'm not kidding you.'

'Get away.'

'Fact, mate, I saw it.'

'Remember the jamboree in '57?' Carl checked each of them to be sure they did. 'When the Queen and Prince Philip visited and Harold Macmillan, and they were all received by the mayor and the councillors at the town hall? Well, I knew the bloke who cleaned the toilets there and he said they had a special leopard-skin toilet seat for the Queen to sit on.'

'My guess is it's her own, carries it round with her,' added Dolly.

'Cheers anyway, Arthur. Good luck for Norwich, mate.' Carl raised his glass of stout and winked a round squid eye at Maggie again.

'Cheers, mate.'

'Your very good health.'

'Way I look at it, best man always wins so nought worth worrying about, isn't that right?' He nudged Maggie in the ribs. 'If I lose it's your fault, matey.'

'Don't tell the kid that, Art. Take no notice. Silly old fool. Cheers anyhow.'

Maggie raised her glass to them and sipped the ginger bubbles. There are worse things, she thought, than staying here in Four Oaks with these, always something worser than the worst. Dolly waved her ruby drink in the air and tipped it between matching-coloured lips.

'That's nice. You get a slice o' lemon here. Look.' She swung it around in her glass.

'You get a slice o' lemon at the Fox and Dogs and all,' Carl said. 'And Muffin's Den. You get a bloody slice o' lemon in all the pubs round here.'

'Course you don't. Blimey, I wouldn't have said if you did, now would I?'

'Tell her, Arthur, for the love of Bob.'

Pop pulled his gaze down from the ceiling, blew out a

jet-stream of smoke. 'I've just multiplied forty-seven by three hundred and fifty-nine.'

'Christ, what for?' Dolly, shrill with incomprehension.

'Go on then, what's the answer?' Pop demanded, draining his pint.

'How the bloody hell should I know? I just found out what a flaming T-junction was the other day.'

'Not you, Doll, daft wench.'

Carl changed his specs for another pair. 'It's where a road meets another road and they make a T shape like this,' he said.

'I bloody know that now, don't I? Another double, Art, if you're going to the bar, ta.'

Pop stood and held his finger up like a referee about to give a yellow card. 'Right, I'll tell you how I did it.'

'They'll never ask that, Arthur.'

Pop leant down close to Carl, lowered his voice.

'They might, mate. We don't know, do we? They very well might and I for one am going to be ready for it.'

Pop's eyes were no longer popping, they were narrowed and determined like Lee Van Cleef's. He was ready for his fifteen minutes. He had heard it confirmed that there was sometimes exclusive ladies' jewellery among the sale items on the show. Maggie saw Iris's eyes rolling and her scarlet door slamming.

He wrote her a letter. He bought expensive paper with ghost words floating in its weave, Conqueror, in the hope she might be convinced subliminally, and sat with a fountain pen swirling ink from left to right until he was satisfied. Maggie delivered it. She pushed it through and then to her complete amazement the door opened. They stood looking at one another.

'Hello,' said Iris.

Maggie ran. She pelted along with her head down and didn't look up until she reached Clarendon Road. She sat on their step panting, with a stitch, not the faintest idea why she was so afraid.

Pop caught sight of himself in the window of the Washeteria launderette and his afternoon was almost completely spoiled. He'd imagined something altogether sleeker; the hall mirror didn't do the job at all apparently. He peered at the strings of hair poking in all directions like a thicket of telephone wires. He took himself off to Truman's the barber with its twirly pole and rug of hair across the chilled tile floor. He emerged clipped and smooth, blinking and flinching in the sunshine, cropped and shiny as an otter.

Maggie stared while a cheekful of sherbet frothed between her teeth. The haircut had snipped away some of his hooligan panache, trimmed his power. It had given him a soft white neck, pretty as one for the guillotine. His hands stroked it in disbelief. His jaw too looked different; a velvety fold hanging off the bone. His ears sprung out, spider-veined and curling, ready to catch the merest question. He looked nude and girly and ponged of spicy cologne. It gave her the creeps. She told him she liked it.

Not previously one to bother about his appearance from one week to the next, he now peered into every reflective surface he encountered and buffed his spoon especially, so he could loom in, bug-eyed and deformed.

Beguiled by his new self, he experimented further. He found himself returning to browse in Brian Hill Fine Menswear, where he picked out a jacket the colour of lichen and a tie blooming with mustard-coloured cuboids. He was persuaded into slacks too, in a cinnamon brown, which he decided wasn't a bad idea in the event of him winning and having to emerge from behind his desk to view the big prizes and their accompanying hostesses with Mr Parsons. It was this new Pop who steeled himself for the big time, neatly clipped and sprucely turned out in decaying shades of autumn.

It was decided they would take the train to Norwich, for the novelty and the opportunity to travel in style and Anglia Television were paying for the tickets. They were all going. Pop had persuaded production assistant Sandra Henson to provide two rooms at the hotel, so Maggie would go in with Dolly and he and Carl would share. He had his entourage and was ready to float like a butterfly and sting like a bee. Blowbroth would stay behind, the disappointment badly affecting his bowels. But the supreme punishment was saved for the car. The Anglia would be left out of the entire proceedings, Pop's sweetest revenge. Its headlamps made disbelieving 'O's up Clarendon Road.

They were going to stay at the Holiday Inn. Pop got out his small blue suitcase that refused to lock and, when finally persuaded, refused to open again. His new clothes were laid in carefully with his comb and hair tonic, brainteasers, crosswords, two cans of pale ale and a photo of Eve. Carl had to buy a suitcase from a shop in the Parade because Dolly had already filled their small brown one with spiked heels. Maggie packed her best cheesecloth shirt and the lucky floppy hat with the cherries hanging off.

They were driven by minicab to the station via the Plough and Harrow to drop Blowbroth off with Ken. One for the road, they decided while they were there. 'Cheers, Arthur. Good luck, mate!' Tatty and Bren raised their pints. Ken's eyes whirled in his putty face. 'I don't believe a bloody word of it.'

'Ta-ra a bit each,' Pop called over his shoulder. The dog lay under a table, tail twitching like a scorpion. They encountered a retching stink he'd left in the minicab when they climbed back in, and had to travel to the station in a flapping hurricane with all the windows down.

At Birmingham New Street station Maggie walked between them through the railway wind again. Her strides were longer now. The screech of metal on the tracks wasn't her mother's cry for help.

On the train Pop limbered up with sudden-death questions, puns and long division until he made himself nauseous from the concentration and had to lie down across two seats. Dolly went to the buffet and came back with an armful of drinks and snacks. They sang, *Why Was He Born So Beautiful?* and *Good King Wenceslas*.

They were met at the station in Norwich by a girl called Kerry who said, 'Hello Arthur, hello Maggie, hello Carl, hello Dolly.'

'*It's so nice to have you back where you belong,*' trilled Carl like the song, bouncing on his toes, filling up so scarlet that Kerry blushed too. Pop asked where the other contestants were, glancing snake-eyed around the station as though they might be hiding behind a newspaper at the shoe-shine.

At the hotel Dolly was sick in the beige and tan bathroom.

'It's me they're broadcasting nationwide, woman, not you,' Pop snapped.

'I'm not used to a matching suite,' she explained.

Maggie churned too. She lay flat on her back on the other twin bed next to Dolly. Through the wall they could hear Pop reciting Wordsworth, Shakespeare, the Highway Code and Wimbledon tennis champions.

Carole

Misadventure they had called it. Maggie knew better. She knew something they didn't. She kept it to herself. Miss Adventure. Her mother's death, technically at least, was due to a lack of balance at a critical moment; this had been her misfortune, her misadventure. Carole had trained briefly as a dancer and was proud of her calves and her ability to glide as if she were on castors. She could pirouette quite easily on one leg, even after a few drinks; it was her party piece.

Slipping and falling. She would have hated it, the ignominy.

Maggie knew something was wrong but she stood in the holding yard of the grey shadow for a while, studying its menace, preparing herself. The garage door was slightly open. It cast a sharp shape, like a dark fin across the concrete. Inside the air was all swallowed up, indistinct shapes merged into one another, dust rained down; Maggie felt it sticking to her. She saw her old bike and some gardening stuff, bags of sand, their previous television set, the tall hair-drier with the pink hood.

Her mother was on the floor, on her side with one knee up and crooked arms, and the little gaming table with the deformed legs and faded green baize was collapsed beside her. A smell of metal and newsprint, stacked pages, the same ones these facts would appear in, a couple of lines about a Sittingbourne woman and the girl, 13.

A flex was knotted loosely around her mother's neck. The plug lay on her collarbone in place of Our Lord on his cross, making Maggie think of the electric lamps you could buy that lit up a plastic version of the preaching Saviour and glowed all night so you never forgot he died for us.

She heard the sound of her own urine on the concrete, and she saw the snipped cable at the base of the hooded hair-drier.

Some of her mother's teeth were broken, fragments like porcelain pieces in the dust. 'I had a dream all my teeth fell out,' she had said. 'Forecasts a season of financial reverses,' her *Dreamer's Dictionary* had informed them, 'check your investments.' A scrunch of tissue peeped out of her mother's sleeve, Maggie knelt and took it to wipe away the tear on her mother's lip. Her jaw didn't look right; it was set at an unnatural angle that made her appear inappropriately sceptical. Maggie straightened the hair fallen around it. 'Gotta grab what life throws at you,' her mother had told her calmly just days before snatching her death in an outbuilding on a summer evening, exactly as she had once described. Maggie untied the knot around her mother's neck and removed the flex and plug. It swung grotesquely on the end, like a body part.

A dark disc of blood was creeping around her head, almost black in the gloom, a drab halo. Holy, Holy, Holy, Lord God of Sabaoth. She took her mother's hand, wrapped it inside her own. She was still holding her hand when the first finger of blood touched the opposite wall.

Maggie hid the flex deep in the pile of grass cuttings, planted it down where the debris and leaves were rotting, *she slipped and fell*, and took herself to the hall table, her mother's perfume still warm on her hands, her mouth turning slack with shock, to dial the three nines on the ashen-grey telephone. My mother slipped and fell.

The Sale of the Century

The studio is hot and stuffy and filled with humming lights, whistling floor crew and bunches of cables taped out of the camera's sight. The audience mumble and shift in creaking plastic chairs on a raked platform and are advised to sit still when the show commences and desist from coughing, heckling or scratching themselves. Pop has excused himself during rehearsal for a cigarette and is now back at the desk labelled ARTHUR in emergency capitals. He is panicking that he cannot hear anything in his earpiece. He calls out to Mr Parsons who is talking to a woman in a pinafore dress with a clipboard. 'Can't hear a thing, can't hear anything at all,' shaking his head, looking around, his tie swerving across his shirt. A technician comes to his rescue and Pop yatters away at him with relief.

A gleaming caravan is parked a few yards to the left under dazzling lights.

A lazy tumble of swinging brass and sunny trumpet plays out while the floor crew semaphore and the cameramen hunch down.

Pop glances about him, picks his nails, sucks his teeth. Maggie feels her breathing plunging in and roaring out. She clings to the horns and piccolos falling through the theme tune, folds herself under their shiny bright optimism. He flinches to the side the way he does when he's going to speak and Maggie panics that he might blast off some 'Gunga Din'. Instead a disembodied voice, richly resonant and disturbingly reasonable, calls out from somewhere else.

'YES, it's the Sale of the Century. Why not go touring with

227

this very modern caravan which can sleep up to five people and at the same time provide all the comforts of home? Usual price, nine hundred and seventy pounds, on sale for eighty-five pounds. This fine, eighteenth-century long-case clock, with brass arch-dial of unusual design. It has an eight-day movement, it was built around seventeen sixty and is guaranteed for five years. The cost would be five hundred and twenty-five pounds in the store, on sale though for just sixty pounds. Or if that doesn't tempt your fancy, how about a fine pair of eighteenth-century Irish silver-gilt goblets? They are nine inches tall and exquisitely engraved. Priced at four hundred pounds, on sale tonight for forty-seven pounds. These are just three of the top sale items on offer to the winner of this week's . . . *Sale of the Century*. And now . . . meet the man who pays the money out to our three lucky contestants . . . Nicholas Parsons!'

Everyone claps, led by a bloke in headphones doing big seal claps over his head. Mr Parsons coasts on, head slightly tilted, softening the room with his ecclesiastical smile. Pop seems not to notice and starts to talk to the contestant on his left, poking through the music with his Midlands mumble.

Maggie feels herself leaving her body; she tries to drift far away, to another studio where they are filming something else, like *This Is Your Life*. Nicholas Parsons has reached the appointed spot and pauses briefly while the applause clatters towards him. He acknowledges it politely and elegantly with a very slight bob of the head and lowered eyes like an equerry of the royal household.

'Thank you very much indeed, hello and er . . . welcome to *Sale of the Century*. Well now . . . our three contestants this week are all senior citizens, so let us first of all welcome the most senior of the three.'

The voice rising and falling, pitching from the pulpit.

'She's had many jobs in her long life, she now describes herself simply as a housewife. She has a grown-up daughter and two teenage granddaughters. She comes from Ditchling in Sussex and her name is Mary Mackintosh.'

Applause. Maggie's palms skidding with sweat. An ample lady with neat, pale hair, a long, crisp nose and a shelf of bosom. Nicholas Parsons's twinkling blue gaze swoops across and down into the audience – busily clapping, enthusiastic now about their task, making sure of their claps – and silences them instantly. His smile, a broad white altar, shining with show business, eases any disappointment.

'Mary tells me she's seventy-seven years of age,' he says, incredulous, a quizzical tilt, leaning into his compassion. 'I hardly believe it,' he adds, returning her the blue gleam of his attention, forgiving her, and the audience, released from the spell, clap again. Seventy-seven. A miracle.

'Our next contestant is retired.' Pop looks up suddenly as if it were a clue. Maggie digs her fingernails in.

'He was formerly a building inspector . . .' A building inspector.

A building inspector? When was he a building inspector? What's a building inspector? Before he enlisted maybe? He's a chippie. What about being a flaming chippie? Maggie's thoughts torpedo left and right. My grandfather the building inspector.

'He is a widower with one teenage granddaughter . . .'

Weightless at the thought of herself, the shock of it broadcast.

'He comes from Sutton Coldfield near Birmingham and his name is Arthur Landywood.' The clapping makes her want to cry. Her hands swim towards each other to make the applause that is due to him now as he is introduced to licence-fee payers and Nicholas-Parsons-fans the length and breadth of the country.

What on earth would they see now as his face fills up the screen? A building inspector no less. He cringes, but the turkey-cock in him soon throws his chin up again to reveal the smile, crooked with amazement, pulling his eyes into diamonds. He swipes at his nose and mouths something to himself. Maggie thinks of the lip-readers.

'Our third contestant tonight is also retired. He was formerly a police officer in the colonial service and he has two grown-up children and two grandchildren. He is from Cheltenham in Gloucestershire and his name is Geoffrey Morgan.' A broad-set man with misaligned brows and spongy curls in pewtery silver. Mr Parsons has reached for his questions even as the applause rises. Pop has seen it too. He straightens the cuboid tie, sniffs, cracks a knuckle, as though the first punch landed on Mr Parsons's nose wins the point.

'As usual we'll begin with some simple questions, valued at a pound, to get you in the mood. So which of you, for one pound can tell me . . . The Bible: What was done to celebrate the return of a prodigal son?'

A fraction of hush, just the celestial lights and then the explosion of a buzzer and Pop craning forward, his pencil lodged behind his ear.

'Arthur!'

'A fatted calf was killed,' he mumbles.

'A fatted calf was killed,' Mr Parsons repeats, stepping in the muddy shapes of Pop's Warwickshire words. Mr Parsons raises his voice an octave, launches his question over the invisible lectern.

'For what is the Scottish engineer John Loudon McAdam best . . . Mary?'

The buzzer rips into the question, the men are left blinking in the dust.

'Roads,' she says, clouting the R.

'Yes, McAdam, roads, well done, Mary.

'What common expression sometimes describes the first day of April?'

Pop on the buzzer, his wide eyes crouched behind. 'All fools day,' he croaks suspiciously.

'April fools day is correct. Can you speak a little louder, Arthur? I can hardly hear you.'

'Jacques-Yves Cousteau – what is he known for? Yes, Geoffrey.'

Pop shifts, embarrassed. His hand goes to his mouth, pulls at his 'tache as though this is the obstruction.

'Underwater diving.'

'And exploration. Well done, Geoffrey, a pound. Where would you find peace in the garden?'

'In the rose bed.' Geoffrey has found his feet.

'Yes, yes, and for a pound which of you can tell me what colour is the rose . . .'

Geoffrey has blasted off on them.

'White, off-white,' he chimes.

'Off-white yes, a lovely white but a very pale one, well done, Geoffrey, a pound. For another pound, on June twenty-fourth, first- and second-class postage rates went up to?' The buzzer.

'Arthur?'

'Four and a half,' Pop says loudly in his best Midlands.

'Rates,' replies Parsons quietly.

'Fourpence ha'penny,' insists Pop.

'There's two of them, what's the second-class?' Through a clenched smile.

'Oh,' he says, brightening, 'thrupence ha'penny.'

'I can't hear you, Arthur.'

'Three and a half,' he shouts in his best bar-room call.

231

'Is correct!' returns Parsons's tombola cry. 'They've all got some more money,' he exclaims hurriedly. 'Let's now offer them an instant sale. They can spend or they can save, what will they do? As we·hear what the first instant sale is here tonight . . .' And he spins around to face the prizes on their podiums under the laboratory lights. The disembodied reasonable voice erupts from somewhere, mysteriously aristocratic all of a sudden. 'And this would be a splendid addition to any home,' it sneers, while a Wurlitzer hurries out a background tune. 'Six pounds will buy this lovely eight-day lever-striking carriage clock in a gilt case. Now this would cost ninety-three pounds in the shops,' it warns laconically, sending Geoffrey's fingers scrambling to his buzzer and winning an approving round of applause. Mr Parsons returns his attention to the audience, soothing them with his sympathetic blue stare, which he directs east, west, north and south to make sure nobody feels excluded. 'So professional,' Maggie's mother murmurs.

'Geoffrey Morgan had no hesitation there,' Mr Parsons explains. 'He was the first one to press his buzzer so he can buy that. Geoffrey, the money's taken away from the money in front of you and you have a beautiful carriage clock. You are now on seven pounds, Mary on eleven, Arthur on thirteen.'

Thirteen. There it is again. Unlucky for some. Maggie has trouble with arithmetic but she knows a thirteen when she hears one. Everything in the universe is mathematical. She tries to catch his eye, she watches his face for clues. He is fiddling with his tie, his pencil, his eyes are not blinking now, they follow Mr Parsons as he glides. She glances at Dolly and Carl next to her. They are set in matching attitudes of surprise, mouths open, muscles rigid, captivated, a couple of quiz-show corpses. Surely now he would lose. Or win. Or pay some terrible price anyway for all the fags and beer and bloody codswallop he'd spouted all these years. Thirteen was not to be trifled with.

'And the questions now go up to three pounds.' Mr Parsons prepares his mouth for foreign pronounciation.

'For what is Albert Schweitzer best remembered?'

Geoffrey's colonial days have it at the buzzer.

'Well done, yes that's right, working with the lepers out there wasn't he, yes, well done, Geoffrey. Originally a Highland chief's attendant, what do we call the man who attends sportsmen when they go angling or shooting? . . . Arthur . . . ! . . . Now listen! The time is up! You can take it or not, Arthur. Do you wish to take it?'

Pop looks Mr Parsons straight in the eye and says, 'A gillie.'

'A gillie,' repeats Mr Parsons, 'is three pounds to you.'

'Who was the Prime Minister at the time of the outbreak of the Second World War?'

All three buzzers go simultaneously.

'Chamberlain.' Geoffrey somehow.

'In which sport would you use a spoon?'

'Golf,' replies Mary crisply.

'What is held in the hands of the figure of justice outside the Old—'

The buzzer grabs it.

'The scales, balances,' Pop interrupts with a wary eye. Mr Parsons does not answer.

'. . . And a sword in the other one,' he admits finally.

'Ohhh, thank goodness you added the sword,' gasps the host, producing soft chuckles from the audience.

'The scales in one hand, the sword in the other. They've all got some more money, let's now offer them our second instant sale. John Vincent, what do we have to offer them this time?' Mr Parsons gazes reverentially up into space where the bright lights hang and the disembodied aristocrat's sales pitch falls down unto him.

'Well, seven pounds is all we want, Nicholas, for this magnificent high-capacity freezer, designed for the luxury kitchen. Comes complete with all the aids to good, modern freezing and would cost you one hundred and thirty-nine pounds.' The last spangling Wurlitzer note hangs quavering before it is washed away by the applause.

'The time is up and nobody pressed their buzzer, the questions are still worth three. What is an archipelago?

'Arthur.

'Yes, a gathering of islands in an ocean is right.

'What do we call a person who is in love with himself?

'Arthur.

'A narcissist is correct.

'What is the largest animal in the world?

'Geoffrey.

'Is correct. You find them in the Antarctic. I mention that because I would like one of you to spell Antarctic.

'Geoffrey.

'Yes. It's the C before the T that confuses some people.

'What is the title of the song that Peter Penn is now going to play?'

The man on the organ pokes a jumpy tune out of the Wurlitzer.

'Arthur.

'*Roaming in the Gloaming* gets you three pounds.

'What is the date of St Swithins day?

'Mary.

'Well done, Mary, three pounds. And what is the well-known saying connected with St Swithin's day?

'Mary?

234

'Correct. If it rains on St Swithins day, it will rain for forty days afterwards. That is the saying or the legend, call it what you will, three pounds. I've never seen people's fingers go so quickly, but of course the first one eliminates the other two. A dog licence, how much do you pay for this?

'Geoffrey?'

Pop is leaning low on his desk; he looks shifty. Hard to believe Blowbroth would qualify as a dog anyway.

'Five shillings, fifteen shillings.'

'You pay it in pence actually, Geoffrey, thirty-seven and a half pence, which if you translate it backwards means seven shillings and sixpence in old money, so I'm afraid you lose three pounds. Let's now have our open sale. Here our contestants can relax . . . they look very relaxed, don't they? So while they relax even more let us hear from John Vincent what we have on offer this week in the open sale.' The organ man takes his cue and begins another whirling dirge, chopped into little bouncing squirls.

'Yes well indeed,' speaks the voice without a body. A warm, clear voice, persuasive and soothing, the voice of benign authority, like God's. As the camera settles on each item, some of them in action like the bubbling pots and pans that are being caressed by a hood-eyed hostess, the voice makes helpful remarks about the bargains on offer.

'The open sale, ladies and gentlemen, is the part of the programme where the items are easy on the eye and the prices are even easier on the pocket. Let's see what's cooking here this evening. A beautiful set of cast-iron pans to enhance the flavour of your cooking, they would cost in the shops thirty-three pounds, in the open sale they're going for just three. And since we're on the subject of food, how about this to take care of the aperitifs? A set of six cut-glass sherry glasses complete with decanter and tray, fifty-four pounds off here and going for six.'

The long red nails of a hostess rap the rim of a twinkling glass while she nods encouragingly at the camera. Maggie imagines them filled with ale, sipped slowly from the sighing settee in the front room.

'Now, waking up in the morning can actually be a pleasant experience with one of these, and even more pleasant when you hear this tea-maker can be yours for only three pounds. And this can give pleasure to anyone from seven to seventy, a portable stereo unit, usually costing thirty-one pounds, going tonight for three. No businessman should be without one of these, an executive briefcase with all the trimmings and the biggest trimming of all is the price reduction, down from forty-two pounds to five.'

The hostess with the nails again, stroking its leather, undoing its locks.

'Keep that summer tan right through the year with this health lamp, the *Sale of the Century* price should bring on a glow too, two pounds. Good companion for the tea-maker you saw just now, eleven pounds worth of automatic toaster, going for just a pound. And this bicycle can be used as a runaround for all the family, it has a basket for shopping and is down from forty pounds to five.' The hostess mounts it.

'Three pounds secures this twenty-nine-pound compact, easy-to-operate, mains/battery cassette recorder. And finally, this double continental quilt and cover will keep you cool in the summer and warm in the winter and it's down to only five pounds from forty-two. And those are the items in the open sale tonight!' Once again the applause scoops away the Wurlitzer's final trembling note. Maggie checks and sees Pop with his pencil between his teeth, bug-eyed with temptation.

'Well, our contestants, as you know, have a chance to spend some of their hard-won money if they so wish. We begin with the one with the most money in front of them. Arthur Landywood, you have twenty-five pounds, do you wish to spend some of that money? If so, now is your chance, in five seconds giving also the sale price, starting now . . .'

Pop is ready. He strings all the words together, getting as much in as possible, finding from somewhere a precision Maggie is entirely unfamiliar with.

'Teasmade three pound toaster one pound record player three pound . . .'

'You started the record player before the five seconds was up, you can keep it, Arthur!'

Mary Mackintosh buys a toaster too and Geoffrey Morgan buys the saucepans and a Teasmade.

'We've taken away from our contestants the money they spent in the open sale, ladies and gentlemen, which gives us Mary Mackintosh in the lead with nineteen pounds, closely followed by Arthur Landywood with eighteen pounds and Geoffrey Morgan at thirteen.'

Unlucky, Geoffrey, unlucky.

'In which country is there an area known as the Valley of the Kings?

'Egypt is right Geoffrey.

'What does a taxidermist do?'

'He does indeed, well done, Geoffrey.

'The Kontiki expedition, what was this?

'Across the Pacific, yes Geoffrey, well done.

'Murrayfield, what—

'Is correct, Arthur.

'Gingivitis—

'Geoffrey, mouth, yes.' The questions spin Mr Parsons

between his camera, his contestants and his studio audience with the wind in his hair.

'For five pounds, can you name the famous architect considered by some to be the founder of the English classical school?'

'Nash, Wren . . . er, eh?'

'Inigo Jones. You lose five pounds, Arthur.

'Where in the human body would you find the thymus gland?

'Is correct, Arthur.

'What is the word which means son of a somebody and is used to describe a Spanish nobleman?

'Hidalgo, well done, Mary.

'For five pounds can you name the famous American runner of the thirties who won the—

'Jessie Owens is correct, Arthur.

'Near which city is Pucklechurch prison?

'Bristol is correct, Arthur.

'*Keep the Home Fires Burning*, who composed and wrote this?

'Ivor Novello is right, Geoffrey. And once again it's time for our fourth and last instant sale! What's the last one we have to offer them tonight, John?'

'Well, nine pounds is all we want, Nicholas, for this highly desirable—'

A buzzer blasts. Pop.

'. . . two-hundred-pound portable colour television set. Pictures wherever you go in fact, and what's more it's fitted with all the modern aids to good viewing.' The wobbling Wurlitzer, teetering on its final note, can hardly believe it.

'Arthur Landywood has bought the two-hundred-pound portable colour television set for nine pounds!' It sounded

238

like a jeer to Maggie but Pop was shining like he'd flown the thing in on a single engine.

'The situation is,' said Mr Parsons, beaming his blues east and west of his congregation, 'that Geoffrey Morgan is in the lead with thirty-four pounds, Mary Mackintosh with twenty-seven and third is Arthur Landywood with twenty-two, and the questions of course still worth five.

'Which professional man would use a theodolite?

'Correct, Geoffrey.

'William Wilberforce, what—

'Abolition of slavery is right, Geoffrey.

'Who was the Prime Minister at the time of Edward the eighth's abdication?

'Stanley Baldwin, correct, Arthur.

'In which Dickens novel does little Nell Trent appear?

'Well done, Mary.

'Bridge: What is the order of seniority of the suits?

'Is correct, Geoffrey.

'Who was President of the United States when they entered World War Two?

'Roosevelt is right, Geoffrey, all jumping on their buzzers.

'For another five pounds, what did the D in Franklin D stand for?

'Arthur.'

'Dehane.'

'What?'

'Dehane. Or Deharne.'

'Delano. I'm afraid you lose five pounds, Arthur.

'With what do you associate the Fabian Society?

'Mary?'

'Well, oh dear, it was started by Shaw, oh dear, dear . . .'

'You're almost there, I'll give it to you, Mary.

'Who was the first woman to fly the Atlantic?

'Arthur.'

'Amy Johnson.'

'Who composed *Land of Hope and Glory*?

'Arthur.'

'Edward Elgar.'

'Can you name the field marshal always associated with poppy day?

'Arthur.'

'Earl Haig.'

'It was British Guiana, what is it called now?

'Geoffrey.

'Guyana, yes.

'Which part of this country was once well known for tin mining?

'Arthur.'

'Cornwall.'

'What was the date of the D-day landings?

'Arthur.'

'June sixth, nineteen forty-four.'

'The artifical harbour that was used then—

'Arthur.'

'The Mulberry.'

'Who was commander of the allied forces?

'Arthur.'

'General Eisenhower.'

'Who is the government chief whip?

'Geoffrey.'

'Bob Mellish.'

'What was the date of the bombing of Pearl Harbor in World War Two?

'Arthur.'

'December seventh, nineteen forty-one.'

'On November twenty-fourth nineteen forty-four what did the Americans begin—

'Arthur.'

'The B-twenty-nine raids on Tokyo.'

'Bunny Austin: What was he well known for?

'Geoffrey.'

'Tennis player'

'*Good Wives*: Who wrote this?

'Mary.'

'Louisa M Alcott.'

'What is ikebana?

'Mary.'

'Flower-arranging.'

'Name the conductor who started the popular Promenade Concerts.

'Geoffrey.'

'Henry Wood.'

'For what is John Logie Baird well known?

'Mary.'

'Television.'

'Who was the reigning monarch during the fourteen–eighteen war?

'Arthur.'

'George the Fifth.'

'Who wrote the opera *Madame Butterfly*?

'Arthur.'

'Puccini.'

'Which famous soldier and statesman lived at Apsley House in Piccadilly?

'Geoffrey.'

'Wellington.'

'Who was Sir John William Alcock?

'Arthur.'

'He flew the Atlantic with Brown.'

'Which country has Caracas as its capital?

'Geoffrey.'

'Venezuela.'

A shattering clash of gong as if Yul Brynner has arrived and Mr Parsons throws his arms up. 'And we have no more time!

'Geoffrey Morgan! Eighty-four pounds! You are tonight's winner!' The applause is joined by some hammering blows on the Wurlitzer.

Maggie watches Pop congratulating Geoffrey. He grasps his hand and leans in to speak in his ear. They laugh suddenly and Maggie feels hungry for those words chosen so carefully for the winner. She feels disappointed for Pop after he did so well but he looks like he couldn't care less, grinning and leaning over his buzzer as though he might answer another question. She looks at Dolly and Carl clapping and gawping like he's gone and won it, clapping and gawping herself too now.

'Well, I don't think I've ever seen so much money between three contestants before. Mary Mackintosh, I think you've done wonderfully well to come third. You have a toaster to take home and fifty-two pounds in cash. Well done, and competing against those two young lads as well.'

Pop lets off a shout of laughter, sticks a pencil behind his ear and applauds along with everyone else. Mr Parsons is on full evangelical burn now, arms wide, gaze shining and commiserations healing, the light warm rainfall of applause soft on his face.

'Arthur Landywood, second with eighty-two pounds, you bought a toaster, a Teasmade, a record player and a portable colour television. We've had *winners* with less than that score,

242

but you take that money home with you tonight. Well done, Arthur, congratulations.'

Pop blinks at the clapping he's waited on all his life. He hears it shatter towards him and swim around his head and when he closes his eyes he sees green, the colour under your feet win or lose. Not a bad score for an away game in the First Division, happy with that, can't complain. Played to the best of our ability anyhow; worse things happen at sea. Walk on.

'Geoffrey, will you care to join me please while we begin now our Sale of the Century!'

Geoffrey moves unsteadily on big turned-out feet towards the caravan, the sauna, the emerald ring, the eighteenth-century oak grandfather clock and the silver-gilt goblets.

The Conquistador

They came home to a foul-breathed Blowbroth and some news.

'The singing cowpoke's riding in. He'll have to leave his ruddy snakeskin boots in quarantine,' is all Pop said about it.

Maggie's father had been contacted in the USA and was returning to England. She pictured him riding along the A446 on a dusty horse, clopping along the Parade and through the Gracechurch Centre, adjusting his stetson and shooting off his Colt .45 in the Pint Pot, blowing away all the toby jugs and nodding 'ma'am' to the yeti, telling his stories to Ken to see if he believed a bloody word of it.

It had taken most of August to trace him and inform him of her mother's accident. She wondered if, on hearing, he'd thought of the Jesus Christ aim-and-fire doors or the early days when Carole sat on his knee in Kent beer gardens.

A dazzling silver drizzle falls steadily in long needles, dashing leaves and streets and windows so that they shine, filling reservoirs, streams and gutters until they shout with water. Everyone wants to feel the rain on their skin. People stroll in their shirtsleeves, carefree as Australians, hands on hips, nodding up at the rainclouds, telling tales of before with the authority of survivors, exaggerating. All become farmers in the Sudan, nomads in the Masai Mara.

Pop stands outside until the rain puts his fag out. He flaps back in, clothes plastered to his skin in smacking folds, 'tache dripping, and lights another one. The smoke hangs in a mist around his damp face as if he is reappearing from a distant past.

There is a letter for him. Blue writing in tight twirls like knitting on small squares of paper. Maggie tries to read it upside down, she manages groups of words. Congratulations . . . did very well . . . what a pity . . . never mind . . . Teasmade will come in useful . . . corresponding this way would be quite acceptable . . . Warm regards.

He sits holding it for a long time. Maggie can't tell whether he's glad or sad. Then he looks up and winks. 'Knew I'd wear her down in the end.'

There is a celebration drink for him at the Plough and Harrow. The lamps are on even though it's lunchtime and the windows glow through the latticework of drizzle. Pop and Maggie lean into a fresh breeze that swerves left and right, snatching at leaves and dying flowers, trailing the damp smell of autumn behind.

Newly arrived from the Faeroes, where tourists are folding themselves into Harris tweed, it will chase the drought back to Africa where it came from.

The door's cry announces Pop's entrance and a quick cheer goes up, dissolving into the jangles of loose change as everyone moves to buy him a drink. He is slapped on the back and punched in the arm, reminded of his errors and his wisdoms, told what this person and the other one thought of Nicholas Parsons, continental quilts and gleaming caravans, berated for not pronouncing the Delano from Franklin D. Roosevelt correctly and teased for wearing a cuboid tie. The pints queue up and Pop spins a few back about the pubs in Norwich, the unclaimed sale items and the hostess with the big earrings.

'I'd've had the pans and the clock, mate, if I'd been you,' Ken says, leaning across his bar, flushed with after-the-fact advice.

Carl stands up, eyes brimming, and raises his glass to Pop.

'Arthur, Duke of Clarendon . . .' He can't go on, too over-come, which prompts another rousing cheer and a game of darts.

Blowbroth has sulked for two days under a table in a fug of flatulence.

'What's wrong with you, soft pillock?' Pop demands on bended knee. A bag of pork scratchings and Dolly on all fours prises him out eventually. The lamps give off a syrupy glaze that along with the ting of the till makes promises of Christmas. Pop grins and lifts another caramel pint.

'Looking black over Bill's mother's.'

'Oh ar, forecast's all rain now, mate.'

'Where's the summer gone, eh?'

'Siberia in a couple of weeks.'

'Nicklaus won the Masters again anyway.'

'Hell of a handicap, him.'

'Bloody daft game golf.'

'Ar.'

Dolly hoovers and dusts every corner of the sitting room, making the carpet and furniture look sorrier for themselves than ever. When she's finished Pop bends low to kiss her cheek and the light gathers on his freshly oiled hair, making it shine. They hear her heels scraping along Clarendon Road, pausing every time she hears a car, dipping to glare at the occupants when one passes.

Pop strikes a match and Maggie watches the quaking in his hands and the folds of his clothes, the same shivers as the day she arrived.

He checks his watch. 'Not even time for a half,' he says, winking at her, tapping his ash into a toby jug so's not to spoil the ashtray.

A clamour of music brings their gazes level and sends Blowbroth skidding for the door, yowling like a jackal. A red minicab, scarlet as a stop light, with a telephone number brazen across the roof, pulls up under the rowan tree. The song on the cab radio is streaming through the open windows. Some bloke knock, knock, knockin' on heaven's door. Blowbroth has to holler louder. A snakeskin boot swings out and a gaunt face rises over it, suntanned, with his secrets carefully concealed behind dark square sunglasses, the mouth a folded, indecipherable line. He bends to pay the driver. 'Keep the change,' Maggie catches, wondering how it is possible that everything he says sounds like a country song. Then turning and short steps as though he's not sure, number ninety-nine growing taller in the gloomy squares of his shades. A spit of rain on his boot and then another and then with every step, as he walks tall and keeps on walking.

*   *   *

They are alone in the sitting room. Pop boiled the kettle and left with the dog, slamming the door with volcanic force, to jog her father's memory.

They don't talk. The toby jugs look on askance. He sits on the sighing settee in his boots. He looks absurd, like having Elvis on your three-piece suite. He takes his sunglasses off and she can see his eyes are small and raw with hurt as he says her name.

He spends the evenings alone in the gloamy bar at the Three Tuns Hotel on the high street, where he has taken a room. He visits Clarendon Road each day with a small gift, like a suitor, prancing away from Blowbroth's snapping gob-flecked snout. He buys Maggie a cake she can't finish in a coffee house called Reflections on the Boldmere Road. He tells a couple of good jokes that make her laugh suddenly, hitching her shoulders up under her ears. She responds in kind. 'Doctor, doctor, I can't stop singing *The Green Green Grass of Home*.' Then they sit in armchairs at the Three Tuns Hotel under the deafening toll of a chiming clock while he talks, closing his eyes every time he refers to God's mysterious plan.

Summer has slipped away in the night, buggered off to the Antipodes. A cool, grey light is against the windows, sending chills along the stone and folding up the flowers. A mantle of cloud hides the wild blue sky that ran across August, dragging its braids of jet fuel and purple evenings. It is white as far as the eye can see, so that the whole sky is milk, soft and sightless. The

247

cloud is battened down on the horizon so that you cannot see Staffordshire now from Sherifoot Lane.

Pop has winter in his bones already. Maggie sees him in a new cowed shape on the stairs. He has his heckle and grin, but he is dulled without the sun crashing over him. He finds his jacket and cap in the place he threw them last April, when the drought sent its first fire-toed messenger on ahead. The damp irritates his cough, wet barks pulling him further and further towards the ground, his eyes surprised above the tide of fluid rising in his lungs. Their shoes slap the streets until they are all behind them, Tower, Clarendon, Worcester. Past Iris's garden, shaggy and spoiled with the beginnings of autumn. Past the dustbins and the dying elms. Past the churchyard where his quiet grave lies waiting. Followed everywhere by the scrape of blown leaves, loud as ironmongery behind them.

The Gum Slade has begun its carpet of leaves in flame colours and their feet make the sound of surf as they go.

Here lies the gentle knight and stout,
Who to such height of valour got
That, if you mark his deeds throughout,
Death over his life triumphed not
With bringing of his death about.

The world as nothing he did prize,
For as a scarecrow in men's eyes
He lived, and was their bugbear too;
And had the luck, with much ado,
To live a fool, and yet die wise.

Don Quixote by Miguel de Cervantes Saavedra.
Translated by J.M. Cohen.

Acknowledgements

I am indebted to Peter Aldridge for his invaluable assistance with research and his enthusiastic support, and also to Mary Aldridge for her quiet faith.